INVASION

Alien Invasion Book One

AVERY BLAKE
JOHNNY B. TRUANT

STERLING & STONE

To YOU, the reader.
Thank you for taking a chance on us.
Thank you for your support.
Thank you for the emails.
Thank you for the reviews.
Thank you for reading and joining us on this road.

INVASION

INVASION

DAY ONE

Chapter One

ON THE MORNING the ships came, Meyer Dempsey found himself preoccupied with drugs, sex, and business. It would have been hard to believe that just six days later, only one of the three would seem to matter.

"You're not listening to me, Heather," he said into the phone. "I'm going to be in LA from Friday to Tuesday. I've already booked time with the studio on Monday. The whole reason I'm coming early is—"

Heather cut him off, probably to feed her need for a zinger more than a reply that couldn't wait. Heather was always "on," never really able to take a break and just be a person for once. It was one of the reasons they hadn't been able to stay married. It was like living with a jester.

"Because you want to do the Walk of Fame?" she said. "Because you love weekends on Sunset?"

"Heather …"

2

"What do you want me to do, Meyer? Telly makes my schedule. I do what he tells me. I've got a gig."

"Where?"

"Boston."

"*Boston?*" Meyer said the word as if he and Boston had an ongoing argument and everyone knew Boston was being an asshole about it. "Cancel it."

"*Cancel it?* This is my living we're talking about."

"Then postpone it."

"You want to see me so bad, why don't *you* postpone?"

"I can't postpone. Lila has a thing. Trevor has … I don't know … another thing."

"Now I know why you got custody of the kids. You're so on top of things."

Meyer rolled his eyes at the empty penthouse. Heather's dry, biting wit had made her career, and it's what had attracted him to her in the first place. He still loved Heather plenty, but too often she seemed incapable of having an adult conversation.

"Do you want me to get the school calendar? I know what the 'things' are. Lila's is a dance. Not prom. The other one."

"Oh, 'the other one.' I remember my Other One. I wore pink chiffon. My date was Jimmy Breslin, and he could only get this powder-blue tux that smelled like cats had peed on it. Or were *still* peeing on it, like it had hidden compartments in the tux for urinating cats to do their thing. He was a total dork, but I gave him head afterward anyway, because, you know, everyone does that at their senior Other One. Because you only get one chance. Well … except for the other Other One."

"Are you finished?"

"I wouldn't ask Lila or Trevor to miss anything,"

3

Heather said, slightly more serious. "But Telly booked this months in—"

"Telly works for *you*, Heather."

"You're right. *That's* why I hired a manager and give him, like, half my income. Because I want to *not* do what he says and make my own schedule. What's the big deal, Meyer? You'll be back."

Meyer had walked to the window and was looking out across Central Park. The weather was pleasant, and he considered going out onto the porch, but the wind looked rough. The roof terrace would be better, but not by much. That was the problem with tall buildings. You got a great view for an exorbitant price, but it's like architects forgot how quickly the weather changed as you climbed higher in the air.

He took a beat before replying. He didn't want to admit how much he'd been looking forward to seeing her. Besides, telling Heather about the ayahuasca ceremony he'd already booked with the shaman (and paid for in full) seemed like a jinx. You weren't supposed to plan surprises for your ex-wife — even drug-related surprises. They both understood that, but the way Meyer sneaked around behind Piper's back made both him and Heather feel guilty. Heather wanted badly to dislike Piper, and if she'd been able, it might have made things easier for them both. Unfortunately, Piper was impossible not to love.

"Fine," Meyer said.

"Just come out, and do your business with the studios, then go home. You don't need to see me. You're not flying commercial, are you?"

"What am I, homeless?"

"So it's not like you need to go those specific dates anyway, if you're taking the Gulfstream. Just go out for Monday instead of the whole weekend. If you'd cleared this with me in advance, it'd be different, but I'm booked, sweetie. When we were getting started working together, would *you* have liked it if *I'd* just bailed on something to run off and screw my ex?"

"You didn't have an ex back then."

But now he was just being juvenile. Meyer sighed. He'd get over it. He'd lose the money he'd already paid to Juha, and he'd have to wait for the burst of mental expansion that always followed a ceremony ... and yeah, that sucked. But what the hell — ayahuasca wasn't the kind of thing you got addicted to. And he could certainly afford it. Not seeing Heather felt like the bigger hit. He hated to admit how much he missed her. Of course he loved Piper, but if there were such things as soul mates, Heather was his. Too bad she was so goddamned annoying.

"I can also meet you in Vail," she said. "I have a thing in Denver in, like, two months. We can check on the construction of your new place and hang out."

"If it's not finished in two months, I'm going to hang myself."

He rolled his eyes for no one to see. The project was already three months overdue, and if the crew dragged its feet much longer, they'd end up building his Axis Mundi in the snow. That would be annoying for the construction crew, he imagined, but it would be far more annoying for Meyer. He didn't particularly want to navigate the back-woods roads on his two hundred acres of Colorado property in the snow. It was private land and wouldn't be plowed unless he hired someone to do it.

But hey, if that happened, he supposed he'd make it work. It would be a pain in the ass, but he'd do it. Any way to ensure the project got finished. Something under his skin — something he couldn't quite articulate, but that he always glimpsed in those ceremonies with the shaman —

had begun to feel very pressing in recent months. He *needed* that place finished, and then he needed to hightail his family out there to make it their new primary residence. Because something was on the horizon. He felt surer as weeks became months. Every day without his Colorado house and the bunker beneath it was another day Meyer felt at loose ends, as if he'd misplaced his keys with no way to find them.

"Then I'll meet you in Vail in two months, and we'll hang out," said Heather.

"I'll want to take Piper and the kids when it's finished." Meyer hadn't told any of them — Heather, Piper, *or* the kids — that he meant to take them permanently. But Heather could feel free to interpret him any way she wanted.

"Then I'll join you."

Meyer almost laughed, but she wasn't kidding. The women had spent plenty of time together before, and he'd played the dutiful, faithful husband every time.

"Fine," he said. But his tone must have betrayed his irritation at having to wait, because in a moment Heather was all over him, mocking mercilessly.

"Oh, baby," she crowed, her always somewhat squeaky voice now exaggerated. "Are you *disappointed?*"

"It's fine, Heather. I'll just meet with the studio on Monday and save the extra days. I'll—"

"You're *disappointed,*" she repeated, laying it on thicker. The thing she was doing with her voice was a babyish effect — something she and her comedy audiences found hilarious but that had always made Meyer want to punch something. "You *miss* me, don't you?"

"Maybe you're doing me a favor," he said, trying to put a positive spin on the situation and realizing he could easily find one. "I'll save three days this way."

And he really would. Ayahuasca wasn't one-and-gone; if he expected to be in his right mind by Monday's meeting, he and Heather would have had to meet the shaman on Friday (as booked) in order to have the weekend to ponder the universe and be generally obnoxious by the outside world's standards. Heather would spend most of that time staring at the ceiling and talking about colors, and she'd humor Meyer when he got his great new ideas and made a few more connections in the cosmic puzzle he felt like he'd been assembling.

He didn't want to skip a swim in the eternal sea, but it was true that he could save a ton of time if he did.

Or — and this was an intriguing option — Meyer could take the trip as planned, but hit Colorado first to check on construction. Given the bunker beneath the main house (already finished and mostly stocked, thanks to his last visit), it was a complicated project and vital to get right. The crews were good, but they were just construction guys. They'd follow the plans, but they didn't share Meyer's conviction that the concrete walls and sealing lead doors would one day be needed to stay alive. Even Heather didn't share that conviction … or Piper, for that matter. Both women loved him and humored what they saw as his eccentricities.

So yes, maybe he should go after all. If he didn't make sure things were right, nobody would — and getting it right felt more essential with every passing day. He hadn't told Piper that he planned to move the family to the ranch once the school year ended, and he definitely hadn't told the kids. Trevor was already growing moody and would probably turn into a drama queen. Delilah would probably profess her undying love to her boyfriend and dig in her heels. Piper would go along with it all as long as the ranch had a yoga studio, which it did.

No one would truly like the idea of moving, but Meyer made the money and that meant he'd earned the right to make the family's decisions. They'd keep the Manhattan penthouse, sure — but after the move it would become like the London place: somewhere to visit rather than live.

"No, you're *bummed out*," said Heather, drawing the final words out into her babyish little girl squeal. "You want to play, and *mean old Heather* won't let you."

"It's totally fine," he said, annoyed.

"But if I don't play with *Sweet Little Meyer*, who ..." She stopped.

"Heather," he said, taking the break as an opening, "I've gotta go. I'll let you know about sending the kids out. But I'm looking at the 17th through the 19th. Just for the weekend. That still good?"

Heather said nothing.

"Heather? The 17th through 19th?"

For a moment, Meyer thought the connection had broken. He shook his phone and was moments from tapping its surface to end the call and try again when he heard her voice: small, distant, and chillingly cold.

"Meyer," she said.

"Are those dates still clear for you? Into LAX. I can get flights that arrive most of the day, but afternoon arrivals work best for me unless I have someone take them to the airport. I'd rather do it myself, though."

Heather said nothing. In the distance, Meyer could hear her television. That was another thing about living with Heather that had annoyed him to no end: the woman couldn't abide silence. She always had noise on, and fell asleep with the TV blazing.

"Heather?"

"Meyer. Turn on the news."

8

Meyer's phone vibrated in his hand: an incoming text or a call. A second later it vibrated again.

"Someone's calling me, Heather. Just tell me yes or no on those dates. I need to have Piper buy tickets soon if you don't want first class to fill up."

"Turn on the TV, Meyer."

"When we're done." Heather's tone sent a chill creeping up the back of Meyer's neck.

"Turn it on!"

Meyer's phone buzzed again.

"Look, I've got another call. Just … I'll call you back."

"Don't you dare hang up on me!"

A third buzz. The phone was a hunk of metal and plastic and indestructible emerald glass, but Meyer thought he could almost hear its urgency, as if the caller was yelling at him just like Heather was right now.

"Okay, okay," he said, flustered. "Just let me get this other …"

The phone buzzed again. Meyer found himself wanting to throw it across the room.

"Meyer, I'm …" Heather began, but he'd already pulled the phone away from his ear and was jabbing at its screen to switch calls. He pushed the wrong button, saw a message that he'd just ended the call with Heather, and felt a sudden urge to call her back before taking the new call. But the incoming ring was from his assistant, Laura, so he raised the phone to his face and said hello. The line was dead. He'd missed Laura too, gone to voicemail.

He looked at the phone, still considering throwing it. Heather had rattled him. She had a way of doing that, but usually in a totally different way. Whatever had just happened was red hot and ice cold at once. Meyer, for the first time in God knew how long, felt his heart thumping in fear.

The penthouse was quiet.

He reached for the phone's surface to call one of the women back, but didn't know who to phone first. He slipped the cell into his pocket and crossed to the coffee table. Then he picked up the remote, tapped the glass to bring up the TV menu, and turned on the screen. He clicked to CNN from the selection screen and caught an attractive female anchor midsentence.

" … from the Astral telescope on the moon's far side," she was saying. The screen changed to show a black square dusted with specks that looked like stars. "These images are streaming from the Astral app now. We're told there are only about four seconds of delay as the signal bounces around the moon satellites, travels through space, and is processed by Astral here on Earth. So what you're seeing is close to live."

Meyer squinted. The screen looked like nothing.

"You can't see much on the light telescope yet," said a piped-in male voice — seemingly an expert on whatever was happening. "But if you go to the radio array, you'll clearly see the objects, like a collection of small pebbles."

Whatever "radio array" meant, the station switched to it. The black screen with light specks was replaced by a much clearer image showing a cluster of small round objects.

"NASA is saying they're meteors," said the woman's voice.

"Not unless meteors can decelerate," said the man.

"And they're on a collision course?"

"An *approach vector,*" the man corrected. "And whatever they are, based on current estimates, they'll be here in five days."

Chapter Two

PIPER PICKED up her rolled blue mat and her small duffel, tossing a wave to Deb and Paulette as they left the Yoga Bear studio. She pulled her phone out to check the time (and maybe Facebook), and saw seven missed calls, all from Meyer.

Piper's heart immediately pounded — faster than it had during the final few seconds of the unusually long Warrior One Greg had forced them to hold, when her tight hip flexors were screaming for mercy. She didn't generally get calls from her husband. Most things earned her a text — maybe a call if he had something more complicated in mind, like deciding where to go to dinner on an indecisive night. But *seven* calls? Meyer was the opposite of insistent. He wanted his way and wanted it now, but blind insistence was, to Meyer, a form of weakness. The worst thing you could do in any negotiation was to admit

11

need, and insistence was exactly that. And for Meyer, life was a negotiation.

She held her thumb above Meyer's icon (a dignified photo from a *Times* piece last year; he'd rolled his eyes when she'd shown him, and she'd thought his reaction was as funny as the photo), then paused. She felt light-headed — too much yoga, perhaps, followed by urgency one wasn't supposed to feel after Savasana's integrating peace.

Piper was bubbly and almost naively optimistic by nature, but in times of crisis she always felt betrayed by her serene mind, going to the worst possible scenarios — so laughably dire and unlikely.

Was something wrong with Lila? Had she fallen and cracked her skull?

Was it something with Trevor? He'd been so moody and distant. Had Meyer found him dead, a victim of teen suicide? These things happened, and the old PBS specials Piper had grown up with always said you never really saw it coming.

Relax. Jesus Christ, relax, Piper.

She touched the icon. Her eyes took in Meyer's serious, borderline pompous (but deliciously handsome) expression before the screen changed from the photo to show a connection in progress. It seemed unfair to see a man so ruggedly handsome and powerful and on top of the world, but still fearing she'd find him crippled, panicked, somehow distraught enough to call seven times during one hour-long yoga class with the ringer off, blissfully ignorant of the world where terrible things might be happening to strong and confident husbands, while …

"Piper, Jesus. Thank God you're all right." He sounded out of breath, as if she'd called him while jogging.

"Me? I'm fine. Why wouldn't I be fine?"

"Have you seen the news? Or Astral? Have you checked Astral?"

Piper was as amused by the Astral app as it seemed everyone was (the makers, Rysoft, credited their app for ushering in "the second great space age"), but it wasn't something she checked compulsively like Facebook.

"Astral?" Piper felt baffled. He'd called seven times, and now he was asking about the space view app? Maybe the calls had been a mistake and everything was fine after all. Maybe he'd simply pocket-dialed her. Seven times.

But no, he was clearly out of breath. Urgent. In no-bullshit mode. No matter what the world thought of Meyer Dempsey the mogul, he'd always been Meyer Dempsey the man to her. He was sweeter than people thought, and strangely courteous. He pulled out chairs for Piper in restaurants, and insisted on opening her car door whenever they went out. The fact that he was so down-to-business now prickled her skin. The threat on his mind was real and present. Piper found herself wishing he'd just say it and get it over with, so that at least it would be out in the open.

"Have you called the school, Piper? I've tried. I can't get through."

"Called the school?"

"If you've already called, I'll stop trying. But I need to get ready here, so I'd like to stop." There was a heave and grunt on the other end of the phone, then the sound of something heavy striking something soft.

"I haven't called anyone. Meyer, what's going on? Why would I call the school?"

As Piper said it, she thought she heard something out in the hallway — a dull crash, like someone slamming a door. But this was a yoga studio, and people traipsed the bamboo floors on slippers and pillows, speaking in whispers. Still, she could hear commotion on the level below.

Looking up, Piper thought she could see some sort of ruckus on the street — the tops of heads rushing by, visible only from the hair up from her second-floor vantage.

"They're saying that …" Meyer paused. "Shit, Piper. Nobody there knows?"

Piper looked around the emptying studio. Cell phones were required to be silenced in class, so during the movements the place was more or less severed from the outside world. Although she wondered now if the commotion outside had been going on long — nothing overt, just a generalized sense of increased energy — and whether Greg's rainforest soundtrack had drowned it out. You were supposed to disconnect from the world and turn inward during yoga. Apparently, it worked too well.

Alan, a well-muscled classmate Piper had been noticing lately with no small amount of guilt, stood just a few feet away. She could see the wideness of his eyes as he looked over, his own cell phone in his white-knuckled grip. Every eye was fixed to a screen — something she'd never seen in the studio before.

"Knows what?"

"There's …" Meyer sighed. "Something showed up on the Astral telescopes. Approaching … objects."

Piper's blood went cold. "Like a comet?" It was a stupid thing to say, and she felt foolish, but she liked old movies and had seen her parents' generation's disaster fetish films. The idea of Earth-smashing celestial bodies had kept her up many nights as a kid.

"No. Like … shit, just trust me, okay? Call the school. Pick up the kids. Meet me at home as soon as you possibly can."

"What, Meyer? What's coming?" Piper was practically shouting. But nobody was looking at her, because others were speaking just as loudly — the ones who weren't staring dumbfounded at their phones, their eyes wide and complexions like flour.

"They think they're ships."

"Ships!"

"Yes. Look. I don't have time to get into this, Piper. Listen to updates on the radio on the way if you have to — I'm sure it'll be on every channel — but you have to get moving. Now. For our kids' sake."

It was a dire way to say it, and a small part of Piper wanted to make fun of him. Meyer was easy to make fun of, and her quirky humor was one of the things he seemed to like about her most, but she couldn't do it. Something terrible was happening, and it didn't matter for a second that Lila and Trevor weren't her biological children. She'd been more like a sister than a mom, but they were family either way, and whatever was happening, Meyer's nerves were infectious. "Their sake" felt accurate, and pressing.

"It can't be real, can it? I mean …" She didn't want to say it. "You're talking about flying saucers?"

"Spheres, it looks like."

"You're not kidding, are you? Please tell me if you're messing with me, ha-ha, I promise to laugh, and …"

"Just call!"

Meyer was gone.

Piper stared at the phone, seriously considering offense that he'd hung up on her. It was a familiar, uniquely female emotion welling inside her. She wanted to wrap both hands around it, run to her nearest female friend, and bitch about how shitty men could be. Anything to shift the air's ominous feeling.

She shook it away and dialed the school. The phone rang and rang, but no one picked up.

Alan looked over. He still hadn't returned the shirt to his tight muscled body. Piper would never cheat on Meyer, but she was an attractive woman at twenty-nine and liked to flirt. She'd normally have returned his look, then engaged in some pointless banter. But not now.

"They're saying that …" Alan began.

But Piper was already grabbing her bag, snatching her mat as if yoga might one day matter again, and making for the door, still clutching her phone. She trotted to the garage, wondering if circumstances would allow her to leave the car and hail a cab. The streets had an odd energy, and she didn't particularly want to be behind the wheel, but something she remembered from Meyer's tone told her he'd want the car, even if she didn't.

She rang the school. Now her phone refused the connection.

She tried again. Same results.

The sidewalks were chaos. It was unusual to see people running here unless they were actually out for a run, but now she saw scampering businessmen and businesswomen, still clinging to briefcases and satchels like useless tokens. Faces were lost. Piper found herself thinking of old footage of 9/11. New York had returned to business as usual since those terror-filled days, but apparently the tendency for panic had never stopped bubbling under the surface. She saw it now, barely contained.

Piper dialed again, trying to reach Constellation's office. If she couldn't reach the school, she'd drive there. Screw getting permission or notifying anyone in advance. Judging by what was happening around her, protocols no longer mattered. There was a security checkpoint at the doors of Constellation like any other school, but to hell with their security if she couldn't reach the secretary by phone. She'd barge in, and dare them to stop her.

She tried again. The phone blessedly rang, and was

snatched up almost immediately by a harried-sounding woman.

"What?"

Piper's brow knitted. "Is this … is this the Constellation School?"

"What do you want?" Now that the voice had said more than a few words, Piper suspected it wasn't a woman after all. If she had to guess, she thought it might be Mr. Hoover, the vice principal, his voice scraped by nerves.

"We're very busy here dealing with …" the Hoover/woman began.

"This is Piper Dempsey. I'm—"

"I know who you are."

"I'd like to pick up Trevor and Delilah early today, if that's okay with the school. I know it's the middle of the day and I don't have—"

"Lady, I don't give a fuck what you want to do. You want to come over here and piss in the fountain, I could care less."

"Who is this?"

"We're just trying to keep things together and fight our natural desire to run out of here and leave your kids to fend for themselves. Damned kids all have cell phones today. Even if we wanted to keep calm, we can't. They all have Astral."

"So there really is something …" Piper couldn't make herself say *coming toward Earth from space*. "… wrong?"

"I have to go," said the voice, impatient. There was noise on the line — either Hoover preparing to slam down the school's old-fashioned hardline or the threat of a disconnection from elsewhere, possibly because everyone in the city seemed to be on their phones. Vaguely, Piper wondered if she'd be able to reach Meyer again if she needed to. The probable answer made her push the thought away, frightened.

"So I can just come and pick them up whenever? Do I come to the office?"

"Everyone seems to be coming," he said with an audible effort to contain himself. "All the parents. Trevor … is he a driver?"

"He's fifteen."

"Then he'll be in the car line. We'll tell them to keep back from the curb, or some of these crazy bitches out there are going to run them over."

"And Lila?"

"She's a senior?"

"Junior," said Piper. "She's seventeen."

"Hang on."

There were distant taps and clicks. Piper could imagine Hoover looking Lila up on the school's computer system. She found herself admiring the vice principal, maintaining his post. Like a captain going down with his ship.

"Dempsey, Delilah. Junior. Homeroom is Dr. Cheever."

"That's her."

Hoover said, "She's not here. The computer says she never showed up this morning."

Chapter Three

Day One, Late Morning
Central Park, New York

Lila looked down at her phone, saw a fresh text from Piper, and slipped it back into her purse.

"What's up?" said Raj. He had mocha skin and dark-brown eyes. Lila found him beautiful. Even today, even given what had happened, she couldn't help herself being deeply in love.

"Nothing."

"Who keeps texting?"

"Piper," Lila said.

"Piper! You think she knows you ditched?"

Lila laughed. "I think that's a safe assumption. She doesn't normally text me at school."

"You gonna answer her?"

Lila shrugged. She was too cool for the world right now, she knew better, she was her own boss and answered to no one.

"Tell her you had a doctor's appointment," Raj suggested.

"Because she wouldn't know if I had a doctor's appointment."

"Well, what's the text say?"

"Which one?"

"She's texted you more than once?"

"Yeah."

"Well, then what do *they* say, Li?"

"You have a little crush on Piper there, Raj?"

"My dad texts me, I answer him."

"See, that's why you're going to be a good doctor some day," said Lila. "You're so responsible."

"I'm not going to be a doctor."

Lila leaned over on the stone bench and kissed him. "You should be a doctor. I want to marry a doctor. They're so good at providing for their families. Keeping their wives in fancy things."

"You don't care about fancy things."

Lila shrugged.

"Your dad is loaded."

"And I want to take charity from my dad forever."

Raj looked distracted. He wasn't happy ditching school, he wasn't happy with how things had changed between them, and he was, frankly, too responsible for his own good. He probably wouldn't be a doctor like his father, but he'd be something respectable.

Lila took his hands in hers. "Relax. Enjoy the beautiful park."

"I wonder what this land is worth?" said Raj, looking around. "If I owned a piece of Central Park and wanted to sell it to a developer, what do you think I could get?"

He didn't wait for her answer. He'd been spouting pointless things like this all day, and Lila kept having to return him to center. He was whistling in the dark, trying not to feel the pressure. But they were both seventeen now, practically adults. She'd been kidding about marrying him as a doctor, but she wasn't kidding about marrying *Raj*, if he asked. They'd been together for three years, had been having sex for two, and both saw themselves as ending up together in the long term. They *could* get married soon; really. Her grandmother had married at eighteen, and that had lasted over fifty years.

"Bajillions," said Lila.

Her phone buzzed inside her purse.

"At least see what it says," said Raj.

"No. I'm here with you." She wrapped both her arms around one of his and leaned her head on his shoulder.

Raj looked around the Ramble again. He didn't like being down here and kept saying it was a gay hookup spot. Lila could have replied that they were here because it was the only place she knew where they could talk in relative isolation, but it was more fun to chide him for being homophobic. Raj was Indian, but his family had been in this country long enough and become affluent enough that he had acquired quite a bit of liberal white guilt.

There was a buzzing from Raj's wrist, shaking near Lila's head. Raj was more responsible than Lila. He looked at his forearm immediately.

"You're such a dork with that thing."

"This is state of the art, cretin," Raj said, tapping at it.

"My dad wears a watch. You're just like my dad."

"I got a message from my mom."

"Is it about being responsible and getting good grades?"

Raj looked up from the device and met her eyes with irritation. He was usually so fun. It hurt her to see him like this, but the recent news had unsettled him. He was torn somewhere between fear and an intensified form of personal responsibility. Now he had a problem to solve, and would remain annoyed until he'd managed to do it — as if it were his problem alone.

"She just says to come home."

"You should call her back. I love when you talk to your wrist. You look like a brown Dick Tracy."

"Who's Dick Tracy?"

"My dad has these old comics, like hard-copy comics, and … well, it's what people thought the future would be like back then. Can we take your hover car back home, Dick?"

"I love you, Li, but I'm not really in the mood for joking."

"What, just because I …" Now her phone wasn't just vibrating. It was vibrating again and again. Apparently, Piper had tired of texting and was calling. She sighed and dug the phone from her purse, looked at the screen, then gave Raj a look. "Hang on."

She put the phone to her ear. "Hey, Piper."

Lila waited for a torrent of guilt. Piper was strange as a stepmother, being just twelve years older than Lila herself, and was ill suited to outright chastising or discipline. Piper usually tried talking to Lila like a sister, saying she remembered what it was like to be a young girl … then infusing those somewhat-dated memories with sage, vaguely parental advice. It was like an older sister trying to help more than a mother interfering. But still, her father stood behind Piper, so Lila usually listened to her requests before they turned into Meyer's commands.

Instead of rattling on about Lila ditching school, Piper demanded to know where she was, her voice hurried.

"I'm …" Lila hesitated, but Piper's concerned tone was

disarming. She found herself blurting the truth, " … in the park."

"Are you near the museum? The Museum of Natural History?"

"I … sure, I suppose."

Lila heard a scream somewhere behind her, followed by running feet. Raj looked over, his eyes wide. Then the feet were gone, and they were back to being mostly alone.

"The West 77th Street entrance. Meet me there."

"When?" But that was far too compliant. "Why?"

Lila listened for several minutes while Piper lost her mind on the phone. When she finally hung up with a promise to be in front of the museum as soon as she could ("though it may take a while for me to get there because the streets are losing their shit"), Lila looked at Raj. She was ready to say that her stepmother had finally lost her airy-fairy, hippie mind, but Raj's expression stopped her. He'd been poking around on that stupid wrist mobile thing of his, using the projection feature to watch video on the bench with the accompanying earpiece pushed into his head. And his eyes were as wide as she'd imagined Piper's through their conversation.

"Aliens," said Raj.

"You can't possibly believe that. You're more rational than stupid crap like UFOs and aliens."

There was another shout. A group of people ran into and then quickly out of sight. Raj clutched Lila protectively, but they were gone before the potential threat could more than register.

"Everyone else seems to believe it," said Raj, nodding toward his wrist. "What did Piper say?"

"She said …" Lila trailed off. It was all too ridiculous.

"Shit, Lila. This isn't good. We can go to my place."

"It's way the hell uptown."

"We'll take a cab."

A crashing, crunching sound tore through the air from somewhere far away.

"Piper is going to pick me up at the museum."

"Let's go," he said, standing. "Think she can drop me off? Think she'll be too pissed that we ditched together?"

"Something tells me she has bigger things to worry about," Lila said. "Just don't tell her you got me pregnant, and I think we'll be fine."

Chapter Four

Day One, Late Morning
Constellation Academy, New York

Trevor stood dutifully in the car line at school for five minutes, then decided that another frozen moment would make him fucking retarded.

The school had held itself together for a respectably long time, but everyone's seams were now showing. Mr. Banks, the principal, seemed to be totally MIA. Mr. Hoover seemed to be acting as a reluctant shepherd. He'd made that "proceed to the front lobby in a calm and orderly manner" announcement over the tablet network, interrupting Trevor's already distracted class by popping onto everyone's screens in a small window in the middle of a lecture about the Protestant Reformation.

When Trevor's group (more or less intact and keeping its wits) arrived in the lobby, Hoover had been there too, shouting loudly enough that everyone decided to gift him with responsible authority. Hoover had brokered the bus lines, seeming to mostly get the right kids to the appropriate places, assisted by the corps of surly bus drivers themselves. To the side of the bus loop, a few of the security officers who'd stuck around managed the car line, continually warning the kids back from the curb as if afraid their manic parents might run them down in their haste.

Nothing in line was orderly. A car at the rear would make a pickup then try to rush forward, cutting everyone off. There was much honking and already two fights.

The car line dutifully formed around the horseshoe and out into the street, but Trevor could see the writing on the wall: anyone who joined at its rear now would spend angry minutes fighting the loop before rejoining what was an increasingly snarled line of traffic beyond.

Trevor hoofed it out toward the end of the line, where new cars were joining. He moved back with the line. The school wasn't as jammed as those downtown, but getting out of here wouldn't be easy — especially once they turned back toward home.

A few minutes later, Piper's distinctive blue Bug pulled up, and Trevor felt his gut sink. Yes, he'd be leaving school and going home. But he'd be riding in the car, alone, with Piper. In the Bug's infuriatingly close quarters.

He flagged her down, raising his hands in a universal "stop, don't pull up any farther" gesture. Then he ran to the vehicle, feeling that odd tumult he'd been recently feeling whenever around his stepmom.

He reached for the door, but Piper was already leaning over to push it open for him. He looked in, and she was still across the seat where he needed to be, her huge, beautiful blue eyes looking up at him with watery concern as if he were only a child. She was wearing a tight top — maybe coming from yoga; Trevor *hated* when she did yoga at home — and her ample boobs were on shapely display, courteously separated and shaped by the bisection of her seat belt.

"Trevor, thank God."

Trevor said nothing. He looked away from Piper and slid into the Bug's bucket seat, setting the bag on his lap. Everyone said the world was ending and aliens were on their way (he'd even seen photos on the app; he had it same as anyone), and still he was getting an inappropriate boner. Perfect.

"Are you okay?" she said, her naturally husky voice sounding somehow uneasy, barely hanging on. "You seem okay. Is the school okay? Are they taking care of the kids who are left? Look at me. Right here."

Trevor reluctantly looked over. Jesus, she was beautiful. Those big, blue eyes, that innocent, usually carefree bearing, that dark and wavy hair with its retro-geek bangs. That seat belt plumping her chest.

"Good, good," she said. Trevor didn't know what was so good. The aliens? The panic? "But Hoover — that was Mr. Hoover, right? — he's taking care of things? Are there any riots? I mean, not riots, but, like, panic, like people fighting and …"

"A little in the car line," said Trevor, looking away.

"Oh my God. Oh my God. Do you think it's okay? Do you think they'll be safe, or—"

"What are you going to do, put the whole school in the back of the Bug?" Trevor snapped, his newly deep voice booming more than intended. He pushed at his glasses, feeling her gaze and knowing they looked stupid and childish. He was fifteen, and every kid he knew had had their vision corrected if it was the slightest bit off. His dad was famous and rich. Why did he have to look this way, with big dumb frames on his face?

He didn't look up at Piper, but could see her shock in his peripheral vision while staring at his backpack. He played with one of the zippers, turning it over and over, back and forth.

"Okay. Okay, you're right," she said. "We'll just go. I'm sure they'll be fine. We can only worry about ourselves, right?"

Trevor thought he'd have to snap at Piper before she'd pull into traffic, but she blessedly looked over her left shoulder, tapped the console, and confirmed that she wanted to merge.

Even her technophobia was adorable. The car, without Piper in it, could have picked him up, and it would have done so without rubbing forbidden tits in his face. And still she insisted on confirming every little move it wanted to make, reintroducing the possibility for operator error into what was otherwise a near perfect system.

Then again, judging by what he'd seen in the car line and what he was already seeing on the streets ahead, plenty of people were piloting manually today. Autocars tended to balk at driving on sidewalks, rear-ending stopped vehicles to make a point, and running over streetside trash-cans to clear a path. And autocars rarely honked: the staple shout of rage for any driver in a rush.

"Did they tell you about the aliens?"

Trevor looked over, watching her profile. She hadn't even tried to soften it.

"*Ships*, Piper. Or maybe just asteroids or something."

"I hope you're right," said Piper. "About asteroids. Or maybe I don't. I don't know if that's any better. Unless they miss. They could miss, right? Because they could be shooting right at Earth, but Earth is moving, isn't it? Do you think that could happen, that they could just fly by?"

"Dunno."

"I was listening on the radio, kiddo." Trevor hated when she called him "kiddo." It implied he was a kid, not her midnight lover as he'd often imagined, doing things he shouldn't do while thinking of his father's wife. "They don't think so."

"Think what?" said Trevor.

"That they're asteroids. Or meteors. Or … what else? Like a comet or something. Or Spacelab." She looked over, and he could see a small, exhausted smile on her wide pink lips.

"What's Spacelab?"

"Maybe it's Skylab. Is it Skylab?"

Trevor shrugged. He had no idea what she was talking about. He kind of wished she'd stop talking. Or that he'd invited a friend to be in the car with them, as a buffer.

"Where's Lila?"

"She's in the park."

"Why is she in the damned park?"

"Easy, tiger."

Tiger, worse than *kiddo*.

"Well, why *is* she?" he demanded. "I had to go to school, and she can just ditch?"

"Don't worry about it. I'll make sure she understands she can't pull stuff like that. And besides, right now all that matters is …"

"We're going to the park?"

Piper nodded. A traffic jam loomed ahead, so she jockeyed around, heading down the next block. There was an abandoned cab to one side. Piper swerved into approaching traffic just long enough to get around.

"Yeah. I told her to meet us outside the museum. I think she's with Raj."

"Fucking hell."

"Trevor!"

"Oh, so she can ditch school, a fleet of UFOs is coming, and it's bad news that I'm swearing. Well *fuck that.*"

Traffic eased long enough for Piper to glance over. She'd gone full manual before the cab maneuver, and as far as Trevor could see without looking up, she looked flushed with the stress of driving.

"You okay, Trevor?"

"Peachy."

"You scared?"

Making his voice as insulted as possible: *"No."* It was the biggest lie he'd ever told, other than the one he told every day by saying nothing, about Piper.

"Well, *I'm* scared." She reached out and tapped the radio. "Radio. News." The car filled with a comforting third voice, droning on about something neither of them probably wanted to hear. "It's okay to be scared, Trevor."

"I'm *fine*, okay?"

Again she glanced over, vaguely hurt. That hurt Trevor in return. He didn't want to offend her, but talking with her was hell. Piper only seemed confused, not understanding why he'd turned on her over the past six months when they used to be such good friends.

"Well, just sit back then. Assuming we can make it to the park, we'll get Lila and then head home. Everything will be fine after that."

Trevor found the statement insulting, but said nothing because Piper was probably saying it for herself more than for him. Still, heading to the top floor of a Manhattan building during a coming invasion was less intelligent than ridiculous. There was no way his father, with all his paranoia, had the penthouse in mind as their final plan. He probably had survival gear stowed somewhere, and they'd head into the subway tunnels to live like well-equipped hobos until the overlords had enslaved the world above.

On the radio, the announcer repeated something Trevor had already heard from his friends' investigations during class, when word about the Astral app happenings had first started to spread: that current projections, crowd-sourced by the civilian eggheads watching Astral, seemed to think humanity had only five days left to pretend it was alone in the universe. After that, the ships or whatever they were would arrive. Then shit would really hit the fan.

Piper reached out and tapped the radio to turn it off, her finger shaking.

Chapter Five

DAY ONE, *Morning*
  The Dempsey Penthouse, New York

MEYER TAPPED his earbud while running around the penthouse with a sense of foreboding. Somehow without knowing at all, he'd been sure this was coming.

All the visions in his ceremonies. Tripped-out haze, lying beside Heather while she talked about the "groovy fucking colors," sharing none of his richer experience in the far-seeing rituals. Ayahuasca was medicine, but Heather just saw it as a helluva time — not unlike the many other substances she'd put into her body and brain. She'd never been truly addicted to anything through all her dalliances, so it seemed ironic to Meyer — who'd really only cared for that most expensive drug of all — that he might have been the addicted one.

Not to the chemicals, but to the puzzle his mind had been slowly solving since his first glimpse of Mother Ayahuasca.

"Incoming call from: Piper."

The mechanical voice pronounced Piper's name as "Pipper." It was simple to correct mispronunciations, but he'd never cared to. And right now, on the eve of an apocalypse, it annoyed Meyer more than anything that his phone still couldn't properly pronounce his wife's name.

He tapped the bud again.

There was a shuffling noise. Meyer heard his son say, "Here."

Piper: "Oh, excellent, thank you, Trevor. *Meyer?*"

Meyer was shoving item after item into a duffel. He'd just packed two similar bags, and most of what they'd need was already in the van downstairs. From the outside, Meyer's packing would have looked less frantic than he felt, owing to the fact that he'd practically memorized his packing lists and kept whatever he could spare already packed, stowed, and ready to go. Only last-minute items took time, and he was already done. Meyer checked mental boxes in his mind as if on an internal heads-up display.

"Are you on your way?" he demanded.

"Oh, thank God. We've been trying to reach you for hours. Well, not hours. A long time, though. Trevor has."

"So Trevor's there? You got the kids?"

A loud clattering preceded a horn's ugly bray.

Far away, Meyer heard Piper yell, "Brother trucker!" Then: "Sorry, kids." A nervous laugh followed, not from Piper. Seconds later her voice filled the receiver, out of breath. "I just hope I can make it there."

"Where are you?"

"Near the park. I just picked up Lila."

Meyer stopped, wrist-deep in a duffel.

"You aren't out at the school?"

"I had to pick up Lila."

Another rustling, and something that sounded like

Piper might have hit something, run someone over, or driven up onto the sidewalk. All were fine with Meyer as long as the passengers in Piper's stupid Beetle survived. But she was a shaky driver under the best of circumstances. She'd been raised in the country, moving to the city only after her campaign on Meyer's crowdfunding platform had birthed her Quirky Q clothing line — and, eventually, their relationship. Piper was too tentative for New York streets, and today was no normal rush hour.

"Jesus, Piper. Put someone else on the phone. Just drive."

"Lila, take the phone." Then, somewhat near the receiver: "I love you."

"I love you too, baby. Just be—"

Trevor's voice: "Hey, Dad."

"Lila, your voice has gotten so deep."

"Lila doesn't want to take the phone," Trevor said. "She doesn't want you to yell at her for ditching school."

"Lila was ditching school?" He shook the thought away. That was well down the list of things that simply did not fucking matter right now. He had to see them safe, then get to Morristown and the Gulfstream. Things were uncertain until then. Once in the air, they'd be okay. He could worry about FAA rules and where they'd land later. They could fly low and land at the compound if need be. But none of that could happen without the city behind them.

"She was with Raj."

"That doesn't matter right now," Meyer said. "Tell me exactly where you are."

"They ditched the whole day so they could go to the park and make out."

Lila's voice from nearby, probably the back seat: "Give me that phone, you little shit!"

"Lila says hi."

"Where are you?" Meyer repeated.

"On 77th. We just picked up Lila and Raj."

"Raj? You have Raj?"

"Yeah. They keep making out in the back seat. It's gross."

"Trevor, you little—!"

"Get *off*, Lila! I'm talking to Dad."

Piper: "Will you two just—"

There was the squeal of tires, a vintage Piper shriek, and, mercifully, no crash. Meyer realized he'd paused his packing. No matter now that the plan might be changing.

"Tell Piper to turn autodrive back on before she gets you all killed." Meyer had been doing some mental theater since he saw the incoming call, and could imagine every noise paired with ridiculous acrobatics from his adorable but not always street smart wife.

"Tried a bit ago," said Trevor. "The streets aren't terrible as far as traffic is concerned, but there are a billion people running around, like, kind of everywhere. Pretty sure we saw some guy get wasted earlier. Not by us. The car doesn't know what to do with them all. It just kind of politely waits for them to pass."

"You're on the west side?"

"Yeah. On 77th. But Dad, it's going to be pretty hard to get all the way around the park and home. It'll take some time."

"Don't try. We're headed to Jersey anyway. Cross to Weehawken. I'll meet you at that gas station where we bought the Twinkies that made you sick. Do you remember it?"

"I remember it," said Piper's voice in the distance. How loud was her phone, and how little attention was she paying to the road?

"You're sure, Dad?"

"You'd be backtracking. Who knows how much worse traffic might get. The panic's only starting."

"You're always in front," Trevor said. "Even when it comes to panic."

"That's right." Meyer smiled in spite of himself. "Take care of them for me, okay, Trevor?"

"Sure, Dad. See you in Jersey."

Meyer hung up, then closed his eyes to inhale the stillness.

He didn't like the idea of meeting away from the penthouse, but that was just him being nervous and selfish. They were halfway to where they needed to go, practically speaking. Whenever Meyer thought about these scenarios ("obsessed over," in Heather's words — sometimes onstage, in her act) getting out of the city was always the choke point. He'd looked into parking a helicopter on the roof for a while, but couldn't secure permissions. Ultimately, New York itself was the problem, which was why they were moving to the ranch. Unfortunately, the apocalypse had come early.

Meyer returned to his mental checklist, still packing. Trevor had been joking; he knew this was far, *far* more directed than panic. He'd bored his kids to tears discussing concepts that the ceremonies had slowly helped him absorb — a distinct feeling that the universe was far more connected than most people believed, and that a great change was coming that they'd all best prepare for.

It was somewhat of a woo-woo idea for a mogul, but Meyer considered himself a Renaissance man. He conducted his business with iron logic, but cared for his body, with daily yoga and massage. He'd redefined entertainment following the studio failures in the first part of the twenty-first century, and yet his kids always came first — to the point that Heather had granted him custody in deference to his "more stable life."

Like most powerful people, Meyer had his quirks. But now the world was learning what he'd known all along: that his preoccupation with, and advance preparation for, the end days had been time and mental energy well spent.

Walking shoes. Electronics and charged extra batteries.

The latter wouldn't last forever, but they could be charged in his Benz JetVan. As long as they had the van and fuel, and the communication networks stayed up, they'd be able to use them.

The earbud buzzed again.

"Incoming call from: Heather."

Tap. "What?"

"Hello to you too, sweetums."

"Are you packed up? Are you out of the city yet?"

"I'm working on it."

"Quickly, Heather. Have you checked the highways?"

"How?"

"Online."

"Oh. No. I didn't think of it. Should I?"

Meyer sighed. "Yes. Of course you should. You want to end up in a parking lot?"

"Maybe I should fly."

"Don't try."

"I checked the flight schedules. United has a direct flight, LAX to Vail. You can meet me there, or I can rent a car."

"Do you think this is a vacation?"

Heather's reply sounded annoyed, but at least she was being serious, for once.

"Oh, but it makes sense to drive. *You're* flying."

"I have a private jet, Heather. And I'm not going to LAX."

"You're going to JFK."

"No, I'm going to Morristown. JFK will be a mess. Like LAX. But if you think it's smart to try and buy a ticket and fight security and crowds on the verge of rioting, go right ahead."

That was a dangerous thing to say. Heather might take him up on it to prove a point. She constantly flew for comedy gigs and sometimes movie work and was away from their old home more than at it. She'd first caught Meyer's attention because she was as arrogant as he was, and Heather Hawthorne wasn't the kind of woman many men would dare to push around. But she'd been with him as his preoccupation had grown, and she knew as well as Meyer just how fully stocked and bulletproof the Vail compound was. He'd even proposed the idea of Heather moving in when they did, in a guest house on the same sprawling property, for "safety" in Meyer's supposedly paranoid opinion.

"Maybe I should stay where I am."

"Jesus, Heather, no, get on the road, and start driving. Gas up the second you can and then as often as you see a gas station that isn't being mobbed. You've got the hybrid; you should be good unless you're fantastically unlucky."

"That's a long drive, Meyer."

"Better than staying in LA."

"I don't know. Right now I have friends nearby. And the basement looks like CostCo."

Meyer had added to the stockpile with every visit. He'd lived in New York since the divorce, but he was still lord of his old manor whenever he flew to LA. He kept buying bottled water, canned food, sometimes weapons. Even Heather didn't know where he'd stowed it all.

"Heather, do I really need to explain this to you?"

"Go ahead. I just love listening to your explanations. Please, make it a long one."

Meyer bit his retort. "New York and LA. Those are the two cities everyone considers attacking. It's where everything bad happens. It's where everyone, every time there's a blip, goes apeshit with panic. People are already losing it in Manhattan. I'm moving as fast as I can."

Heather's voice changed, suddenly worried. "The kids. They're with you? Did you get them from school?"

"Piper did. But then she came all the damned way back to Central Park for Lila."

"Why was Lila in Central Park?"

"She ditched. But look, I literally just spoke to them. They're fine. I sent them over the bridge and am going to meet them in Weehawken."

"They're not with you?" Now Heather sounded near panic. He'd *never* heard her like this. It was disorienting, almost terrifying.

"They're fine. They're in a better position than I am."

"But *you've* got the Mystery Machine."

"Her Beetle's more agile. She can go manual if she has to. The JetVan's a behemoth. It was always meant to be a Colorado vehicle. Honestly, I don't know how the hell I'm going to get it out of the city. And I won't if I don't hurry."

Saying the words made Meyer's blood prickle. He resumed frantically packing.

Extra socks. Identification papers. Taser.

"Shit, Meyer. I am so not into this."

"You'll be fine. You're outside the city, already facing the right direction. Just start driving. Check the traffic first and avoid the bad spots, but don't rule out the expressways if they seem clear. Just be super careful because if you get in a jam, you'll be stuck. I'd stick to surface roads. You have a good traffic app?"

"I have TrafficCopter."

"And your car charger. And a few external batteries."

"Last time you were here, you put enough mobile batteries in my purse to power my vibrator without a wall socket."

"Good. So just …"

"Almost."

"Go. You may not be able to reach me on the road, so head for Vail, and we'll meet you there. Even the foothills are better than LA. You'll be fine. We'll be fine. Okay, Heather?"

For a moment, Meyer thought he'd lost her.

"Heather?"

Sounding exhausted: "Okay, Meyer."

"Try to call as long as you have steady power, like from your car. They say we have six days. Maybe the networks will stay up."

"I will."

"Take care, Heather."

He thought she'd hung up and was about to tap his earbud when Heather said, "I love you, Meyer."

"I know."

Meyer ended the call and packed faster, knowing how quickly time, in Manhattan's barely-held composure, was thinning.

Chapter Six

Day One, Afternoon
  Weehawken, New Jersey

It took Meyer an hour from the time he loaded the duffels into the JetVan and drove out of the garage until he reached the Weehawken rendezvous point. He'd had to go manual immediately, taking the wheel between his hands and forgetting that he was supposed to be one of New York's most respected private citizens. He'd ridden half on and half off of curbs; he'd annihilated two flimsy trash cans to circle obstructions; he'd nearly cut a homeless man in half when he'd been trying to sneak around some asshole who'd decided to load a U-Haul in the middle of fucking Hudson. As he'd passed, some other angry motorists had been arguing with the U-Haul's owner — a man who seemed to be rather flagrantly loading flats of bottled water into the back with a dolly. Meyer wasn't entirely sure, but he thought that just after he'd passed, those motorists may have seized the man, dragging him from the truck toward the curb.

Things were quickly going to shit.

Meyer's prior assumptions seemed to be holding true: Everyone would panic, and their best chance was to outrun that panic. Trevor, ironically, had nailed the concept: *They, as a family, had to panic faster than everyone else.* Screw the seven stages of grief. Screw denial and bargaining and all the things the populace must be thinking about the strange spheres drawing ever closer to Astral's radio telescopes. There was no time for any of it. The only way out was to be prepared and get the hell out of Dodge without flinching.

Only about an hour had passed since Meyer first heard the news. He'd already screamed out of the underground garage in his apocalypse-ready van. The general population had merely managed to run around waving their hands uselessly in the air like a Kermit the Frog freak-out. Knee-jerk fear wasn't hard to skirt. It was the sure-to-come mass exodus that would be impossible to wade through.

Both halves of Meyer's NYC family — Piper and the kids in the Beetle and himself in what Heather called the Mystery Machine — were well on their way out of town, packed and prepared, by the time Manhattan's slow sigh began. Traffic was slow, but in a strange middle ground: normal workaday flow had dimmed due to the news, but panic was creeping.

He took the Lincoln Tunnel, feeling nervous. In concept, there was little difference between a tunnel and a bridge out of the city, but in the dark — especially if the power grid failed; hey, it could happen if the wrong people left their stations at work — people were edgier. Fear would be thicker under the Hudson, and if someone stalled, there would be no option to simply break through the barricades and push them off into the water.

Meyer seriously considered taking one of the bridges on the island's east side and circling around, but the loss of time outweighed the bridges' superior open-air advantage. Besides, he knew Piper would take one of the tunnels. If there was a backup, he might be able to find his family. The converse was true, too — if he went around and escaped scot-free but they were held up, what good would it have done?

Fortunately, the early traffic out seemed to share Meyer's mindset: prepared, paranoid, but overall more interested in getting out safely than quickly. The crawl was slow but proceeded through the tunnel without incident. Soon he was on the river's other side, prepared to count the blessings of a god he'd never really believed in.

He pulled into the gas station just shy of Tonnelle and sighed with relief at the sight of Piper's familiar blue Beetle parked beside a pole that had probably, once upon a time, held an ancient pay phone. A massive propane tank inside a high fence read, *LEAVE EMPTIES OUTSIDE PAY INSIDE FOR NEW WITH DEPOSIT.* Beside the fence, below the sign, was a picnic table. Lila was sitting on its top with her feet on the bench, eating a sandwich. Trevor was on the far side, possibly pondering something. Piper was emerging from the station carrying a coffee. Beside Lila was someone Meyer had entirely forgotten about.

Piper saw Meyer, dropped her coffee, looked at the dropped cup reproachfully, then sprinted toward him. The run was shameless and full of youth. A moment later, her petite arms were around him, her head coming only as high as his neck, squeezing almost tight enough to sever his breath.

"Thank God. Thank God, Meyer!"

"Any trouble?" he said, looking around. He'd left the door of the JetVan open beside the Beetle. The engine was still running. It was a waste of gas, but something in Meyer told him they wouldn't want to be here longer than a minute.

"No. There was traffic, of course, but it was mostly civil."

Meyer looked around. The area was still reasonably urban, but the worst of it was behind them. Soon they'd be out past 95 and into suburbia. From there until Morristown airport, things would get easier.

"We've been here for *ages*, Dad," said Lila, her mouth full of sandwich. He had the provisions in the van, which meant she'd bought the sandwich from the station. He wasn't sure whether to take it as a good or bad sign. On the plus side, the station was conducting proper business instead of being raided. On the negative, it was a fucking gas station sandwich.

Meyer stepped forward and hugged his daughter. Then he straightened and extended his hand to the boy beside her — a boy Meyer approved of, but who for some reason wouldn't meet his eye.

"Raj."

"Mr. Dempsey."

"I didn't realize you'd be accompanying us. Where's your family?"

"Home, I assume."

Meyer's eyes went to Piper. She shrugged, so Meyer turned to Lila, his eyes taking in the scene. Past Lila, beyond the big propane tank, a group of kids her age were milling. They looked over. Meyer looked away.

"So, Raj," said Meyer.

"Yes, Mr. Dempsey?"

"We're taking a little trip."

"Okay."

"To the airport."

"Sure."

He wasn't getting it. "Meaning we're leaving New York. Jersey, whatever."

"Okay."

Meyer's eyes fixed on the Beetle. "You can take it if you'd like."

"Take it where?"

Lila picked up Raj's hand and squeezed it. "He's coming with us, Dad."

"His family is here, Lila."

"You want me to take the Beetle *back into the city?*" said Raj, aghast.

"You should be with your family. They'll be worried."

"Maybe we can meet up with them later," said Raj.

The kid wasn't understanding. It was as if he'd started the day with one objective — apparently to ditch school with Meyer's daughter — and hadn't yet cottoned on to the shitstorm's obvious gravity.

"There's no later. We're headed out right now. If you stay with us, you'll end up in …"

"Dad," said Trevor, arriving at Lila's side.

"Trevor," he turned back to Raj, " … in Vail."

"Cool," said Raj.

"Dad," Trevor repeated.

"Hey, kiddo." He wrapped an arm around Trevor's shoulders, but the boy stepped out of the embrace. Back to Raj: "You can't just fly away from your family. Not right now, of all times."

"So he should go back into the city?" said Lila. "Dad, that's stupid."

"Don't tell me what's stupid, Lila. It's right. He can take the Beetle." He took the keys from Piper and gave them to Raj. "Here. It's yours. You can have it. Merry Christmas."

"Dad!"

Meyer looked at his son, tipping his head as if indicating something to one side.

Meyer followed the gesture and saw the group of teens approaching. As they neared, Meyer could see details he hadn't noticed before: one held a bat and the other a gun.

Meyer spoke to Lila and Piper without moving his eyes from the approaching kids.

"Get in the van." He pushed the keys into Raj's hand. "Raj, take the car. Hurry. And be careful."

Raj looked up at the nearing group. They all did. The group had seen them, and was changing course accordingly.

"Take the car, Raj."

"I'm coming with you."

"No, you're not."

Lila was dragging Raj through the JetVan's open side door. Trevor followed, and Piper, keeping her eyes low, made for the passenger seat.

"Hey!" yelled the kid at the head of the group — the one with the bat. Beside him, the one with the gun (a girl, Meyer realized) was raising it.

"We don't want trouble," said Meyer, skirting around toward the open sliding door. Lila made to close it, but Meyer gave her an almost imperceptible wave, asking her to keep it open.

"Just wanna talk to you," said the kid.

"I have to go." Edging closer.

"Let us talk to you first."

"I'm sorry." Now Meyer's eyes were flicking between them and the door. They were fifteen yards off now, not running but moving with purpose.

"Nice ride you got," said the girl with the gun. "I'd like to check that out."

"Hey!" came a shout from the gas station.

Meyer fought the urge to turn toward the yell, diving for the door and scrambling into the driver's seat while Trevor pulled the door closed behind him instead. The kids had all flinched toward the sound and now spun back, weapons up. They ran. Meyer braced for a shot, but the girl must have been too stunned to fire. He slammed the van into manual drive and stepped hard enough on the pedal to shoot gravel from behind the wheels.

They were away, safe but with five hearts thumping.

Meyer jockeyed the van onto the road from the shoulder, keyed autodrive, and closed his eyes.

He hoped things at the airport would be smoother. But he already had a niggling suspicion that this was only the beginning of an end, and that from here on out, things would only get harder.

Chapter Seven

DAY ONE, Evening
Morristown, New Jersey

THE DRIVE to Morristown should have taken about an hour. It took nearly four.

In the van's lush rear, the three teens lowered the seats to beds and slept. Despite it being just before three when they set out, Meyer wanted to sleep too. The day had been draining. He felt his body telling him to give up, lie down, and let whatever was going to happen, happen. The effort to fight the urge, even after all the thought and planning Meyer had given this moment, was enormous.

Piper stayed dutifully awake beside him, laying a comforting hand on Meyer's arm as light bled from the day. With the sun down, everything seemed more peaceful despite the line of traffic — and, at the same time, much more ominous. They'd stopped just once, at another gas station, during a short stretch of clear road. The station had been deserted. The houses in the surrounding area were lit but graveyard silent. The feeling was one of waiting — as if those inside didn't know what they'd face in the morning, but wouldn't peek from their hidey holes in the meantime, just in case.

The station was, blessedly, fully automated and fully operational. Unlike the previous station, this one had no clerk — and therefore no one to rob. Payments were electronic; there was no cash on-premises. The foodmat inside was equally automated and light on provisions. In time, if things unfolded without peace prevailing, pirates would perhaps break into the foodmat and siphon gas from the station's tanks. But for now, that wasn't happening. And as Meyer topped off, he thought that this could be any night, anytime, anywhere.

But the highways were another story, and despite what he'd told Heather about surface roads, highways still seemed like the best way to travel. The van was well-stocked, but it wasn't otherwise as end-of-the-world prepped as it should have been. It had tires that could be punctured, windows that could be broken, and plastic side panels that could be shot through. The freeway was crawling. But surface roads, as they looked into the shadowy and streetlight-lit neighborhoods beyond, looked dangerous.

They didn't have far to go. Sleep, for the passengers, made time tick quickly. Meyer had his running thoughts, and Piper seemed to feel her only job (which she was happy to do) was to be by his side. The time spend was fine. They didn't have an assigned flight time like commercial fliers. They wouldn't have to go through security or even through the airport itself, small as it was. All that mattered was that they arrived whole, that the plane was still there, and that the pilot was ready to fly. And thanks to the still-functional cell network, he was able to confirm the second two just fine. As long as Morristown stayed peaceful, there was no reason for Nick to hop into the jet and fly off on his own. He was well paid, and despite the day's events, money still seemed very much to matter.

There had been scant new information. The van's radio had been on and tuned to a satellite news channel the entire trip, and as the evening had rolled on the station had taken to replaying the exact same half-hour in an excruciating loop.

Ships were still approaching Earth, same as they'd been this afternoon.

The president was still urging calm.

NASA was still predicting an arrival in approximately five days.

And the special interview guest — a man named Bertrand Delacroix, who sounded like a conspiracy nut to Meyer but who apparently had some sort of legit credentials — was still saying that if not for the public availability of the Astral app, the government would be covering all of this up. They were forthcoming now, he scoffed, because there was no way to lie. Somehow this was good news, but Meyer could only intuit that from Bertrand Delacroix's tone of voice, and the interviewer's reaction.

Ten miles from Morristown, Piper reached over and touched the radio, turning it to music.

"That's enough of that," she said.

"We need to know what's happening, Piper."

"We know it. Like six or seven times, we know it by now."

"Something might change."

But Piper wasn't listening. He'd thought she'd fallen asleep, and now she closed her eyes and looked it. She took his hand. He'd had them folded in his lap for most of the trip but had remained sitting in the driver's seat in case a move to manual proved necessary. So far, it hadn't. A line of traffic was a line of traffic, and everyone had to wait their turn. The autocar could do that much fine.

"It's crazy to think there's still music, isn't it?" Piper said.

"On the radio?"

"In the world." She sighed. Piper loved music and was more current on trends than Heather ever had been. It was one of the things Lila loved about her stepmother, and a tiny source of jealousy with Heather. "All that's happened, all this fear and fighting, and someone is still out there playing music."

"I'm sure it's programmed."

She sighed, not wanting to hear him.

Meyer shook his head at the line of traffic. "We're almost there. I'm going to be so glad to get out of this van."

"After all the time you spent stocking it?"

"The Axis Mundi is better stocked than the van."

"Why do you call it 'Axis Mundi'? The ranch, I mean."

Meyer considered explaining, but despite her spiritual bearing, he felt that Piper didn't understand any of the spirituality that actually mattered. She didn't participate in the ceremonies. She hadn't seen Mother Ayahuasca. He didn't resent her for it, and she didn't resent him, but it robbed them of common ground. Her parents had been religious and believed in a bearded savior in the sky. Meyer, on the other hand, had more or less predicted everything that had happened today. It was a decisive victory, he thought, but he wouldn't waste breath on explanation. Some places were holy. That and the fact that he'd wanted one of his own was all she needed to know.

"Why are we doing this, Meyer?"

"Going to Morristown?"

"Going to Vail. Shouldn't we stay put? We don't even know anything yet."

Jesus. It was the same thing Heather had said. He hadn't been able to reach her again due to the over-crowded network, but if he had, he'd conference the two women so they could be ridiculous and shortsighted together.

"We know enough."

"What do *you* know that nobody else knows?"

Piper looked at him with those huge blue eyes. It was rhetorical, basically a joke. But he'd already known enough to prepare, and could still feel the puzzle assembling some-where inside. He couldn't see it, but you didn't need to see a black hole to feel its pull.

They needed to be in Colorado when it happened, whatever "it" was. That was the only safe place. If this had only waited another few months, they'd have been living there already. *Then* they could have stayed put. *Then* they could have bunkered down and kept off the roads. But staying in New York — the city in which all sorts of bad shit always happened first — because they hadn't had time yet to make their big move? That was just stupid.

"We're almost there." Meyer looked out across the sea of brake lights. He patted her hand to soothe any possible reproach he might be broadcasting without intention and gave her a forced smile. She smiled back. He felt something release inside.

"And we can just fly away."

Meyer nodded. "One of the perks of owning your own plane."

Despite the awkwardness between them, Piper pulled Meyer's arm toward her enough to lean uncomfortably atop it. They looked like a stretched-out picture of lovers side-by-side at a romantic movie.

Meyer reached out and poked the radio. They were approaching the exit. Once off the expressway, everything would be faster.

Piper moaned.

"I just want to check before we get there," Meyer said.

The radio program had changed. Apparently, there was fresh news after all. But none of the reports had to do with Astral or the ships or anything else. It had to do with government preparations and the people's safety.

Meyer listened. He heard the announcement that made him shout as the airport came into sight, the terminal and gate slowly being surrounded by flashing blue and red lights.

Trevor jerked awake in the back seat. He blinked. "What? What's wrong?"

"The FAA just grounded all flights," said Meyer, pinching the bridge of his nose. "We're a half hour too late."

DAY TWO

Chapter Eight

PIPER WOKE with a soft vibration under her head. At first she didn't know what it was.

She'd been having a dream where she was on a roller coaster with Meyer's ex-wife. Heather was wearing an outrageous red dress that turned her average-size boobs into respectable and decidedly Victorian-era cleavage. It wasn't the kind of thing Heather wore in her lesser comedy shows and certainly not in any movie (released by Meyer's Fable Studio or otherwise) that Piper had ever seen.

They'd been climbing a hill for most of the dream, a half-minute trip yawning to hours in the way time stretches like taffy in the reverie of sleep. The dream's only common thread from beginning to end was Piper's ever-mounting terror. She'd woken just as they'd crested the first hill's top. The last thing Heather said before tipping down was, *Hang on tight, baby. It gets bumpy from here.*

Then Piper was awake, vibration under her head, and no true awareness (for the first few moments, anyway) of where she was. For a crazy second, she was sure Meyer's ex was still around. Only Heather Hawthorne would stick a running vibrator under a sleeping girl's head as a gag.

She blinked, yawned, and rolled over to see Meyer still behind the wheel. He wasn't holding it, though, and his feet weren't on the manual pedals. The van was on auto, apparently able to handle the light traffic. He'd scooted the JetVan's luxurious leather seat back a foot and turned it slightly into the cabin. The radio was tuned to a whisper, Meyer tapping around on his tablet.

"Have you been up all night?" she said.

"I thought we might need to run someone over."

Piper wasn't sure whether Meyer was joking. He looked serious enough, his head mostly down, giving her lip service without moving focus from his tablet.

"Where are we?"

"Pennsylvania." Meyer nodded toward the window, and what seemed to still be nighttime. A glance at the console clock: 6:23 a.m. "America the beautiful. Should I wake the kids to show them what fields look like? They look the same in the dark as they do in the light, more or less."

Piper looked into the van's rear. With the blinds closed, it was easy to believe the vehicle's name — to see it as more jet than van, and to imagine they'd somehow reached the Gulfstream after all. Trevor was closest, his head canted sideways to lean against the window, his eyes closed and his large black eyebrows less troubled-looking than they'd seemed lately. Lila and Raj were asleep in the very back, past the faux-marble console, in a bench seat, leaning against each other like two poles in a teepee. Piper wasn't sure she liked that. They needed each other, yes. But every mile farther they drove from Raj's family in New York was one degree more difficult it would be for Lila to give him up. The way she was clinging to him now, the idea of sending Raj home felt like ripping a cherished teddy bear from Lila's arms.

"Where in Pennsylvania?"

"The middle."

"Not toward New York."

Meyer looked up at Piper and gave her the look that had made him his fortune. Meyer Dempsey seldom wanted something he didn't eventually get. Including Piper, who'd only meant to use Consensus rather than meet (or marry) the man who'd created it — a girl who'd had a simple goal of crowdfunding her tiny design project rather than part-nering with the handsome entrepreneur behind it.

"West." Meyer's look was at once stern and almost condescending. He had his chin mostly down, his light-green eyes rolled up to meet hers. The grim expression of an authority — *explaining* rather than bargaining, asking, or attempting to justify.

They were going on a road trip. Discussion over.

She decided to weigh in anyway. Straightening, fluffing her hair where the seat had flattened it, she said, "I still think it makes sense to go back to New York. What are we going to do out here in the open, Meyer?"

"Drive west."

"You think something's coming."

"I've thought it for a while."

"Then we should be home. Not out here in the boonies."

"Nobody's going into the city right now. There's a reason. New York is always a target. Of everything. Nobody wants to be there right now, unless they literally have nowhere else to go."

"We don't have anywhere else to go."

"Vail. LA. London."

"Yes. Let's fly to the London apartment. That makes just as much sense. Hell, Meyer, it's probably about the same length as flight. We can make it on the plane that's grounded!"

"Keep your voice down. The kids are asleep."

"You need to sleep, too, Meyer."

"We can take shifts keeping an eye on the road. I'm not stopping at a hotel."

"It's not just about being physically able to sleep. We all need a break. If we just stop for a while, finish the night …"

"The further west we get, the … fuck."

The road had been making a gentle turn. Meyer paused, exhaled, and swore. The van moved to a courteous stop behind the rear of a car that, in the dark, appeared to be a light-blue Toyota electric.

"How has it been?" she said. "Traffic, overall?"

Meyer shook his head. They'd been driving along steadily when Piper had woken, but now the road looked like a parking lot: red lights as far as the eye could see in front of them, and nothing but white to the left.

"On and off. I keep thinking we're free and clear, but then something happens. A few accidents with no clear cause, like people are just rushing, going manual to try and get past blocks, then running into each other. A few cars off the road, and everyone stops to rubberneck. This just looks like traffic. There's a city ahead. One with more than two freeway exits. Maybe everyone wants McDonald's."

"Can we go, Dad?"

Piper turned. Trevor met her eyes for a moment then flicked rapidly away, focusing all attention on his father.

"We're going."

"I meant to McDonald's."

"That was a joke, Trevor."

"I'm hungry."

"There's a bunch of dry stuff and bars in the back."

"I don't really want kelp bars and soy burgers."

"I didn't pack soy burgers, Trevor."

"Okay, I don't want kelp bars."

Lila was stirring in the back seat. "Are we talking about stopping to eat?"

"No," said Meyer.

Piper shrugged. "Might not be a bad idea, Meyer."

"No. We have to get to Colorado."

Lila sat up. "Wait. You were serious about that?"

"There's an exit right there," Piper said. "Let's take a break. This traffic isn't going anywhere anyway."

"We're staying on the road. Don't you remember what I said about outrunning the panic? Something like this happens, speed is our only advantage. We have a bathroom, food, water, even entertainment. We stay on the road until we're there."

"That's like three days, Dad." Lila shook her boyfriend. "Wake up, Raj. We're driving all the damned way to Colorado."

"Try Raj's parents again," said Meyer. "He's not going anywhere."

"So you're just going to drop him off at a gas station and hope he isn't attacked by bandits and rape gangs?"

"There are no rape gangs, Lila," said Meyer.

"Not yet," said Piper.

Trevor smirked. "Nobody's going to rape Raj. Maybe we can use him to shoo rape gangs away."

Raj rubbed his hands across his chest. "You're wrong. Everyone wants a piece of this."

"We'll *call his parents,*" said Meyer.

"Because they're out here, right, Dad? Not in New York or anything. They can just ride out and get him."

"I offered him the Beetle."

"Well, that didn't work out, though, did it?"

Trevor made a face at his sister. "Oh, like you wouldn't have thrown yourself in front of the wheels if Dad had pushed him into it and those people hadn't come. You're not letting Raj go anywhere."

Raj was still rubbing his hands across his chest. "Can you blame her?"

Piper looked at Meyer, then shot Lila and Raj a look. She understood; she'd been a stupid teenage girl in love once, too. But Lila's father hadn't been, and somehow Piper imagined Meyer's teen dalliances as more calculated and strategic than head-over-heels foolish in love.

"Try them now," Meyer grumbled, his attention still half on the tablet. Piper hadn't seen what he was looking up, but now he was using it as a crutch to avoid facing his children head-on.

"Who?" said Piper.

"Raj's parents."

"They won't be awake yet," Raj said helpfully.

Eyes still on the tablet, Meyer said, "I'm okay with waking them."

Piper could hear his restraint. Meyer needed sleep. He was as thin as the rest of them, but refused to rest and recharge. He was always a tempest. All that changed, between his calm and anger, was the strength of armor holding it back.

Raj shrugged, then tapped at his wrist. Piper had a strange desire to ask if she could see the device because she'd never used one before, but now wasn't the time.

"Nothing," Raj reported.

Meyer still seemed to be seething.

Piper said, "They don't answer?"

Raj shook his head. "No signal."

"The network is down?"

Trevor: "Probably just flooded."

"We should get a hotel," Piper suggested. "Let traffic clear out. Maybe the networks will open up."

She looked at Trevor, the last to use a phone. He looked away as if angry. Maybe he resented her for something. Piper didn't know, and had been trying for weeks not to be bothered.

Lila said, "People aren't going to make fewer calls as the aliens get closer."

Raj wrapped his arm around her, and pulled Lila closer. "You don't know they're aliens."

"Just empty ships from outer space, then," Trevor said. "That are flying themselves."

Piper thought, *Flying*.

"That doesn't mean that …"

Piper turned to Meyer, but she spoke loud enough to stop Raj in the back seat. "Wait. How far are we from Morristown?"

"Like, nine or ten hours."

"How *far*."

"Thirty, forty miles?"

"Well," said Lila, verbally pouting. "I guess we'd better settle in for a long trip."

She pushed her body even harder against Raj, then glared at the side of her father's head. Lila and Trevor got along with Meyer, but they were still teenagers. Piper, recently a teen herself, tried to understand, but often there was no use. Somewhere around your twenty-second birthday, teenagers started sounding like melodramatic idiots no matter what you did.

"That's another reason to get a hotel room," Piper

said. "They might let planes fly again. We can take the Gulfstream."

"They're not going to unground flights. Not any time soon." He shook his head. "I knew they'd do it, too. Only makes sense. Something coming from the air, military craft heading up in droves, people down here freaking out and storming the airports because *everyone* has to go *somewhere* when panic strikes, even if it doesn't make sense ..."

Lila said, "Good thing we're smarter than that."

Meyer seemed to consider shouting, but only mumbled. "This is different."

Lila laughed. But when Piper shot her a glance, she settled, having made her point.

"We've all talked about this," said Meyer. "Whenever I'm ... well, *when I think about it* ... it's been clear to me for a while that *something* was coming."

"Come on, Dad," Lila said.

He'd talked all their ears off about this. The maddening thing was that coming from Meyer Dempsey, talk about the end of the world never really sounded crazy. He put it in terms of change and inevitable consequences and how it was stupid *not* to be prepared when you had the financial means to do so. Piper didn't understand where Meyer's mind went on his Ayahuasca trips and had never wanted to partake herself, but there were two things Piper knew for sure: Meyer believed what his inner eye showed him, and she trusted him no matter what.

Trevor said, "Kind of hard to say Dad's full of shit right now, Lila."

"Trevor!" Piper snapped. "Watch your mouth."

"We have to get to Colorado," said Meyer, returning his eyes to the road. Cars were starting to move — slowly, but steadily. Piper could see the singularity of purpose and knew the futility of arguing. "The ranch is mostly done, and the part that matters most, in the vault, has been finished for over a month. I had it stocked last time I was there. We have an isolated power source, air filtration, plenty of supplies in food and water, concrete walls and lead doors …"

"Everything the modern paranoid survivalist needs," Lila said.

It was hard to call anyone paranoid when his fears came true, and hard to argue with the need to survive.

The cars stopped again. The van, still on auto, stopped without ceremony. Piper watched Meyer's eyes, seeing how they were scanning the roadsides and median. She didn't know if the JetVan could do off-road, but knowing Meyer, he may have had it specially equipped.

A diffuse red light appeared on the horizon behind them — the first rays of a pre-dawn morning. In the dim light with her night-adjusted eyes, Piper could see the cars ahead casting scant shadows.

Car doors in front of them opened, and both the passenger and the driver got out. The same thing was happening across the stopped traffic, one car at a time.

"What's going on?" said Meyer.

But Piper saw. She pointed.

"That," she said.

Chapter Nine

DAY TWO, Morning
  Las Vegas Outskirts, Nevada

HEATHER WAS ALTERNATING between cigarettes and joints in the small cabin of her PriusX, wondering if combining a stimulant and a depressant was somehow a bad idea, like driving an old-fashioned car with the brake applied. She'd done that once, back when she'd been learning, when most people who rode in a car alone still had to be driving it.

Driving with the brake on for most of an afternoon had done incomprehensible levels of damage. Her father's mechanic had told her that he'd never seen four brakes stripped so completely. Her father had made Heather pay for it out of her part-time income, and had suggested that she spend a bunch of time praying for salvation. Not from God, but from him.

She'd smoke a cigarette to its butt, toss it out the window rather than into the wet-compactor below the stereo, then start in on one of her pre-rolled joints. The smokes kept her alert, and the pot made her not care so much about whatever the cigarettes had caused her to notice. It was a perfect combo.

She picked up her phone. Dialed. Was told that the party she was trying to reach was unavailable at this time.

That's how it had been all afternoon, all night, and all morning so far. She'd learned to trust Meyer even if she thought he tripped out a bit too much on plant juice — more because he had excellent instincts than that Mother Ayahuasca was laying some knowledge on him whenever they drank and purged. Heather never felt the "deep understanding" that Meyer claimed, but if he thought he saw other planes while high, then good on him. That was the goal of any drug, after all: to alter your states enough to free you from the boredom of everyday life.

But Meyer had sent her on this errand, and he'd done it a bit like a kid pushing a toy boat out into a wide lake. Heather was the boat, and now that she was away from her home base in LA, the kid who'd given her that shove was no longer around. Despite trying every fifteen minutes or so, she wasn't getting any midtrip updates. He'd ordered her to the compound outside Vail, so that's where she'd go. But if Meyer fell into a hole in the road, she'd never know. She'd simply arrive to find his stupid "Axis Mundi" empty, then spend the apocalypse alone. What a stone-cold bummer.

Heather felt a slight sideways sensation. She looked up to see her Prius pass a red car that had seemingly broken down. There was a man standing beside its steaming hulk, waving his arms overhead as if trying to flag her down. For the briefest of moments, Heather considered stopping. But how exactly would that work if she did? He was one guy, alone.

He might steal her car.

He might rape her.

Heather took another toke, holding the smoke a moment before exhaling into the already-fogged cabin. Yes, that seemed likely. Aliens were coming, but men never really stopped being rapey. If the aliens had already landed those big balls somewhere and were marching forward with their ray guns up and that same guy tried to knock Heather clear of the blast, she'd still probably worry about his dick. Once in the ditch, who's to say any savior wouldn't take what he wanted? Anything to forget all the tentacles and probing of an alien invasion. She'd been in the spotlight — a confident and not-at-all-unattractive woman with risqué material and strong opinions — for long enough to know how threatened men were by girls like her.

Well, except for Meyer Dempsey, who the press seemed to think must wield a pretty thick prick stick. And that wasn't his dick itself (which was impressive), but just his general manly boorishness. That's what the *New Yorker* had implied; it's what the *Times* and *Newsweek* had both implied; it's what *Saturday Night Live* portrayed in its parody. Everyone seemed to think that Meyer was an arrogant asshole just because he was successful, had revolutionized film, had taken the Internet for a ride back in the gold rush. But success and confidence alone didn't make a person a bully or a bitch. Heather knew from experience.

She watched the stranded motorist disappear in the rearview, assuaging a prickling of guilt by telling herself that she would have stopped for a family or a woman. It wasn't true — this felt like an every girl for herself sort of situation, and right now she had a vehicle and some supplies. But telling herself helped. A little.

She picked up the phone, tried again, and was told that service was unavailable at this time.

Deciphering the various ways in which her phone could fail had become a road game, similar to the way she used to catalogue state license plates or play I Spy on long rides with her family. She set the phone aside, thinking.

"The party you are trying to reach at this time" meant that something was jammed on Meyer's end but that hers was working.

"Service is unavailable at this time" meant that she wasn't getting a signal on her end. This one only counted toward her road game if she could see bars on the display and knew, contrary to the phone's opinion, that she did, indeed, have service. "Service is unavailable" probably meant too many people trying to call at once.

Sometimes she got "Your call cannot be connected. Please try again." Of all the ways Heather's phone could fail, this was her favorite. For one, it was an optimistic failure, urging her to never give up. Second, it was blunt and honest, like Heather's comedy act. That message wasn't bullshitting her about "at this time," like it was an error of unfortunate timing. No. It just said that your call couldn't be connected, no bullshit beyond that.

You know what, bitch? No, you can't make this call, so move on. But hey, there's always tomorrow, so don't lose hope.

Twice now the phone had simply failed to light up. Those times, she'd let the battery run out while using the GPS. That one didn't happen anymore because she'd plugged the phone into the universal port.

It was a stupid game, but Heather had to pass the time somehow. Leaving LA had been tricky, but Meyer had been right; she was to the east of the city and, by moving quickly as he'd insisted, she'd been able to avoid the worst of the panic traffic.

After dark, as she'd moved into less populated areas, staying off highways for the most part, Heather's pace had picked up substantially. She had her phone's GPS on for curiosity (the one built into the Prius didn't have a wide view and had a bitchy English accent), but she'd never have wanted to try the tangle of roads she'd taken on her own. But what did she care? The car could make those decisions. All she had to do was sit back and smoke.

But it got boring. She lived in movies and wanted none of them. She had all sorts of old TV shows loaded into the Prius's juke, but she'd already watched four episodes of *Three's Company* and five of her hands-down favorite, *Friends*. She'd had enough watching for now. And really, they'd probably do nothing but watch *Friends* when she got to the bunker. It was one of the things she and Piper shared, even though Piper was young enough that she almost had no right even knowing the classics. It was infuriating. Part of Heather wished Piper was a brainless bimbo — a midlife crisis seized upon by a forty something man to follow his failed marriage. But Piper was hard to hate. Impossible, really. It would suck spending forever underground alongside her, knowing that guilt about sleeping with Meyer would prevent her from doing it in such close quarters.

She let the thought go. Tried dialing again and was told that she couldn't have her way … but that she should try again later. She gave a little cheer for nobody to see. Phone-related car game: *won.*

For the past hour or so, she'd been seeing signs for Las Vegas. At least that was some variety to look forward to.

Part of Heather was excited. She'd played Vegas a dozen times in the past few years (her last three annual specials were filmed there) and Vegas was always a good crowd. She arrived by air, never by car, never through hills and mountains. Still, the hook was strong. It was something she knew. She had fond memories there. And right now, after a night alone in a stupid little car with nothing to look at, the idea of being somewhere familiar — some speck of the life she'd so recently loved — was undeniable.

She should probably avoid Vegas proper. It was a big city, and even during the best of times it was packed with crazies. Crazies and old people. No good could come of that as the five-day countdown (now down to four days; the radio loved to remind her) neared zero.

Aliens in Vegas? Hell, they could turn that into a show on the Strip. Charge admission. Sell shitty souvenirs and nine-dollar bottles of water.

She'd asked the car to avoid 15 in a nice big halo around the city itself, if the car was thinking of getting back onto 15 at all rather than staying in the hinterlands. But Heather wanted to get close enough to see the lights, assuming they were still on.

But when Vegas appeared on the horizon, the lights were somehow different.

The city was on fire.

Chapter Ten

DAY TWO, Morning
  Pittsburgh, Pennsylvania

LILA FELT SICK.

She hadn't had time to read up on pregnancy specifics while trying to pretend the microscopic bun in her oven didn't exist, so she wasn't sure if it was normal to be sick this early. Morning barfing was one of the first signs of TV pregnancy, but sitcoms (from contemporary to the oldies her mother and Piper both liked) also showed birth as taking approximately fifteen seconds from the onset of pushing to the baby being out and totally clean. But one day in Los Angeles, because her mother had been a bit tipsy and thought it was hilarious and wrong, Lila had seen the video of her own birth. It had gone on forever. "Like taking a dump for days," Mom had said.

TV didn't get everything right. The Internet tended to, on average, because enough serious eyes were on the biggest websites, kicking out the contributions of assholes and jokers, but Lila hadn't looked. She'd been bored enough to get past her denial last night, after Raj and Piper were both snoring and Trevor was looking moodily out the window as if waiting for a lost lover. But she couldn't get an air signal on her phone, leaving the van's wireless as her only option. That signal was plenty strong for some reason, but Lila wondered if the van stored her search and browse history. Dad might use his tablet to find an Arby's and see her prior search for morning sickness. Shit would hit the fan.

Still, it was morning, and Lila felt ill. She'd never been great during travel, so this might be plain old carsickness. But she had been sleeping, not reading or doing anything much with her eyes. She hadn't felt ill last night, even after hours of driving and looking at her phone for a signal — even after enduring the tense silence following Meyer's decision to turn away from the airport they'd spent an evening trying to reach.

If this was morning sickness, she might barf. She didn't feel it yet, but that kind of thing could sneak up on you. Lila wanted to be prepared. She was looking around when Raj met her eyes.

"What are you looking for?" he said.

"A bucket or something."

Raj looked puzzled.

Lila pointed. "There. Crawl up and grab me that rubber thing." She didn't know what it was, exactly, but her dad (or someone) had filled it with more of Meyer's gross snack foods. Subtly emptied of its contents, it would do.

"You want a snack?"

"I want the container."

Raj's head cocked. "Why?"

"I have to throw out this tissue." She had one stuffed in her pocket. Overnight, with the lights out, the world had suddenly and unexpectedly seemed hopeless. She'd spent a few minutes quietly crying. She was knocked up and didn't know how to tell her dad — either that she was knocked up, or that she and Raj had been having sex. He probably knew the latter because Meyer was an adult and not stupid, especially given how she'd dutifully obeyed his "no dating before sixteen rule" and hence had earned some freedom. But the fact that she'd been letting Raj drop loads inside her was, in retrospect, bafflingly stupid. It had just seemed so hot at the time. You tell a guy to go ahead and cum in you, and it makes him that much happier and sweatier. Like a horny puppy.

It had all hit her around 1 a.m. She had Raj, yes. But really, she was alone. She'd have to tell her dad she'd been having sex, and she'd have to admit she'd been being stupid about it.

Oh, and apparently aliens were coming to destroy the planet or something.

"Let me take it," said Raj, reaching for the tissue.

"I want to throw it away."

"O … kay."

He reached for a shower caddy they'd been using as a garbage can. It was latticework, like a basket.

"Ew, no. I want that one."

"But this is the garbage."

"I want *that* garbage."

Trevor turned. "Jesus. Will you two shut up?"

"I'm sorry. Am I breaking your concentration on …" she looked to see where Trevor was gazing, " … on the back of Piper's head?"

"Shut up, Lila!"

Lila blinked. Wasn't she supposed to be the one with mood swings?

Trevor returned his attention to the front — not past

Piper. Without turning, he said, "Aren't you even a little concerned?"

"Concerned?"

"You know, about Dad?"

Lila rolled her eyes. "Dad's right there. Three cars up."

Trevor apparently hadn't seen him, but changed the subject to avoid his failing.

"Riots spread pretty quickly in a situation like this, you know."

"Like what, Trevor?"

"Panic."

"Uh-huh." Lila looked toward the column of smoke they'd seen earlier, up ahead. It seemed to be in the road and was fairly wide. It was black, like a petroleum fire, but there didn't seem to be any flames. "I'm not seeing any panic."

"Give it time," said Trevor. "It could happen. You don't know what happened up there."

"Broken down car," said Lila.

Raj shook his head beside her. "Look how black that smoke is. Something's burning."

"Why would something be burning?" said Lila.

Trevor looked back derisively. He and Lila had always got along well. It was a shame that he'd become such a temperamental little shit. Just six months ago, she'd have told him all about her unexpected motherhood. But now, it felt like she could no longer trust him with her secrets.

"You're right. Let's look at 'why would' rather than what's right there in front of us."

Piper looked back. The van was long, and she seemed very far away.

"I'm sure it's nothing," she said.

"See, Trevor?"

"She doesn't know any more than you do!" Trevor spat.

"Settle down," said Piper. "Just ... it might be nothing."

"Or it could be a riot." Trevor shrugged. "Traffic jam, someone throws a Molotov cocktail, others pull guns, spreading back toward us until ..."

"Stop it, Trevor!"

Duly chided, Trevor lowered his chin and looked out the side window, away from the windshield where Meyer was marching back toward the van.

He sat heavily in his seat and closed the door.

Piper looked over, waiting for him to speak.

"Something's on fire up there," he said.

"See," said Trevor, his voice spiteful.

Meyer looked back curiously, but said nothing. He continued. "Talked to a guy just now who walked up and helped put it out. Nothing wrong; just a crappy car, too much idling, and a lot of leaking oil. Engine just caught fire. They threw dirt on it."

Piper sighed, sitting back.

"Well, there's more."

"What?"

"The fire, no big deal. Ordinarily, they could just put it in neutral and push it off the road so we can get past. But it's on the bridge."

"Push it off the bridge, then," said Lila.

"Yeah, just chuck it into the Ohio River," said Trevor, rolling his eyes.

"I meant off one end, dumbass," said Lila.

"Lila ..." Piper began.

"Ordinarily, that'd be no problem," said Meyer. "But there's construction, too. Bunch of orange cones up ahead. Someone must have wiped out the merge signs; I saw them lying down up there. But it's three lanes going to one across the bridge, and that's why we were so jammed up to begin with and what caused this guy's engine to go, but now he's smoking up there right in the middle of the single lane."

"Push him forward," said Lila. Trevor shot her a look but said nothing.

"Can't, buttercup. He's packed in, and the guy I talked to said his transmission is frozen. It'd take a tow truck. And even then it'd need to get in, and ..." He trailed off.

Lila's stomach lurched. She caught the swell of illness without giving much sign, but she saw Piper eye her before looking away.

"So ..." said Piper.

"We're going to have to go around."

"How?"

"We'll have to go north." Meyer shook his head, eyebrows drawing together darkly. "That's the thing about coming from Northeast Ohio. Just when you think you've gotten out, it pulls you back in. Like the mafia for Michael Corleone."

"Who's Michael Corleone?" said Trevor.

"You kids today," he said. "Anyone wants to take over Fable in their adulthood, you're going to have to get more steeped in cinema."

Piper was looking to the left, where traffic in the other direction was still creeping past. Lila thought she might say something about making that line of cars stop and using the other half of the bridge. Instead she whined a single word. "Honey ..."

Meyer looked at Piper, then at the eastbound cars.

"No," he said.

"It's like something is telling us to go back. We don't have to go all the way to New York. But I know people in Pennsylvania."

"Pittsburgh is probably a secondary target. Same as Cleveland. I feel like we're wearing a bulls-eye right now, just sitting here."

"No, back east. Fifty, sixty miles. Nice and isolated."

"Who?"

"Yoders."

Meyer laughed. "The Amish?"

It took Lila a minute to make the connection. In the years she'd known (and been financially backed by) Lila's father, Piper's Quirky Q clothing line had made her into a minor celebrity in trendsetting and fashion circles. It was always funny to see where that fashion touched, but one of Piper's favorite stories was about the Amish matron who ordered her dresses by mail, had them shipped to a P.O. box, and wore them secretly under her long black frock. Apparently, her husband never saw her change, and they had sex in the dark, so it was a perfect secret. Rebecca Yoder said the dresses made her feel "alive," but not alive enough to risk a shunning.

"Why not?"

"How are you even going to explain that to her husband? And what are we going to do, Piper? Milk cows until the end of time?"

"They're good people," Piper said in a small voice.

"I'm sure they are. But we have a *bunker*, Piper. An honest-to-God *bunker*, which will shelter us completely — versus hiding out in a grain silo like Harrison Ford in *Witness*."

This time Trevor said nothing, and Lila didn't either, but Meyer still rolled his eyes. Hey, she'd tried. She'd watched all his favorites, both old and somewhat less old: *The Matrix, Memento, Canvas, Bright Lies Big City, The Fountain of Truth, Inception, Eternal Sunshine of the Spotless Mind, Dark City*. She actively liked *The Beam*, which was still airing. But her father was an encyclopedia of entertainment, and his teenage children couldn't be expected to keep up with it all.

"We're not going to hang out with farmers. We need to get to Vail."

"But …"

"End of discussion, Piper." He put his hand over hers — not a cheap gesture for Meyer Dempsey, who seldom showed affection in public. "I love you, and I respect your opinions. I'll do anything for you. You know that. But you have to trust me."

"I do trust you. But …"

"Trust that I'm smarter than the idiots on the radio," he clarified, then glanced at Lila, Raj, and Trevor in turn, and Lila felt some unknown context pass in that look. "And trust that whether or not you believe what I keep telling you — about the puzzle — I believe it. And I know it's true."

Quietly: "What's true, Meyer? What do you think is going to happen?"

"Something," he said. "Something that requires we make it to Colorado, no matter what."

Lila watched the two adults, still feeling that churning in her gut, waiting to see how the power struggle would unfold. Finally Piper sighed and gave a small, press-lipped smile.

"I trust you," she said.

Meyer gave her hand a final squeeze, then tapped the console and rolled the car into manual. He gripped the wheel, shifted into reverse, and expertly jockeyed the JetVan through traffic.

Two minutes later, they'd crossed the median and were heading east — for just a little while, before heading north, and into the unknown that made Lila want to scream.

Chapter Eleven

Day Two, Afternoon
Rural Ohio

TREVOR LOOKED to the right-side front seat, where his father was finally sleeping. It was disarming. Trevor had to keep reminding himself that his dad would be of little use to anyone if he didn't get some rest. He hadn't slept the night before, fueled by nervous energy alone.

Up until running into trouble in Pittsburgh, they'd been stopping at gas stations whenever they found one that wasn't too busy, had its lights on, and didn't seem likely to be harboring more teen hoodlums like they'd encountered back in Jersey. Most of those stations were automated, without so much as a clerk to wave a gun and tell them the provisions were his. But despite the fear of me-first roving gangs and shotgun-wielding clerks, they'd only found a single ransacked Circle K. People were behaving for the most part — something that, again, his father had seen when the bridge had become blocked. There, he'd spoken to others civilly without a single person getting knifed. And despite the way Trevor had been goading Lila, he was glad for it.

Whenever they stopped for gas (keeping topped off for the seemingly inevitable moment when the power grid failed and the pumps stopped working, or gangs took the land), Meyer grabbed coffee. It was all brewed fresh, payable with a swipe as if nothing strange was happening in the world. Caffeine pushed him through the night and well into the second day. But despite appearances and what Trevor felt about his old man, Meyer Dempsey was not an unstoppable machine. He was his son's hero, as cliché as that was, but just another man in the end. Seeing the anchor in their storm unconscious — even necessarily so — made Trevor uneasy. And judging by the others in the car, he wasn't alone.

Lila and Raj were talking secretly, keeping to a two-person huddle. Watching them, Trevor suppressed a bubble of jealousy. He and Lila had always been close, and seeing the way she'd shut him out in favor of Raj hurt more than he wanted to admit. They seemed to be working on something, and twice Raj (not Lila) had asked Trevor if his phone had data coverage. It hadn't either time, but the question piqued Trevor's interest. He'd assumed they kept checking phones to try and call Raj's family, but what was the data for? The van had all the entertainment and connectivity they'd need, thanks to the Mercedes satellite.

Despite the jealousy he'd never admit to — and the loneliness that came with being shut out — Trevor found himself adjusting to the idea that Lila's boyfriend might be with them to stay. Everyone had tried to call his parents — and Mom, for that matter — but no calls were going through. They had data in the van and had tried to send messages that way, via messaging and mail, but there was no sign that Raj's parents were receiving. As usual, Trevor assumed his father had been right. According to the news, the major cities were sparking with chaos: looting, riots, crime. Apparently, there was a big fire somewhere, but he couldn't remember where. So who knew what New York would be like now — in terms of survival, not just Internet service. Thank God they'd fled when they had. Thank Dad for all his plans and decisive actions, whether Trevor bought any of his more new-age fears about culmination and consciousness or not.

The sticky question of Raj Gupta seemed to have ended in permanent stalemate. It was a mistake to take him from home, but they wouldn't leave him alone on the delusion that it was somehow better than simply keeping him with them. Every mile they put between New York and themselves, the more firmly they drove Raj into their family, for better or for worse.

If they made it to Colorado (*when* they made it, he amended; Trevor trusted his father more completely than he'd ever tell Lila), Raj would be moving in with them. They'd stay in Dad's Bunker of Fear, probably eating beans and stale crackers while the world went to shit, with nothing to do but sit in front of Piper's dumb old TV shows and watch Lila and Raj make out.

He looked forward, his attention waning. The road ahead, now that it had grown dark again, offered little of interest. Traffic had thinned, and they'd mapped out a path that skirted Cleveland and the outlying suburbs while still keeping them high enough to get around the problems in Pittsburg and the halo of disorder that seemed to have sprouted around it. Maybe traffic would pick up again. Trevor almost wished it would. Right now, this just seemed like any car trip, with the autodrive tooling along at a

AVERY BLAKE & JOHNNY B. TRUANT

conservative sixty-five despite Meyer's insistence that they haul ass while he was asleep. It was easy to believe none of the past day and a half had happened.

Piper had mostly turned around so she could cross her legs. He'd successfully ignored her while watching his sleeping father in his almost fully reclined seat, but now she saw him facing forward and looked up.

"Hey." She smiled.

Trevor forced himself to meet her eyes, then detour his focus to somewhere near her left shoulder. His crush had always been inappropriate, but the past thirty-six hours had made it clear just how unseemly continuing that infatuation would be. Piper was twice his age; she was married to his father; she was, for shit's sake, his *stepmother*. But that didn't stop her from being the most beautiful woman Trevor had ever known in person, and it didn't help that she doted on him, paid him all the attention he'd ever want.

Trevor was with her for the duration. He was with his father, with Lila, with Raj. Assuming Mom wasn't waylaid, she'd be halfway to the ranch, and blessedly, Trevor was with her for the duration, too. They were all in this together. Their own little ecosystem. He had to make peace with the idea that he'd be locked in with Piper, and that his chances to find another girl and forget her were practically nil. Hopefully, the ranch had porn on the juke. He could form an unhealthy attachment to some slutty actress who took it in all holes. Wouldn't that be a pleasant change?

"Hey," he replied.

"How are you holding up?"

Trevor looked back. The van's relative quiet made it feel like they were alone together, but they weren't. Lila and Raj were up. In their own world, but awake.

"Okay, I guess."

"We'll make it, you know."

"You mean, like, stay alive?"

She laughed — a delightful sound that was as much throat as it was air.

"I meant we'll make it to the ranch."

He glanced at Lila. Then, not wanting to speak but wanting to move things forward and needing to talk to *someone*, Trevor said, "Do you believe him?"

"Your dad?"

"Yeah."

"About the ranch?"

"Yeah. That we have to get there and stuff."

Piper shrugged. Her answer was only half serious. The other half was the pacifying answer you give a kid who won't know a brush-off for what it was. "Where else are we going to go?"

"Somewhere that's not days away." They'd all heard the update on the news. The original estimates held. NASA and the Astral people were in agreement. They had four days before first contact, and that left little wiggle room. It had taken them almost thirty-six hours so far, and they'd only reached Ohio. They were supposed to have taken a plane. They were supposed to be there already. When that was the plan, this made sense to Trevor. The idea of driving changed his opinion in the extreme, trust in his father notwithstanding.

"Where?"

"Anywhere. Get a hotel."

"Your dad doesn't want to get a hotel room."

"Well, maybe we could talk him into it. Somewhere out in the middle of nowhere. Or Canada. Aliens never go to Canada."

"You have a lot of experience with aliens?"

"In movies, I mean."

"Maybe in Canadian movies they go there. Are you sure? Do you want to check?"

She was humoring him. He was slowly moving from infatuated to infuriated.

"I'm serious."

"I know you are, kiddo. But he's doing the best he can. He's a smart guy, and I trust him. Do you trust him?"

Trevor looked back. Now Lila and Raj were listening. Lila nodded first, probably without even realizing it.

"Yeah."

"Then we have to go with that. None of us knows what's going to happen. Your dad was prepared so far, and he'd tell you that in some way, he did know what was going to happen — at least enough to start building a bunker, buy and stock this van, and all that. We owe him a lot right now, whether we understand it or think he got lucky or not. And yeah, we can't know for sure, but it's better than what I knew — or what I'd know to do now on my own."

Trevor nodded.

"We've said what we think," Piper continued. "And we should continue to. We will continue to. Of course. He'll *want* us to. But in the end, he's driven to take us to Colorado come hell or high water, and, well …" She trailed off.

Trevor sighed, then nodded again.

The van was quiet for a long few seconds, save the hypnotic hum of their wheels on the road.

Then Meyer's phone, silent since Jersey, started to ring.

Chapter Twelve

MEYER BLINKED awake to the sound of his ringing phone. For the first moment, he didn't answer. He just stared at his family and Raj. They were all looking his way, vaguely guilty, as if they'd been doing something they didn't want him to know about.

The spell broke, and he snatched his phone, registering that it was Heather when he saw the screen, though his mind didn't really make the connection until her voice was in his ear: decidedly higher-pitched than Piper's sexy rumble, a bit squeaky, rushed with adrenaline as if she were high.

"Heather?"

"Meyer? Thank God. Where are you? Are the kids okay? Hell, is fucking *Piper* okay?" She didn't stop to let Meyer answer. "I've got a little bit of a problem here. Actually, I've got a lot of problems. I forgot to bring my Vellum, for one. When I get to Colorado, will Piper share hers? I mean, if she doesn't mind me seeing her porn or whatever other embarrassing books she has on it. She wouldn't mind, right? Better than sharing her husband." A small, uneasy laugh.

Meyer lowered his voice, peering at Piper, hoping she hadn't heard that. Heather had built a career on inappropriate jokes, but that one was way too close to the bone.

"What's the matter with you?"

"Nothing. Nothing at all. Everything is just great. I'm not even counting days until the world ends."

"Are you high?"

"They're going to get my car, Meyer."

Meyer looked again at Piper. It wasn't clear either way whether she was hearing any of this.

"Who is?"

"Angry gamblers. Elvis's ghost. Those white tigers the gay guys used to perform with. Siegfried and Ron. Was it Ron?"

"Roy."

"See, you understand. This is all very logical to you. So tell me, when you were seeing the bright and swirling colors and the spirit in the sky or whatever told you to dig a hole and get ready for aliens to show up, was there any information on me being *fucking gang-murdered in Las Fucking Vegas?*" Her voice rose into a shriek, seconds from losing control. That's what it took to finally shove Heather out of her on-stage persona: terror.

Piper had heard that one. Her eyes went wide. She started to say something, but Meyer shook his head. He looked out the window ahead, watching anonymous miles of Ohio roads spool out before them. He'd have to check the GPS to be sure, but they were probably somewhere between Cleveland and Toledo. He suddenly resented being woken. The idea was to drive through Ohio at night, ideally while sleeping. He didn't want to see it.

"Calm down. What are you talking about?"

"You know my car?"

"Yeah."

"And you know how I own it? Because it's *my* car?"

"Yeah."

"You know how if someone got it from me without my permission, maybe by stabbing me to death, that would be them *getting it?*"

"How about you just fucking answer the question for once?"

Meyer closed his eyes and exhaled, forcing himself to calm down. He'd kept it together so far. They all had. But they were teetering on a precipice, and at some point someone in the van would stare reality in its unblinking eye. It was easy to pretend there weren't ships approaching from outer space — and to pretend they wanted to reach the Vail compound for an early ski season — but there were harsh truths that all of them had so far managed to nudge aside. He wasn't as immune to that knowledge as he'd managed to seem, and was in danger of showing it now. Heather was in trouble. Beneath Meyer's calm veneer, his fear for her was a blood red warning.

"Is that Mom?" said Trevor. "Is anything wrong?"

Meyer waved him away, then turned forward, now trying to speak quietly, to listen without being overheard. What he wouldn't give for an office door to close.

On the other end of the phone, Heather sounded like she was crying. Not helpless crying — terror crying. Closer to hyperventilation than a quiet sob.

"Where are you? Specifically? Tell me what happened."

Heather spoke again, her voice still hitching but more

contained. For once, she sounded both composed and serious. A good sign. No panic and no jokes — so far, so good.

"Just outside Vegas. I don't know the road. It's all desert."

"Vegas." Meyer took the phone from his ear and squinted at Piper, asking a silent question. They'd heard something about Vegas. Something that, as he thought about it now, tickled the back of his brain with bad news. What was wrong in Vegas? *Something* …

"It's burning to the ground. There are squads of people walking around — not running, but walking, like they're on patrol — and just general fuckery from one end to the other."

Piper was pointing at her tablet's screen, showing Meyer the news update he'd seen earlier, about Vegas.

"You should have gone around it."

"I *went* around it. And …" There was a crashing sound. Heather shrieked, then fumbled the phone. Meyer waited, hearing ambient noise, wondering what might have happened. The line was still open, but what had happened to Heather? A minute later, she was back.

"What do I do, Meyer?"

"You haven't told me what's wrong."

"Because you interrupted to yell at me for getting too close and not following instructions."

"Okay, fine."

"But these … these three Big Daddy Roth cartoons came out of nowhere, all supercharged hotrods with engines poking out of the top and shit, bunch of toothless motherfuckers hanging out all over the place, hooting at me like they wanted to drag race, beat me to death, and peel off my skin, whatever."

"What, they came after you? From Vegas?"

"Two behind me at first, coming up on the side, waving

and hooting and yelling. Then one more pulled up in front and ..."

"Why didn't you stay out in the desert? You got too close to the city."

"Let's talk some about what I should have done! Let's rehash all the shit I did wrong during our marriage! You're always right! You always know best!"

"Calm down."

Another bang. Another small gasp from Heather.

"They're herding me back."

"What does that mean?"

"They're herding me like a fucking cow, Meyer! That's what it means!"

"Where?"

"I don't know. Toward the Strip?"

"Can you outrun them?"

"I'm in a Prius. They're burning premium and testosterone."

Meyer wondered why in the hell anyone driving around Vegas in hotrods would want Heather's crappy little hybrid, but he refrained from asking. *They want the driver, not the car.*

"Are you at least behind the wheel?"

"No. I left it on autodrive. The car keeps beeping courteously at them, asking if they wouldn't mind staying in their lane. And asking me if I'd like to stop at the Arby's up ahead. And that's really the worst part of all of this, Meyer. Why does it think I would ever, in a million years, no matter how many alien ships show up ..."

Meyer felt a strong need to cut Heather off before she finished the sentence.

"You'll have to ..."

" ... *ever* want to eat at Arby's?"

" ... to lose them," Meyer finished.

"Have you ever eaten at Arby's? Like, ever in your life?"

"Stop joking for a goddamned second, will you?"

Meyer's pulse had quickened. He was sweating around his collar. He wanted to wipe his forehead, but that would mean declaring defeat to the universe. Heather was a dozen states away, and this was the only call they'd managed in a day. If she was going to be overtaken, he'd only be able to hear it happen. It was rare that Meyer met a situation he cared about but couldn't control. This was one.

"How am I supposed to lose them?" Not really a question, more a yammering of desperation.

"Where is she, Dad?"

Meyer shook his head at Lila as he'd shaken off Trevor.

"Is she okay?"

"Heather? You're not holding the phone, are you?"

"Dad! Is Mom okay?"

"Yes. I'm also writing an essay and flipping through my dad's old filing cabinet."

"Heather ..."

"Dad!"

Meyer spun. "I *hear* you, Lila! Will you just hold on a goddamned second?"

Lila shrunk back, wounded. Trevor's eyes were wide, shocked, scared. Meyer felt his gut plummet. He was losing control. He was supposed to be the rock, but the boulder was crushing them all.

"Of course I'm not holding the phone. I have the earbud."

"You're in the Prius?" He winced, determinedly avoiding Lila's penetrating gaze from behind, waiting for Heather to make another stupid joke. She'd already told him that she was in the PriusX. She was being surrounded by highwaymen in a high-speed chase, and still she'd take any comedic opening he gave her.

Instead she said, "Yes."

"There's a gun in the glove compartment."

"There's ... no, there's not."

"Just get it, Heather. Put the car on auto, and get it."

Sounds. A clicking noise.

"Why is there a gun in my glove compartment?"

"Because I put it there."

"You know I don't like guns." It was one of Heather's things. Meyer didn't particularly like guns either, and they'd had talks, after some recent school shooting or other, about gun control and waiting periods and the other things that made the NRA so furious. But liberal convictions didn't come in handy when the world was burning.

"You're going to like it plenty right now. Do you see it?"

"Jesus, Meyer." But then, with perfect timing, one of the other cars must have struck her, and there was another gasp. Then she said, "Okay, I've got it. Where are the bullets?"

"In the gun."

"You left a loaded weapon? Right there in my glove compartment?"

The lecturing, naughty-naughty tone of her voice unhinged something. Meyer snapped, "It doesn't do a hell of a lot of good without bullets!"

Piper leaned forward, her head cocking like a dog's. Piper was even more liberal than Heather, tending toward "peace-loving hippie." But there were guns in the van, too, and she'd need to make her peace with them soon enough. It was them or the people trying to attack them. The sooner everyone woke up and smelled the goddamned coffee, the better. The days of peace and love were over for a while — at least until the ships arrived, declared any intentions they may have, and humanity had a chance to get used to it. Or die in fire.

"How do I use it? Just pull the trigger?"

"There are bullets in the clip but nothing in the chamber …"

"What does that mean?"

"If you'd shut up for a second and let me explain, I'd tell you!"

"Okay, okay." There was an odd reversal in the air. Heather was the one with men on her tail, and Heather was the one who'd called in a panic. Meyer was safe, and yet he was the one coming slowly undone. The lack of control was getting under his skin.

He breathed. Tried to reset.

"Hold it by the grip with your left hand, finger away from the trigger. Then grab the slide — the part on the top — with your other hand and pull it back until it clicks, then let it slide forward. Just like in the movies."

There was a loud racking sound on her end of the line.

"Okay."

"There's a little switch on the side. Above the grip."

"Looks like a little toilet flush lever."

"Yes. Keep your finger off the trigger and flip it."

"Now I see a red dot."

"That means the safety is off."

"And now I blow into the end where the bullet comes from, right, like this?"

"Stop it, Heather."

"I'm kidding. Lighten up."

The idea that she was telling him to lighten up, now, was too absurd for a reply.

"Now what?" she said.

"Point it at whatever you want to go away. Then pull the trigger."

"I can't just ... what's that beeping?"

Meyer heard it too. He looked around, then found the source. It was coming from his phone, blinking with a message that said, LOW BATTERY.

He grabbed for his phone, then scrambled for the cord. But the phone had been giving him problems for months now, and he didn't want to send it in to have the battery switched because he needed it. On cold days, it barely worked. More than once on his morning runs as the air had grown chill, he'd slipped the thing inside his shirt to warm the battery enough to keep it alive.

"Meyer?" came Heather's voice, tinny with distance. He could hear her from far away as the speaker left his ear, as he tried to mesh plug with port. "Meyer, they're shoving me off the road. They're making me pull over!"

"Hang on!"

"Meyer, are you there? There's one in front, and I can't get around him, and he's slowing down and—"

"Don't let them pull you over! Don't let—"

The phone's screen went black as Meyer was still fumbling with the cord and port.

The call was broken, and Heather was gone.

Chapter Thirteen

Day Two, Evening
Bowling Green, Ohio

IT WAS LATE.

The roads were quiet, almost deserted. It reminded Piper of her youth, of open skies away from the bright lights of the big city. They'd skirted Toledo to the south and remained on two-lane country roads. The only real signs of activity they'd seen, save the scant illumination inside the living rooms of single houses, was a parking lot's worth of lights on an artery called I-75. There were a few twinkles coming from the south that seemed to be a burg Piper had never heard of called Bowling Green. But otherwise they could have been anywhere.

Piper was still in the left front seat, and Meyer was still in the right. If there was a need to take over manual driving, Meyer would have done it, but so far there hadn't been, and they'd stayed put. Little beyond polite, almost hushed requests had been traded between the van's occupants since Meyer's phone had dropped Heather's call. The ensuing silence seemed to be an unspoken moratorium, or a period of respect, like a moment of silence to honor the dead.

Piper tried to make Meyer feel better. She told him that Heather had a gun. She had it cocked, armed, and ready. Meyer had done that much. Thank God that call had gone through. It was almost too good to be true, as if someone above had made it happen. They hadn't kept the line open, but Meyer had told Heather what she needed to know. There wasn't more he could have done, anyway. If the call hadn't dropped when the phone died, it would have merely offered an auditory window into whatever happened next. It wouldn't change a thing. Meyer couldn't help any more than he already had.

And there was an unspoken corollary that Piper didn't want to say aloud, though she hoped Meyer was aware enough to understand: Yes, they might have heard Heather's victory over her pursuers. They might have heard her vanquish the bad guys and get away. But there was also a fair chance that they'd have heard her beaten, robbed, raped. Hearing that would do nobody any good, particularly her children. If bad things were destined to happen to Heather (and Piper did believe in destiny, whether she admitted it to Meyer or not), then it was best for those things to happen where no one could hear them. It sounded terrible, but it was true: if today was Heather's day to die, it was best that she die alone.

Meyer wouldn't speak. He wouldn't answer her well-meaning consolations. He stared out at the dark road, into the cone of the headlights, his square jaw set, his green eyes hard and forward. A tiny part of Piper was jealous of that stare: of her husband holding vigil for another woman. But that was selfish thinking, and the larger part of Piper knew better. Of course Meyer still loved Heather, in a way. They'd been together for long enough to have two children. They were still great friends. And although it hurt Piper deeply to think about it, she strongly suspected they weren't as separate, romantically speaking, as they strictly should be. Meyer took a lot of business trips to LA, and he always came back with news of Heather for Trevor and Lila. She'd called his hotel once when he'd been on a trip, guiltily, knowing she should give him his privacy. The clerk had confirmed Meyer Dempsey's reservation and rung her through to the room, but Meyer never answered despite her night of trying. She was sure he stayed with Heather. Or maybe that had been petty jealousy talking and she should grow up. Be better than this.

She looked over at him now, unsure whether she should take his hand, lean on his arm, or otherwise try and tell him that none of this was his fault. He hadn't kept the phone plugged in, no. But he'd shepherded them out of New York. He'd urged Heather out of Los Angeles. He'd even inadvertently managed to save Raj — and Piper was indeed beginning to suspect that was a "save" situation. She'd tried to keep the van radio off out of concern for frightening the kids, but she'd been surfing news on her tablet compulsively, and felt sure that Raj was in a better place now than he'd otherwise be. They all were.

Las Vegas was burning, from one end of the Strip to the other.

New York had decayed into riots. According to reports, about half of Manhattan's power grid had failed. That fueled the riots further.

The major cities had all reported looting, especially once night fell. There were a lot of people in those cities, and many had nothing more than a small home or apartment and barely enough food to get by. If the power failed and stayed off, it was only a matter of time before the water stopped flowing or became unsafe. Everyone wanted food; everyone wanted water; everyone wanted fuel. Those were the commodities people needed when the bedrock underfoot became uncertain, as it was now. Some hoarded what they could. Others fought to take it away, to make sure that if only a few could survive as new supplies stopped circulating, they'd be among them.

Haves versus have-nots, reduced to the level of eating or starving.

And yet here they were, in their luxury van, touring the country in style. Despite seeing little to fear out here in America's hinterlands, Piper couldn't help but feel they were wearing an enormous target on their backs. Tomorrow would mark forty-eight hours since Astral had first seen the ships approaching. The resolution of the images the telescope continued to show (the government couldn't stop them if it wanted; that particular cat was quite far out of the bag) only made the arriving objects seem that much more ominous. They were visible on some of the light telescopes now as recognizable objects, no longer relegated to blurry radio images. But even small and distant, the ships (if that's what they were) were horrifyingly neutral. They weren't all edges and turrets and flashing lights. They appeared to be perfectly round, perfectly smooth spheres — gray, if the colors on the distant images could be trusted.

Tomorrow, if estimates held, there would be just three days left. People would wake (if they managed to sleep) with the feeling of wasted hours. They'd panic a bit because of the time that had passed, the miles covered by the approaching armada in their sleep. And soon, they might start to notice the big flashy van. They might start to hoard fuel from more and more gas stations, siphoning from the tanks of even the remote, fully automated stations they were lucky enough to keep finding.

It wasn't a matter of *if*, but *when*. They'd run out of gas sometime, finding themselves unable to fuel without an audience. Maybe once or twice, they could manage to get their gas and go. But as more time passed, those crowds would consider what the clean, fed, well-dressed family in the rich-man's van had that they didn't. Then there would be problems.

Meyer seemed to be thinking the same, and in the past half day he'd taken to buying a few extra five-gallon jugs of gasoline whenever they stopped at a station that stocked them. Those extra cans were in a storage compartment in the back, but even that made Piper nervous. What if they were rear-ended? Didn't all that gas make them like a bomb on wheels? And even if they did have the gas, how would they use it if the streets filled up? You couldn't fill a tank from inside. You had to get out, so they'd need to find isolated spots to do it. What if they simply drove through an area too congested to pass? Then the fuel wouldn't matter; crowds could surround them and take the van, fighting among themselves for its spoils. And come to think of it, how did you gas up from a can? Did they have a funnel?

She shook the thoughts away. Those were worries for another time. Or maybe for never. If they stuck to small roads, maybe they could drive all the way to Vail without incident. Maybe they could avoid the crowds entirely. She tried to do the gas calculation in her head, wondering how many extra jugs of fuel they'd need before they stopped needing gas stations at all. But the wheels' song on the road made her tired, and the night's pall was heavy. She could figure it out later, or let it go and trust Meyer. He'd been right so far.

"I'd like to drive," he said. She realized that he'd been watching her for a while.

Piper looked at the console. The car was driving just fine by itself.

"I need something to do." Then, heartbreakingly, he added, "Please."

Piper stood without speaking, feeling something come undone, and switched places with him. Meyer was polite, but never begged. Piper wouldn't have refused him the driver's seat under any conditions, but even at the most extreme moments — in far bigger negotiations over things that actually mattered — Meyer didn't plead. If he couldn't have what he wanted, he let it go.

His "please" sounded like an appeal.

Piper's feeling of assurance — of trust in Meyer — slipped a notch closer to desperation. Once behind the wheel, his control restored even in the most useless of ways, he seemed to straighten and harden. Within minutes, it was easy to forget the pleading eyes he'd had earlier — not about something as silly as driving, but about his guilt over Heather, over fears he couldn't and wouldn't dare articulate. He was Meyer Dempsey again. And Meyer Dempsey always got what he wanted.

They drove that way for an hour. Two hours.

As the dashboard clock approached the wee hours, traffic started to swell — some unknown Indiana city on the horizon, perhaps. With more cars on the road, Meyer seemed desperate to drive faster. The van kept beeping to warn him about his speed, and he ignored it with a steely gaze forward. The kids were asleep in the back, but they woke to his aggression.

He cut in. And out. And in again.

Horns honked. Tires screeched.

He was driving like he had something to prove.

"Dad …" said Trevor. But then he stopped, and said no more.

Piper gasped as Meyer cut between a car and an SUV that had been dutifully sticking to their lanes. Meyer grumbled as if their adherence to proper driving and safety was a hassle, or a weakness.

A horn blared behind them.

"Honey," said Piper.

"These fucking people," said Meyer.

"Maybe if you just ease back, and …"

"The sooner we get there, the sooner I can ease back."

"But we're nowhere close. We're just in Indiana."

"Exactly. We're nowhere close. Which is why we have to make up time."

"Maybe we should rest." Then, inside her head: *Maybe you* should rest. *Maybe we should all just step back for a bit.*

A near collision with the rear of a Buick. The van swayed, then surged into a gap. From the back, Lila lost a tiny scream.

"You're scaring us."

"It's not me doing the scaring, Piper. I'm trying to do the saving."

"Then you need to slow down."

"Slowing down doesn't get us where we need to be. I'd rather you were scared now. Because we should all be scared of what's coming."

Piper was usually docile, but now she felt her eyebrows bunch, her forehead wrinkle. "Shh. You'll frighten them."

The van nudged the rear bumper of a silver car ahead. The car swerved, corrected, then drifted far away from the big vehicle and its crazy driver. When Piper looked over she could see the woman on the car's right side looking over with big, vacant eyes.

"Oh, I'll frighten them, huh?" Projecting: "Hey, kids.

Guess what? Aliens are coming, and we're hauling ass to get to our doomsday bunker." He shook his head at Piper, lowering his voice. "They know it already, Piper. Pretending nothing is wrong will only make us stupid."

"And do stupid things like driving like a maniac?"

Meyer laid on the horn, then cut left. A second car swerved to avoid him. Piper was reminded of her father driving years ago when she'd been little, back when all of the cars had been manual, and the true test of a man's patience had been to put him behind the wheel in heavy traffic. Her father had consistently failed that test, and Meyer was failing it now.

"Let me handle this, Piper."

"You'll handle us into a collision."

"I'm trying to get us where we need to be."

"You're angry."

"I'm angry because we're not where we need to be, and everyone here is out for a Sunday drive."

"Slow down, Meyer."

"Every minute we waste ..."

"The bunker in Vail doesn't do us any damn good if we're dead in a pileup, Meyer!"

Meyer looked over, his fugue momentarily broken. His eyes hardened again, now fuming atop the rage.

"This is my van, my plan, and I'm the only one here who's willing to ..."

"Look out, Dad!"

Meyer's eyes snapped forward as Trevor yelled, and he saw the back of an enormous RV looming ahead. It was stopped. The entire line of traffic had stopped, and Meyer hadn't seen it coming. Nobody had.

He wrenched the wheel hard to the right, apparently deciding that rolling the van was preferable to smashing it into the RV's back end. But they were skirting a hill that climbed to the right, and the wheels rose as momentum tipped in the same direction. The two forces seemed to cancel out, and the van remained on its spinning rubber feet. Meyer hit the brakes and jockeyed the wheel back to center, holding tight, letting up between brake pumps to prevent an imminent skid. They struck the guardrail and grated along it for maybe fifty feet, raising sparks and a grinding noise like the end of the world.

Then it was over. The van had stopped on the berm still six feet from the dead line of traffic. A man in a tan Oldsmobile was staring at Meyer as if he'd just committed a crime.

Meyer laid his hands on the wheel, his head on his hands.

The road had turned into a parking lot.

They were all going nowhere.

DAY THREE

Chapter Fourteen

MEYER IS STANDING in the middle of a plain filled with long grass so green it's almost neon. It flows with the wind, but the motion is too perfect. It's moving in waves, but the waves seem artificial, as if in a computer-generated effect in one of his movies. Only instead of producing this movie, he's in it. He's the star. He's in this field of perfectly waving grass, and the grass is so green it's almost lit from inside. The whole world is green, except for the sky, which is a perfect uniform blue from edge to edge, bunkering against the edges of this infinite field.

A caricature of reality rather than reality itself. A landscape drawn by a child.

There's someone beside him. It's Heather. Company on his journey, possibly holding his hand in the real world, beyond this vision. Meyer confronted his demons as he always does, facing his mother and father, who he watches die every time. This time he watched himself slit the throat of Sam Blackwell, Heather's comedian friend. Not new, but never pleasant. He doesn't always murder Blackwell, but he's done it often enough.

The medicine is supposed to wash you clean, but first it must dredge the worst of what's inside you to purge it. In real life, Meyer is never jealous of Blackwell or the way the media acts like he's in dalliances with Heather when they share a stage. And he shouldn't be, because he has a new wife, and Heather should be able to sleep with whomever she wants — not that he believes she's sleeping with Blackwell.

But he must be jealous somewhere deep down, because more than once he's found himself wrist deep in Blackwell's blood, pieces of spleen and heart clinging to his shirtsleeves. More than once he's taken Blackwell's head entirely off, and once he saw himself reach up through the ragged neck of the severed head, somehow meeting gray matter from the brain below.

This time, merely slitting the man's throat feels like a vacation.

"It's so beautiful," says Heather, her small hand in his, her voice light and more serious than it is outside of ayahuasca's kiss.

"It's too beautiful," Meyer replies. "It's not real."

Heather smiles. "Of course it's not real."

"It's not real in reality," he says.

Heather smiles again and walks away. She's never understood.

This isn't even the real Heather; even deep in the medicine's grip, he knows their minds haven't truly connected. Heather, unlike Piper, likes to experiment. Piper won't travel to Colorado to see Shaman Juha with him. She wasn't interested in his soul trip to Peru, seeking the source. But Heather always has, and finds ayahuasca to be a real gas. But she's never believed the way Meyer has. She's never seen. His connections (and the months of clarity that follow) always seem to lift the veil for him, but never for Heather.

The scene changes. Now he's not in a field. He's on a path above Machu Picchu. He's never been to Machu Picchu, but all places are the same once you realize that no things are actually real in reality. Once you learn the trick of cinema, it's easy to go anywhere at all. Seeing a movie of New York every day, seeing a movie of Machu Picchu the next. There's no difference. The only reason he's never "been to" Machu Picchu, he now suspects, is because he's never *decided, within the privacy of his own mind, to be there instead of New York, or anywhere else.*

Heather is beside him again. Now she's naked, but the thought isn't arousing. It's simply how things are. Heather's skin is no more who she is than her clothes. His own skin is no more who he is than this is Machu Picchu in front of him.

"You found your axis once," she says, her black hair swirling in a gentle wind. "Now find it again."

The cliffside doesn't crumble. It simply vanishes. And he's falling, falling, falling ...

His EYES SNAPPED VIOLENTLY OPEN, as if they'd been glued and he'd just won the battle to see. He felt a sense of departure — of being robbed of something that mattered. Meyer remembered something, just now, about Heather. He'd been with her. She'd been nude, as she'd been beneath him the last time he'd been in LA. Her body was different from Piper's. Good, but not as young, as toned, as firm, as gravity defying. But their connection, even from the beginning, had always been more mental than physical. They had their fun times, but Heather often joked that if only their minds could fuck while their bodies stayed put, she'd be up for trying. It would beat the burden of guilt, as if mental cheating wasn't a lie.

Must've been a sex dream. He'd woken with a cast-iron boner.

Piper was looking over at him. She was just to his side, up on one elbow on the makeshift bed in the converted berth, the partition curtains drawn. Meyer hadn't loved the idea of closing the curtains when they'd pulled into the park last night, taking the exit at Piper's insistence to wait out the line of stopped traffic and get some rest. He'd thought Lila and Raj might use the opportunity to get dirty, but Piper reminded him that Trevor was back there too. And nothing cockblocked quite like a little brother.

"I see you're happy to be awake," Piper said.

"I'll be happy when we're driving," he said, rising.

"The kids are still asleep," she said. Her fingers were walking across his chest, down his flat belly.

"That doesn't matter," he said.

Her walking fingers reached his erection.

"It matters a little," she told him.

Chapter Fifteen

Day Three, Morning
  Rural Indiana

THEY WERE on the road a half hour later, the curtains
back, the bunk reconverted. As predicted, the kids hadn't
stirred even a hair. Piper had peeked through the partition,
and Meyer, a little concerned by the close quarters, had
looked back too. She'd told him that no matter what, he
needed to relax. She'd joked that if aliens were coming, the
human species might need their help. He'd reminded her
about his vasectomy, but she'd climbed atop him anyway,
promising to be quiet.

They were out of the RV park and onto the two-lane
road below the highway before Lila, Raj, and Trevor so
much as lifted their heads. Meyer had traced the road's
course last night after they'd pulled into the park, theorizing that they might be able to get down and around the
obstruction through some tricky turns and creative naviga-

tion. It would cost them distance, yes, but might save them time.

They didn't need to test that hypothesis; the highway turned out to be entirely clear. Piper worried that it would simply fill later, and that they'd find themselves stuck between exits if it did. But Meyer, having traced the long route around, decided the risk was worth it. The sooner they made Chicago, the sooner they could get past Chicago — something that, due to the metropolis's sheer enormity, gave him pause. But once they solved Chicago, they should be home free. There would be people who decided to cross the flat heartland bound for nowhere, sure. And once they reached the mountains, it was true that a blockage could be crippling. But chances on those roads — to Meyer at least — seemed far better. They'd be over the hump with maybe sixteen hours left to drive at highway speed. Plenty of room to spare if they ran into trouble.

They'd slept later than Meyer would have liked (he chided Piper for not waking him earlier, but it was hard to stay mad when he could still taste her), and by the time they were on the road the sun was strong behind them. Meyer let the van do its own driving, turning into the cabin to avoid the light flashes in the rearview. Then he waited, content for the first moment in what felt like forever.

It won't last, he thought.

But nothing *lasts*, said a countering voice inside.

There was something else, too. Something about what he saw rather than felt — about reality rather than lasting and persistence. Maybe something from his dream. Maybe something to do with the haze of his latest ayahuasca ceremony still percolating in his blood. It was the only drug Meyer took, but it was plenty. The effects lasted, and lasted, and lasted. Months afterward, he'd feel above the fray, looking down on his life, able to see connections that were obviously true, but that had somehow remained invisible before.

This was like that. He'd been putting something together behind a curtain for years, it seemed, but he had no idea what it was. He was like an inventor working with a blindfold. He knew he was building a grand contraption (in this case, a vision of previously unknown truth), but until the blindfold came off, that contraption would remain invisible, and the truth unknown.

With the thought, he thought anew of Vail. Of the compound he'd been compelled to have built. Of the van he'd been compelled to purchase and stock — a second vehicle to his everyday ride. Of the plans he'd been compelled to make. Of the move from New York he knew they'd make once school was out. Of the paranoia he'd felt for too long.

Had he really known this was coming, or was it coincidence?

"Hey, Dad," said Trevor, blinking awake. He yawned and stretched. A strange thought struck Meyer: For almost two entire days, Trevor had been sitting in that same chair, rising only for the bathroom. None of them had even left the van last night. They'd locked down, and someone had stayed awake at all times. Even at gas stops, Meyer had been the only one to exit the van since Jersey. Could it be bad for Trevor to sit for so long? He was a growing boy, after all.

But that was just morning reverie. Dream hangover. Nostalgia, perhaps. Meyer was forty-three, and sometimes it was hard to believe he wasn't twenty years younger. And yet he'd somehow aged, with a daughter nearly as old now as he felt deep inside.

There was another vague flash from his dream —

something to do with Heather's nakedness, her skin, his skin. But it was gone like dandelion fluff in a breeze.

"Hey, kid," Meyer said to Trevor. Then he looked at Lila, who'd woken in Raj's arms. She straightened. He added, "Morning, princess."

"Dad," she said, smiling. "Don't call me that."

"I can call you anything I want." He returned her smile.

"Dad," said Raj.

"Don't call me that," said Meyer. But for some reason Raj's joke struck him as funny, and he laughed a little. They really must be exhausted. Not spent in terms of needed sleep, but emptied by fear. When you heard an alien invasion was on the way, you freaked out. But as nothing new happened hour after hour (except for people in cities losing their shit — different issue), that freak-out state became harder and harder to maintain. A person, it seemed, could get used to anything in time.

They drove all morning. Through noon. The kids demanded to stop for food as they had the past two days, but Meyer still refused. The van was stocked, and they could add to the stores whenever they found more opportunities to stop for gas. The idea that restaurants would be doing business now was ludicrous anyway. Was he just supposed to pull their survival van up to a McDonald's drive-thru, roll down the window, and order four value meals? Anywhere they stopped would be closed at best, likely raided, and possibly lousy with desperate people looking to take what they had the moment the Dempsey family gave them a chance.

They picked at the van's provisions, complaining. Watched more movies and TV shows from the van's juke, bored and restless.

Finally, as they began to skirt Chicago and traffic

started to swell, Piper said what Meyer had already been thinking.

"Maybe it would be a good idea to check in on the news. Just a little."

Meyer nodded. He didn't need convincing. *She* was the one who kept trying to protect them from unpleasant truths.

Piper touched the screen, then tapped the news station. An announcer's voice filled the van in a rush, and she jabbed frantically at the console to lower the volume.

" … in scattered locations," the announcer began midsentence, "but the National Guard reports that incidents of crime have been 'within expectations and manageable.' Spokespeople for the Guard have praised the population in general for their 'restraint and level-headedness.' Still, fires continue to burn out of control in Las Vegas and parts of Chicago. Here's William Quincy, National Guard."

"Chicago?" said Raj.

Meyer shushed him. He was more interested in what they had to say about Vegas, as a heavy ball of guilt returned to his gut. He wasn't superstitious, but suddenly his dream of Heather last night felt like an omen. When was the last time he'd dreamt of Heather? Her appearance in his dream now seemed ill timed. Was she dead? Was she a ghost, returning to warn him like Jacob Marley shaking his chains?

It's just because she's on your mind. Don't be stupid.

And that, at least, was true. He couldn't go five minutes without thinking of Heather and what might have happened to her. It was a real-life cliffhanger. He found he didn't enjoy them nearly as much in the flesh, and needed resolution more desperately. And the worst thing? If something had indeed happened to her and she didn't show at the ranch, he'd probably never know. What news outlet would report on one woman shanghaied when the planet was crumbling?

The station cut to another speaker — apparently a snippet of a previously recorded interview.

"We believe several fires were set deliberately — particularly in the Hard Rock Hotel & Casino and the Luxor. Due to its pyramid shape, the Luxor fire seems to have remained within the hotel's walls, but the Hard Rock fire spread readily, caught dry vegetation outside, and was deliberately perpetuated as rioting increased, building upon itself. Now it's kind of become a free-for-all. Police and Guard are focusing mostly on containment and crowd control, and a staged plan to isolate one area at a time and allow fire crews to do their work."

The station cut back to the original announcer.

"Meanwhile, the president's office has issued a statement promising the 'full cooperative powers' of all aerospace and space agencies to the United Nations. The UN is meeting today to enact emergency measures not just to prepare for contact with the approaching objects, but to ensure that all civilian needs are attended to globally, and that citizens are given 'all appropriate assurances' that this matter is being looked into at the highest levels."

"That's a lot of words that say nothing," said Trevor.

Meyer couldn't help but smile. His thoughts exactly.

"Further analysis of the approaching objects by NASA scientists have revealed new information about their shape, size and number. NASA has reserved some of that information in the interest of national security, but appears to be sharing data globally. Here's NASA Spokeswoman Holly Fletcher."

"At this point, we can tell that there are approximately two hundred objects approaching Earth, each about the same size, spherical, and thus far seemingly featureless, with a diameter of around two or three thousand feet each."

"Shit. That's about a half mile," said Meyer.

The radio continued. "At this point we're unwilling to speculate as to the origin or nature of the objects, other than that they first came to NASA's notice about the same time they were spotted by Astral Laboratories and disseminated broadly to anyone using the company's application, just beyond Jupiter's orbit. It's unclear at this time whether the objects were in transit beyond that, but as Jupiter itself is made of gas and exhibits a rather strong gravity well, it seems unlikely that the objects originated from Jupiter itself, as some Internet 'experts' have claimed. We can neither confirm nor deny whether they came from one of the moons at this point and are unwilling to speculate.

"However, given their tremendous speed — somewhere between three and five million kilometers per hour — it seems possible that they may have a source external to our solar system. Among the questions we're similarly unable to speculate on are whether the objects are manned, and if so, how beings with a constitution remotely similar to ours could survive such a trip. In space, relativistic considerations aside, velocity itself is trivial, but it's clear already that the objects are decelerating, and the G-forces on anything braking that fast — plus any effects that whatever is *causing* them to slow (boosters, rockets, whatever) might have on Earth — would be exceedingly arduous for …"

"That's enough," said Meyer.

"No it's not, Daddy," said Lila. "I want to hear about the aliens."

"They said they 'won't speculate' on aliens."

"There *have* to be aliens," said Raj. "What, they're just giant space marbles? Someone had to build them."

"What if they are just giant space marbles?" said Trevor. "You know, nobody in them, but …" He made a marble flicking gesture with one hand and then made the other hand appear to blow up — a remarkable demonstration of someone cue-shotting Earth from the sky.

"It said they're slowing down," said Raj.

"Maybe they'll just slow down enough. Then …" Trevor made the flick-explosion gesture again.

"They're only a half mile across," said Raj. "Not big enough. Although if they were moving fast enough …"

"And there's two hundred of them," Trevor said.

"Could be like with the dinosaurs. How big was *that* meteorite?"

Trevor: "I thought it was a comet."

Raj shrugged. "Well, whatever, same deal. They could just raise a big dust cloud. Kill all life on the planet."

Lila's eyes were huge. They were looking at Meyer, pleading for something. It was the look of a lost little girl, not a seventeen-year-old who seemed to increasingly crave her independence and distance.

"Raj. Trevor," said Meyer. He patted the air, easing them down.

"Not us, I mean," said Raj with the air of correcting a big misunderstanding. "We'll be underground. Unless one hits right on top of us …"

"But man, three to five million miles an hour? That's …"

"Kilometers per hour," Raj corrected.

"Whatever. Point is, how does something that big brake that hard? They'd have to fire boosters, right? Wouldn't that — just the boosters! — knock the Earth out of orbit or something?"

"The Earth is huge, man. Do rockets taking off from the ground push the Earth out of orbit?"

"Yeah, but these are bigger and faster."

"Maybe their boosters will just burn our faces off," Raj suggested.

"Boys!" Meyer shouted. He inclined his head toward Lila for Raj's benefit then spoke calmly, mainly toward Trevor. "We can guess all day long, but even NASA doesn't know. All that matters is that we need to be prepared."

"But for what?" said Raj. "Annihilation or occupation?"

"Or both," said Trevor.

"Doesn't matter," said Meyer. "You can't know, so stop guessing. You'll make things worse. You're scaring your … your stepmother." He looked toward Piper, apologizing for deferring to save Lila embarrassment. Piper was equally horrified.

"I'm just wondering what the plan is," said Raj.

Meyer looked at the boy for a long moment, considered reminding him that he shouldn't even be on this trip, then decided to let it go. The chance to drop Raj off had vanished a long time ago. He was with them for the duration, and if the Guptas survived and life somehow returned to a parody of normal later, he could return their son then, safe and sound.

"The plan is to drive until we …"

The van was slowing.

Meyer turned.

They were in the middle of the expressway, every lane slowing to a stop. A Volkswagen pulled into place beside them. A Land Rover settled on the other side. Meyer glanced at the rear camera's screen and saw a wave of vehicles slowly closing them in from the rear.

He'd thought they had another hour at least before reaching anything remotely resembling Chicago traffic.

They were nowhere near the city limits, and the land around was still mostly suburban, bordering on rural.

They'd been planning to exit the main road far in advance and detour around, taking winding roads through the boonies. It would cost a lot of miles, going that far around Chicago, but it was better than being stopped like … well, like this.

Meyer looked to the cars ahead, to either side, and piling in a long metal line behind them.

They'd entered Chicago's orbit while the car had been on auto, discussing the end of days.

They were boxed in, and this time it looked permanent.

Chapter Sixteen

DAY THREE, Early Afternoon
  Outside Chicago

THE NIGHT HAD BEEN COOL. The day was warm. Somehow, the van's heat and the proximity of other cars radiated into the cabin enough to make Lila sweat.

Or maybe it was the hormones.

She wasn't sure. It was terrible, feeling all the changes inside herself and having no idea what to do. Was this what it had been like for her grandparents, growing up before the Internet? How had they answered all their questions about the world? Back then, if a girl got knocked up, she'd have to ask her friends (who might have bad information) or her mother (with obvious downsides), or she'd have to hit the library and find the right book. Even then, the lost little girl with a bun in her oven would need to fear being seen and discovered or stay ignorant. Like Lila was now.

Did you get hot flashes when you were pregnant? If so,

did it happen this early? She knew women got uncomfortable later in their pregnancies, when the baby's internal heater turned on inside them. But did it happen so soon?

This was intolerable. Lila might have to risk searching on one of the tablets. If Meyer saw she could say she was … researching to write a book or something.

A cruel joke. Lila had known all about sex since she'd been thirteen, had played around at fourteen when she and a boy could be sure of being alone (mostly over-the-clothes stuff, though a few times she'd let guys feel boob) and had finally popped that cherry at seventeen. Given the way most of her friends had dated from fourteen and started having sex around fifteen or sixteen, she thought she'd done a damn good job. How could her father be upset with her restraint?

Except that she'd been knocked up in a kind-of-preventable way. They'd been spontaneous that first time, and blowjobs didn't require birth control. So Lila wasn't on the pill, and they didn't have condoms. They could have simply stopped and not done it, but that option was only obvious in retrospect. At the time, it would have been absurd. You didn't stop when you felt that itch between your legs. You found something to put in there to scratch it.

Which were, interestingly, probably the exact same words her father would use when berating her for being so stupid. He'd never call her a slut or a whore, but he might call her idiotic. Or retarded. Or "smarter than that." That last one was the worst of all. Many of Lila's friends didn't get along with their dads, but Lila had always adored hers. The idea of disappointing him was far, far worse than angering him.

To make things worse, Lila was sort of a hypochondriac. Not in a big, ridiculous way, but she did tend to be suggestible. Once she'd seen a TV show where a character had a brain tumor. She'd decided she might have one, and had developed headaches until she'd scheduled a scan. She always exhibited flu symptoms when her friends did. Lila was the kind of girl who gets thirstiest only when she realizes her bedside glass is empty.

They hadn't moved in hours. She pulled the phone from her pocket, mentally reminding herself to charge it again soon, and looked at the time.

FOUR hours. They'd been stuck in this prison of vehicles, surrounded and totally unmoving, for four whole hours.

Being trapped in the van when they were moving was boring. They'd been in here for three days now, and she'd felt restless after one. But if being trapped while driving was bad, being trapped while stuck was so much worse. She felt a creeping sense of claustrophobia, almost unable to breathe. That might be part of the warmth.

Partly because it was warm.

Partly because she was pregnant.

And partly because she was a mental basket case and didn't like the walls around her.

Jesus. What kind of a mother was she going to make? It looked like that's where things were headed, like it or not. She and Raj had ditched school and absconded to Central Park to talk it out, but the talking had mostly been on Lila's side. She'd told Raj she was against abortion (for herself, anyway) in one breath, then changed her mind in the next. Her personal pro-life stance had always made sense, but then again she'd never been pregnant.

Regardless, it's not like she'd have a choice to be "pro" about. If they didn't get crushed from above, become enslaved, or have their faces burned off by alien braking rockets, she'd be spending the next several years underground. Where she was sure her claustrophobia wouldn't be a problem at all. Where there weren't going to be any abortion doctors.

Maybe she could use a coat hook. Or fall down the stairs.

Both ideas sounded painful and gross, and besides, it's not like she wanted the baby gone quite that bad. She'd just have it. No big deal. One of the upsides of the apocalypse was that she'd be shut in with babysitters twenty-four/seven. Piper loved babies; she'd love to watch it. And on the plus side, her boobs would get bigger.

Meyer said, "We have to leave the car."

Lila looked up. Trevor said, "What?"

Piper picked up the same refrain. "Leave the car? We can't leave the car."

Meyer shook his head. "There's no choice. No other way. We're blocked in."

Lila said, "We can't just go out there, Dad."

"We can't stay in here either."

Lila's pulse started to rise. He was serious. How could he be serious? He'd stocked this van for the end of the world. This was his paranoid bunker on wheels until they could reach their permanent paranoid bunker. If they left, they'd not only be stranded — they'd be vulnerable. They'd be exposed, subject to whoever was out there and whatever hardships awaited. They'd have to carry food and water on their backs. They'd never reach Colorado.

"You wanted to get to Vail," said Piper, as if he hadn't remembered.

He raised his hands to gesture around at the traffic jam, at the van, at the world. "What do you want me to do, Piper? It gets harder to get to Vail without the van, yes. But if my choices are moving slowly and having options or staying here forever, I'll take moving slowly."

"But how ... ?" Piper began. There was no more to say.

"Look," Meyer said, addressing them all, "I don't want to leave it either. But we have to face facts. *Four hours*, it's been." He tapped his wrist, but wasn't wearing a watch. "And that's four hours *since we moved last*. It didn't just slow; it *stopped*." He held up one of the van's tablets. "Traffic reports aren't exactly to the minute, but I did find an hour-delay Google Earth shot that shows a river of metal all the way through Chicago from around here. We can take our chances and hope that it's moved since that shot was taken, but I kind of doubt it, and I don't think it's going to start moving any time soon."

"So we go around," said Trevor. "Like Pittsburgh."

"We're boxed in, Trevor. Even the berm has filled up. A million cars behind and a million cars ahead. We're in the center goddamned lane. I don't know how we'd get out even if everyone agreed to set aside their personal needs and try. Everyone's impatient. Almost literally bumper to bumper. When I was out walking around before, I could barely squeeze between cars." He shook his head. "This van would have to be a tank to get out of here, and shove everyone aside."

"No chance you were quite that prepared, huh?" said Raj.

A tiny smile touched Meyer's lips. "Not quite."

"But ... all our stuff is here!" said Lila.

"We'll have to carry what we need."

"And we're ... we'll never get to Colorado that way. Where will we stay?"

"We'll find a car. The world hasn't ended, Princess. People are just scared. It's not like money's lost all meaning."

"Don't call me that!" Lila blurted.

Everyone looked at her. Were mood swings typical this early in a pregnancy? Another thing she didn't know. Maybe she was getting her period. But then she remembered that wasn't exactly possible, and couldn't believe there would ever come a day when she'd actively miss the Red Menace.

"I know it's scary," Meyer said carefully. "But it's our only choice. This car will be here for weeks if it's not here forever. And we only have days."

Piper put her hand on Meyer's shoulder, speaking quietly. "We'll have to stay here somewhere. Find … I don't know … an abandoned barn or something."

Meyer gave a half nod, but Lila had seen that face on her father before. Tacit agreement, meant to get what he wanted in the short term. She'd bet money that he hadn't come close to surrendering his quest. He was doing whatever it took to get them out of the van now … and get them to do the rest of what he wanted later.

"Sure," he said.

"Better than the van, stuck in traffic," said Piper.

"Of course."

"Wait a sec," said Trevor, and Meyer almost rolled his eyes. "Is it? If we're going to bunker in a barn, why not just bunker here? Four walls —" he knocked on his window for emphasis, "— stocked pantry. Bathroom."

Meyer shook his head at Trevor. "For now, but there are two problems with that plan. Eventually, even with the gas in back, we'll have to stop the engine — for no other reason than that the people behind us won't tolerate choking on our exhaust forever. And without gas, the batteries will run down. That's the entertainment, the plumbing, the heat, and A/C."

"So? We'll still have all our supplies."

"That's the second problem with your plan," Meyer said. *"We'll still have our supplies."*

"What about it?" Trevor asked.

"Eventually, someone else is going to look at this big, fancy van and think the same thing."

Chapter Seventeen

Day Three, Afternoon
  Outside Chicago

BY THE TIME they exited the van, the rather mild-mannered, everyday people in the stopped line of cars were looking at the Mercedes with interest. To Trevor, they looked like dieters facing a pile of donuts.

Those people were mothers and fathers, office drones and carpenters, people who worked for the gas company checking meters, and people who laughed at awkward jokes in romantic comedies. They were the people Trevor had lived among all his life and passed every day. And yet, two days wiser about the ways of the universe and the fact that humanity wasn't alone in it, he thought their resolve was crumbling. They were civilized folks with ordinary lives, but something inside seemed to be telling them that the van was full of what the world might soon be fighting over.

They looked hungry. Right now, they were holding it

in. Right now, they were on their diets. But that might not last, and they might turn from ordinary people into animals.

Trevor's pack was surprisingly comfortable. It was well-balanced, the weight inside it close to his body and low. His father had cinched the shoulder straps tight and told him to fasten the extra strap around his waist. With everything tight and adjusted, Trevor found his shoulders and hips carrying the weight, not his back. He could walk this way. Which was good, because he'd had to.

Everyone wore a pack. Meyer had handled everything, from end to end. He'd retrieved the packs from the JetVan's compartment; he'd stocked them; he'd made sure everyone was cinched tight and carrying enough but not too much. Meyer carried the most. But he told Trevor quietly that he was carrying the second most, and in the moment Trevor found this strangely touching. Raj was seventeen, but skinny and sort of a whiner. Only Trevor, at fifteen, could be trusted to be the group's second man.

Meyer told everyone what they had in their packs before they stepped outside, but it was a blur to Trevor. He knew that his father's paranoia was at work again — although he'd packed them as a unit, everyone had enough to survive for a while even if they ended up on their own. There was food, water, a filter or a purification kit or something … Trevor couldn't remember. Survivalist shit. A packing and preparedness list straight from websites prowled by his father, stirred with all he knew by being Meyer Fucking Dempsey.

Lastly, everyone carried a weapon. His father's was a pistol, out of sight tucked under his shirt at the small of his back. Trevor waited for his own gun, excited even during this exodus into the End of Days. But Meyer said he didn't want Trevor "shooting his own ass off" or otherwise providing enemies with potential threats or weapons to use against him. He gave Trevor pepper spray, same as Lila, Piper, and Raj. It stole wind from Trevor's sails, and made his pack seem heavy, not necessarily responsible.

They exited with packs on their backs. Heads immediately turned. None of the ordinary folks sitting on their cars' hoods and trunks asked if they were leaving, but their eyes did. Still, they said nothing, attempting to stay ordinary.

Meyer locked the doors, but left the transmission in neutral in case traffic began to move and others decided to push the JetVan out of the way. He stuck rocks under two of the wheels as chocks to keep it from rolling without permission.

Then they squeezed toward the berm, past the double line of cars that had massed on the road's edge when traffic froze and ambitious drivers tried to pass. Heads turned, but only for a moment. They weren't the first to leave their vehicle and walk. They were just the best equipped, with their four matching backpacks and a fifth that didn't quite belong.

They followed the highway for a while — long enough, Meyer said, to get a feel for the gridlock. If he'd been wrong and the traffic jam ended a mile up, they could still turn back. If there was an obvious way out, they could try again, waiting for traffic to figure it out. But so far, nothing.

Trevor watched his father whenever he began to feel nervous. He did the same thing on airplanes when turbulence shook the cabin. Bumps made Trevor anxious, but as long as the flight attendants were calm, everything was probably okay. Same with his father. If he seemed calm and in control, they were fine. For now.

The mood was strange. Dad had been right about what he'd told Lila earlier: Nothing had really happened yet, people were just scared. There were no aliens around the planet. Nobody was enslaved or decimated, nobody'd had so much as a single anal probe. Nothing had crashed into the Earth's surface, raising a dinosaur-killing cloud of dust to block the sun. The planet hadn't been knocked off its axis or sent hurtling into the nearest star.

It was a lot of people trying to get from one place to somewhere else. That was it. The Dempseys were headed to their reinforced bunker in Colorado, but where were all these people going? Why didn't they stay home? What about a few photos from a space app made them think that Duluth was better than Des Moines? Why did they want so badly to get from Toledo to Muncie?

It was fear, making people do something so they wouldn't have to sit around doing nothing. His father said it gave them the illusion of control in the face of something unknown and uncontrollable. The same reason they'd hoard gasoline. Why did people run to gas stations when strange new things happened? Were they planning to run the doomsday generators that nobody actually had?

Well, nobody but Meyer Dempsey.

After an hour, they took a break. The GPS said they'd gone just four miles, but given Dad's determined jaw, that was good because it was four miles closer to Colorado.

Only 996 miles to go.

But surely this was just part of the plan. Phase One, as it were. Meyer must be planning something else — some other way to get them moving. What it was, Trevor didn't know. But he knew that the nods he'd given Piper earlier, when she'd suggested bunkering down in a barn, were his way of humoring her. He'd get them to Colorado. Or — and Trevor feared this was literally true — he'd die trying.

Still, Trevor could see his father's mental wheels turning. He was running a ceaseless calculation, based ultimately on making their destination. Every minute they spent stopped or walking was a minute lost on the drive. If they were stopped now, it was only so they'd be able to walk faster later. And if they were walking at all, it was only so they could find a new vehicle as quickly as possible. Everything was a trade. A giant game, where beating the clock was their ultimate goal.

Wait now, hurry later.

Or try to hurry now … but ultimately remain stuck.

There was a balance, and Meyer was always working it. Bide their time to find the perfect transportation at the ideal time. It would be worth slowing down now to move fast later. But they didn't just need a car. They needed a way out of Chicago.

Every minute spent checking the GPS for alternate routes was chewing through battery power — which was no longer unlimited, and would last only as long as the external batteries they all carried.

After a few minutes high on the banked berm (Trevor thought his father was allowing distance in case someone broke formation and decided to come at them), they rose, reshouldered their packs, and walked toward a freeway exit ahead. They were only halfway down the exit ramp before Meyer stopped. The rest of them stopped behind him.

Piper looked at him.

"What?"

"We're closer to Chicago than I thought."

Piper looked to the city center clearly visible on the horizon. "We knew that."

"I screwed up. We should have left the highway a long time ago."

Trevor looked into the sky, where the sun had passed its apex. They'd come to a stop over five hours ago now, and it was into the afternoon. "A long time ago" could mean anything — distance or time.

"And?" said Piper.

"These neighborhoods are far too urban." He looked down the exit ramp. "I'd rather stay on the highway, now that we're this close to the city."

"Isn't that a little racist?" said Lila.

"It's about population density, Lila. And resources. We don't really want to be caught hiking through somewhere low on resources but high on people while wearing these packs."

Raj looked ahead at the highway's parking lot. "Lots of people up here," he said.

"Lots of stocked cars," Meyer replied. "Lots of people from out of town. A crowd always defaults to its average, Lila. The people up here still have what probably feels like enough. Down there? Maybe not. All it takes is one group to decide they should take what isn't theirs. It's like tossing a match. Flick that match into an environment like this highway, I don't think it'll catch quite. But a lot of these neighborhoods are dry grass. Someone decides to start a riot, others are likely to agree."

"I think we should go through, hike away from the city, and keep going until there's some open land," said Raj. "Wasn't that your plan?"

"Sure. But I thought we were farther out. We spent too much time arguing about the end of the world and weren't paying attention."

"Meyer ..." Piper began.

"I think we should go," Raj said, looking down the exit ramp. "It's still pretty bright out."

"No offense, Raj, but I don't really care what you think."

Raj looked up, offended.

"Feel free to go down there. But my family is going to keep following the expressway. We'll take one of the other arteries south. Another expressway. For now, there's still safety in numbers."

"There's only five of us," said Lila, holding Raj's arm.

"I meant numbers of cars. Of people driving on the expressway."

"You mean white people," said Lila.

"That's not what I mean, Lila."

"I agree with Raj. You said it yourself. Nothing has even happened yet. Everyone is worried about themselves right now. They're not going to do anything to us."

"Exactly," Meyer said. "Everyone is worried about themselves right now."

"The sooner we leave the highway, the sooner we're away from Chicago. You want to go closer. Look, Daddy!" She pointed toward the city center, where Trevor could clearly make out the Sears Tower. The expressway seemed to curve directly toward it.

"Not yet," said Meyer.

"You're the one who said we'd buy a car! How are we going to even *use* a car up here?"

"We'll buy one later, Lila. But if we're dead, a car doesn't ..."

"Hey," said Piper.

Meyer stopped, but his eyes stayed certain.

Raj faced him, looking defiant. Lila was at his side. They looked like they fancied themselves as Romeo and Juliet: two lovers facing off against authority, knowing stubborn love would conquer all.

"I'm going this way," said Raj. "It's stupid to keep walking toward the city."

"Suit yourself."

"I'm going with him, Daddy."

His voice was even, cold. Trevor knew he was calling Lila's bluff, but his words still chilled Trevor to the bone. "Go ahead."

They stared at each other for a few still moments: Raj and Lila on one side and Meyer on the other. Piper and Trevor were neutral, watching with wide eyes to see what would happen.

Finally Raj shook his head, exhaled dramatically, then marched up the ramp past the others. After a bit, Lila followed. They were ten feet farther down the packed expressway before Raj turned and said, "Well?"

Meyer began walking without expression, but when Trevor looked up he could see him smirk.

"Dad?" Trevor said after they'd been walking for a while, once Lila and Raj were ahead and out of earshot. "Not that I'm questioning your idea or anything, but we *are* walking right into the city … ?" He let the sentence hang, his final note begging an answer.

"For now. We can cut south in a bit, on one of the big expressways; I'd have to check to see which. We can cut down to 80. If that's not clear, we can get off then. It should be safer, assuming the shit will keep from hitting the fan for just a little longer."

Trevor felt another note of respect radiating from his father. First he'd given him the second-heaviest pack, and now he was casually swearing. He sometimes swore around his children, but it was rare that he'd swear when talking directly to them — the way he might talk to an adult. Or a colleague.

"You're not worried about getting off the road then, assuming the sh …" But he couldn't echo the word to his father, not yet. "… assuming that doesn't happen quite yet?"

"There will be less of a crowd. There should be more people who aren't desperate."

"But they could still be … you know … going crazy?"

"Yes, but more numbers means more problems, all other things being equal. Not just because there are more hands to hold weapons, say, but because people are stupid when they're in crowds, Trevor. They stop thinking for themselves and just ease into whatever everyone else is thinking. We need to stay where people aren't thinking too crazy yet, or where there are fewer people."

Trevor looked at the never-ending line of cars. He knew Lila and Raj had already raised this objection, but it sure seemed like the expressway was the wrong place to be if they were looking for smaller numbers.

"It'll be fine." Dad wrapped his arm around Trevor's shoulders. "Nothing bad will happen to us up here. Not with all these out-of-towners with full cars, in broad daylight."

But he was wrong.

Fifteen minutes later, the riot started.

Chapter Eighteen

Day Three, Afternoon
  Outside Chicago

THE RIOT BEGAN WITH A CRASH, then blazed like wildfire.

Meyer was walking the berm, Piper in front of him and Trevor far off to the side as if avoiding her, sullen as usual. Lila and Raj were twenty or thirty steps ahead, still quiet and radiating defiance. Raj had been beaten down about the exit, so he was pretending to lead the group to reclaim what little he could of his dignity. He had Lila beside him. Right now he'd be warring for her attention, trying to establish himself as the superior male. But Meyer was mature and patient enough to see it for what it was: pomp and chest-pounding. Let Raj fluff feathers for his girl. What Meyer said went, and would continue to go. Raj wasn't supposed to be here. He could stay and enjoy Meyer's supplies ... but only if he kept his head down and obeyed when it mattered.

Without warning, an engine flared to violent life somewhere in the middle of the jammed traffic ahead. A high-pitched squeal of rubber on pavement was followed almost immediately by a muted crash. A grinding noise, then another squeal of tires — this one slightly less piercing — and another crash.

Heads were turning all around, peering toward the commotion like fans in a stadium. Profiles become the backs of heads. To the edges, he could see faces: dumb, vacant, vaguely frightened yet somehow intrigued. He looked back toward the commotion, where those closer were beginning to swarm like insects. Someone shouted. There were a few smaller banging sounds — many metallic, like striking sheet metal with a sledge. Many were more muted: a wooden bat striking wood. Or dirt. Or meat.

There was a high-pitched scream. Pain or desperation.

They skirted the watching crowd. Meyer had one arm around Piper's shoulders within seconds. He put his other around Trevor once he'd dragged Piper over to reach him.

They had to stay back. The something was none of their business.

The crowd shifted, and Meyer saw what had happened. Someone in one of the middle lanes seemed to have reached his breaking point. He'd revved his engine and plowed into the vehicle in front of him. Then he'd reversed and struck the car behind. Meyer watched the car lurch again, striking the red sedan from the rear and making it jolt forward, butting into a white SUV two cars up. The sheer momentum of the kamikaze was opening a hole in traffic.

Now the car seemed to be jockeying around, trying to edge sideways. As if he could barrel his way through four rows of cars and escape to the berm, where he'd have to off road for his life.

Again, someone screamed.

Under it all, Meyer thought he could hear a low, furious, animal growl: the car's driver, screaming, out of his mind.

Most of the people around the hole in the crowd had backed up, but some had been bold and moved forward, striking the car with whatever they could find, even if it was only their fists. One man in jeans and a light jacket jumped on the car's hood, then held on while it attempted to shift around. But it was stuck somewhere; the engine roared, and the wheels spun in place, now raising a thin line of black smoke.

The man on the windshield pounded the glass, which was already webbed and starting to shatter. For a few moments, he was alone — the lone man among the spectators willing to act. Then his will seemed to spread, and others climbed on the car, like ants on a lollipop.

Whatever had been pinning the car broke free with a clang. It skidded forward, this time canting sideways. It struck a small car to one side. The impact's force threw the vehicle sideways.

There was a woman's scream. Meyer could see activity different from the rest: flailing arms, a head whipping dark hair around in pain. She'd been pinned.

"That woman is hurt!" said Raj.

But Meyer was watching the crowd shift. More people were moving forward. They weren't precisely coming to help. They were coming forward because others had, and because it was what the group mind had told them to do.

"We have to go," said Meyer, now looking toward the berm: a gap in the freeway sound barrier.

"That woman is pinned!" said Raj.

A cold switch flipped inside Meyer. "Not our business," he said.

Someone had retrieved a tire iron from his trunk.

Meyer watched the man run forward and smash the battering ram's window. People near the inner circle watched it happen, then moved. Other trunks. More tire irons. Meyer saw baseball bats, possibly fetched from children's luggage.

Individuality in flight, the previously separate minds in the crowd were becoming a hive.

"But she's hurt!" Raj was already moving forward.

"Come on." Meyer was up on the berm, holding onto Piper and Trevor as if he might drop them. He made his hand, around Piper's upper arm, into a beckoning wave. "Come on, we have to get out of here."

Raj threw a venomous look back at Meyer. "We have to help her. If we don't, nobody will."

It was true. The woman was still screaming, but she was already mostly forgotten. The surging crowd's attention had focused on the car, which had now stopped, engine running, windows smashed in one by one. Hands reached into the cab. Dragged the driver out and down to the concrete. In circles around the commotion, others began to move.

Someone else started their engine, apparently inspired. Another crash. Another surge of angry retribution.

They had minutes. Seconds, maybe.

It was going to erupt. Very, very soon.

"Raj!" Meyer shouted. "You can't do anything!"

The woman had stopped screaming, and could very well be dead. She might have been nearly cut in half by the collision, or stomped to death by the hands converging on the troublemaker. But the freeway's motion wasn't all altruistic. More engines were starting. More people were now trying to smash their way out, hoping to break clear and outrun the crowd's ire by storming down the berm. Each time they did, people turned toward them, now instructed by the group mind as to a defector's appropriate fate. And while some tried to run and others taught them bloody lessons, a third group began to creep around abandoned vehicles, toward trunks left open after weapons had been grabbed.

Looters. Opportunists. Apparently, not everyone felt they had enough after all.

Raj threw Meyer a final angry look, then sprinted into the crowd, headed for the epicenter. Meyer's eyes met Lila's. He dragged his two prisoners forward. He could see brainwashing taking hold in Lila's brown eyes. She watched Raj depart. She watched her father.

Then she ran after Raj.

"Shit! *Lila, get back here!*"

But she couldn't hear. A gun fired. It must have been to the right, because Meyer watched a bubble form as people scooted backward. But the bubble lasted only a moment before the bubble became a huddle. There was another shot before the pile formed, but then the crowd piled on, and if Meyer had to guess, he'd assume the shooter no longer held his weapon.

New movement in the line of cars had compressed the gaps to nothing in places, opening wide spots elsewhere. Lila was climbing over hoods, chasing Raj, who was far more nimble. She seemed to be shouting his name, but Raj either couldn't hear or wouldn't listen.

Meyer rushed forward, leaped over a hood, and nearly managed to get Lila by the back of the shirt. If he could grab her, he'd treat her like cargo, drag her back, kicking and screaming. He'd force them all away, and Raj could fend for his motherfucking self.

But he missed. She squirmed past.

Trevor was yelling from behind. Piper was behind him, her hands on his shoulders. Both had flinched to follow, but

Meyer shouted and gestured for them to stay back, to stay far back.

The crowd surged like a monster. Meyer could feel the ebb and flow, its collective lack of intelligence like a swarm waiting for something to sting. Ripples had spread as far as he could see, and now nobody was really just standing around.

Some were stealing what they could.

Some were defending what they had.

Some were desperate for escape.

And some — perhaps obeying some deep-seated instinct of forced conformity — were chasing down the runners, taking them to the ground.

Nobody was just a mom or a dad anymore.

Nobody was just an office drone or an employee of the gas company.

Now they were fingers under the control of some collective beast.

"Lila!"

Her head twitched, but she surged forward. Ahead, Meyer saw Raj trip as he tried to cross a stopped car and fall. He'd be trampled. If he was, so be it. For Meyer, it was good news in a twisted way. She'd stop after reaching Raj.

Another gunshot.

Another broken window.

A small woman, perhaps in her late fifties, ran past with a flat of bottled water. She tripped. A moment later, two other women were over her, kicking and grabbing for bottles.

"Lila! Goddammit, forget him! We have to get out of here!"

Meyer had studied riot behavior, and knew he was doing exactly the wrong thing. You didn't run toward the center. You didn't go against the flow. You didn't move more quickly than you had to. You were supposed to keep your head down, keep your emotions under control, and move steadily toward the surge until you could slip away. But he wouldn't leave without Lila.

Something grabbed Meyer's shoulder. He turned to see a man with three days' stubble, a duffel over his shoulder. In one hand, he had Meyer. In the other, he had a knife. It looked like a kitchen knife, nothing meant for fighting.

Meyer didn't hesitate. In a situation like this, logic and emotion were awful ideas. He didn't look into the man's soul and wonder if he was a good person who always donated generously to the local orphanage. He didn't try to reason. The man was holding the knife as he probably always had: in preparation for cutting a steak. Meyer, however, had trained.

He grabbed the man's wrist and twisted hard, then used his free hand to punch the man hard in the gut — the place that would incapacitate him most completely but do the least damage to Meyer's hands, which he anticipated needing in the days ahead.

The man fell. Meyer plucked the knife from his hand and planted it in the side of a man approaching from the other side, wielding a pipe overhead.

He climbed over the last car between him and where Raj had fallen. But he didn't have to leap the last vehicle; a brown streak was racing toward him. Meyer raised the knife again, its tip red, but the streak was Raj.

He didn't seem to see Meyer. But he did have Lila by the hand.

"Raj!"

Raj scrambled. Climbed. Meyer climbed at him. Into another flow. Panicked. Not being invisible; not obeying the rules of a riot.

"Raj! Lila!"

140

Lila turned. She punched Raj's arm, and for a moment he looked like he might keep pulling forward, ripping it off as he dragged her behind.

Then he stopped, chaos erupting around them.

"Keep your goddamned head down," Meyer hissed. "Move with them, not against them. Don't make eye contact. And don't fucking run. You'll make yourself a target."

Raj nodded slowly. They followed the crowd like a river. Then, with an exhale of relief, they found themselves free, to the side of the road, safe to dart back through the noise barrier as soon as they found Trevor and Piper.

"Dad!"

Meyer looked up to see Trevor running at them. His eyes flicked to Raj, who was dirty and smudged with what might have been someone else's blood, and at Lila, who seemed knocked about but unhurt.

Meyer swept Trevor forward, shepherding the three of them like sheep that might yet flee.

"Get back." He pointed. "That way. Stop once you're outside the wall, Understood?" Meyer stared into each of their eyes in turn, forcing them to acknowledge and nod. They were mere feet from the line of cars. So far, they weren't interesting to the crowd. But that would change.

"Okay," said Trevor.

"Where's your stepmother?" Meyer's eyes scanned the berm, the short grassy hill rising from the gravel's surface, and finally the wall behind which Piper must have hidden.

A horrified look crossed Trevor's face. He glanced into the growing riot.

"She went in after you," he said.

Chapter Nineteen

Day Three, Late Afternoon
   Outside Chicago

PIPER KEPT her arms close to her body, huddled tight around her core, trying to present a small and innocuous target. The surrounding crowd, in the two minutes or so she'd spent in its center, had grown into something alien and ugly. She'd listened to Meyer's diatribes about human nature, rolling her eyes in a way he claimed to find charming. But now she believed every word.

Civilization was a slippery slope, built on a fragile consensus.

Everyone on the highway had behaved for as long as they thought everyone else was doing the same. No threat meant no need for defense. With everyone so obedient, there had been no need to question whether enough was enough. Society would continue. There would always be stores full of food and Starbucks with overpriced coffee.

But the bubble had popped. The first person had

disobeyed, and one by one those around them had realized their security was thin gauze atop a gushing cut.

A man came at Piper. She thought he might hit her, but he was only trying to pass. She turned to watch him, thinking that might have been the direction where Meyer and Lila had fled. But the man tripped in his rush and fell forward, racking his face on a car's bumper. He didn't miss a beat; he hadn't fallen completely down and when he resumed running Piper thought he must not have struck the bumper after all. But then he turned to look back, his eyes vacant, and she saw that his mouth was a mask of blood, teeth black in his maw, tilted inward as if punched that way.

Her heart was beating like a hummingbird's. She looked around, afraid to move, waiting for Meyer and Lila to show of their own accord. She didn't see them, then stepped forward again and found the object the running man had tripped over: an old man, his white hair painted red, reclining in a small puddle of blood.

She resisted the urge to scream.

Stay calm. You have to stay calm, Piper.

But she couldn't stay calm. Piper hadn't meant to be a hero; she'd started forward only because she'd seen Meyer almost snatch Lila by the back of her blouse. He'd had her for a fraction of a second, and in that fraction Piper had meant to move forward and help, to grab her from another angle, to haul her back.

But then someone hit her from behind as they passed. She'd moved away, then moved away again as the crowd surged in a different direction. Behind Meyer, an opening formed, and she followed, feeling it safer to stay with him than attempt to cross the newly formed river of rioters to her rear. Piper thought he knew she was there, figured they'd stay together or at least fall together. But moments later, that proved untrue. She screamed for him to wait, but a wash of looters surged between them. Once they were through, Meyer was gone.

She'd turned, looking for the best way out. That had been a mistake.

She'd rotated back to front, and lost her orientation. She hadn't noted the cars around her and had no landmarks. There were too many people, and Piper wasn't tall enough to see above them.

Get up high.

But how?

The cars. Stand on one of the cars.

Piper clambered onto the trunk of a Chevy Delirium, pausing to let a family squeeze by.

Piper put one foot on the bumper, heaving upward, suddenly very aware of her own presence. She was a small woman, twenty-nine years old, not angry or even confrontational by nature. What if the other rioters noticed her, and saw that she didn't belong?

The thought was bizarre enough to be funny. Nobody here belonged. There was a fat man in a cardigan to one side. A group of teens wearing concert tour shirts to the other. Screaming men and women who looked like accountants, clerks, out-of-shape office workers.

Her breath short, fighting panic, Piper climbed. She was above the crowd for less than two seconds before her ankles were grabbed. There was a yank, and she fell hard, landing mostly on her ass, feeling her teeth rattle.

"You're on my car," said the man who'd tugged her down. He looked as mild mannered as they came, wearing a light-blue shirt and a tie with cartoon dinosaurs, as if this were just another quirkily dressed day at the office. Piper found herself wondering about him, fascinated in spite of her terror. This morning, the world had awoken knowing ships were arriving from outer space. Had he not heard? Or was this how he dressed every day?

"I … I'm sorry."

"You can't ride with me." His voice was uneven, as if throttling his terror. Behind him somewhere, a shot was fired. He wore small round glasses. His manner was precise, almost polite. This man had knocked her down? It was impossible to believe.

"I was just trying to get a look around."

She edged back, nodding at him, their discussion over.

He moved forward. "I lost my wife."

"I'm sorry."

"I don't know if she's dead. I mean I *lost* her."

This was bizarre. She wanted to flee. She wanted to find Meyer and Lila. She never should have come into the crowd. She'd been up for long enough to know the berm was behind her.

Piper glanced back to see if the way was clear, but when she looked forward again, the man was in front of her.

"You look like her."

"Who?"

"My wife."

Looking back. No openings. He took her by the hand, almost tenderly. She snatched it away, and a snarl formed on his face. But then it was gone.

"I can get you out of here," he said.

"I'm fine."

"Really."

Piper didn't reply. She pushed forward, but was rebuked by a man with a bat. He didn't come after her; he brushed past. Somewhere nearby, a new engine started, then roared.

His hands were back on her, harder. This time she couldn't shake him off.

"You can ride with me. It's okay. Come on." He began to drag her backward.

"No."

"Come on." The car she'd stood on was either his or he thought it was. He took one hand off her wrist, then used the other to open the back. It was a smaller model where, in autodrive, the front seats could rotate backward to make a conversation space in the middle. The seats were that way now. Plenty of room for Piper in the middle.

She tried to kick at him. He dodged.

"It's okay," he said. "I have room for you. I'll save you."

"Let go of me!"

"Shh," he said. "It will be okay."

Something large barreled through the space. It hit the man full-on, hard. He fell to the ground under the newcomer, his head rapping hard on the concrete.

"Run!" Meyer shouted.

The man's hands were flailing, trying to free himself. He landed a strike in Meyer's crotch — cheap shot, but enough to give him a shoulder off the ground. They rolled. The hands struck at Meyer's bigger form. Then they came out with something else — something the quiet man had found in the small of Meyer's back, under his shirt.

The gun.

Meyer didn't slow while the man raised the weapon, fingers fumbling in a knowing way at a switch Piper assumed was the safety. He raised an elbow and planted it hard in the man's neck. The pistol skittered toward Piper. She picked it up — safety off and loaded, if she'd understood Meyer's earlier instructions to Heather.

She remembered something else he'd said and racked the slide, moving a bullet into the chamber.

The man had moved atop Meyer, his forearm across Meyer's throat, squeezing.

Piper got to her feet. She held the pistol forward with both hands.

"Get off him!"

Meyer kicked, moving the man's forearm off his throat.

The man with the tie seemed to notice something he hadn't seen before and reached for it: broken glass — from a bottle or something, not a car window. He snatched it and swiped at Meyer's face, nicking the side of his neck, drawing a small red line.

"Shoot him!" Meyer shouted. He pushed with his foot, levered into the man's chest, and raised him enough to present Piper with a clear target. She'd never fired a weapon and didn't like them at all, but doubted she could possibly miss.

His arms were long enough to slash, despite his disadvantaged position. He opened a fresh wound on Meyer's shoulder through his shirt, then barely missed stabbing his eye. The man's face stayed strangely precise, as if he were trying to thread a needle rather than opening a throat.

"Shoot him, dammit!"

But she couldn't.

Piper moved forward and kicked him instead. It was a poor strike, distracted by a crashing noise close by. It knocked the pinning hand away for a moment, but the hand was back a second later.

The man's gravity must have shifted enough to give Meyer what he needed. He rolled his assailant to the side with a heave and slammed him against the car's open door. Meyer scrambled up, glanced back to see if the man was down enough not to follow, then snatched Piper by the arm and dragged her into the current.

Thirty seconds later, the fray was behind them. The man in glasses hadn't followed. They were up the berm and through the gap in the sound wall after another thirty, their backs to the riot, temporarily safe.

Piper looked over, her breath coming in giant gasps.

"How did you find me?"

"I saw you stand up. On the car."

She wanted to ask other questions, to say more. Instead her vision blurred with surprising tears. He'd found Lila and Raj. He'd retrieved Piper. He'd come back and saved her life. He'd done all he'd promised from the start, and more.

Piper gripped Meyer in a death hug, burying her face in the comforting smell of his shirt, his body, the adrenaline sweat of fear and aggression.

"Something you need to understand, Piper," he said.

She looked up, her vision still blurred. His handsome face, his hard jaw line, his serious green eyes.

"The rules are different now," he said. "Any time you hesitate, you fail. Any time you don't do what you should at this point, someone dies."

In her mind, she saw the man with the tie and glasses — an ordinary fellow driven to madness. He didn't seem like he'd normally have hurt a fly, but if not for Meyer's intervention, he would've hurt her plenty.

She hadn't been able to pull the trigger. To end a life.

Even though he'd have ended hers, and almost ended Meyer's.

It seemed for a moment as if Meyer would wait for her to agree, but instead he offered them each an echo of his earlier look, following the exit ramp argument. The look that asked if the group agreed to follow his orders, without second-guessing.

"Let's go," he said.

Piper looked at the group, somewhere between a second authority and a true follower. Raj had somehow lost his pack. Lila and Trevor had kept theirs, so had she despite all the tussling. But Meyer's had been split and mostly emptied somewhere along the way.

He looked back once, his eyes repeating the summons.

Then they set off through the rundown neighborhood on the outskirts of Chicago, their supplies half-gone, as the first signs of evening brushed the sky's light.

Chapter Twenty

Day Three, Evening
  Chicago

LIGHT FAILED SOONER than Lila expected.

At first, she hoped it was only the clouds and that daylight wasn't bleeding from the sky. She looked at Trevor, seeing him meet her eyes, maybe thinking the same. A message seemed to pass between them. She was looking to her brother rather than Raj, as she always had until he'd entered his moody phase. Trevor's face made her regret the reversal.

Her brother was as nervous as she was. And just as afraid of the dark.

Remembering her father's earlier warning, Lila walked the streets warily, fingers tight on her tiny vial of pepper spray. She kept pressing the trigger's top ridges into the meat of her finger, ready to spray anyone who approached. Ready to defend her family, while staying together.

She wasn't sure what had passed between Dad and

Piper in the crowd, but his warning about hesitation seemed to carry weight — an unspoken agreement and a stern reminder to someone who'd done wrong once and should be careful not to do wrong again. And even though the message wasn't really for Lila's ears, she was determined to heed it.

Things really had changed. For two and a half days, the world's air had seemed electric with potential, but until now it had remained *potential*. The riot proved that things were falling apart. And if it really ever did come down to her family or someone else, Lila was all too willing to defend her family.

Her left hand stole to her belly, almost of its own accord.

All of her family.

Still, despite what Meyer had said at the aborted exit ramp, the neighborhood around them had thus far been much quieter than the highway had been even before the riot's eruption. Houses were small and shoddy, paint peeling and windows hung with mismatched curtains. The power was still on, and at least that was something — some reminder of the civilized world Lila felt they were increasingly leaving behind. But the people stayed inside, if indeed they were even at home. It was possible they'd all fled.

They heard a few shouts on two separate occasions as they crossed the massive sprawl, both times they steered far away, content to never know what might be brewing.

A few other times, they'd almost run directly into groups of people out in public without knowing they were there. They'd skirted these too, but with far less warning. To Lila, as they passed and peeked between homes and across yards bordered with jangling chain-link fence, they looked like *gatherings* — the diametric opposite of what her father had warned them about, in terms of roaming, rioting, looting groups. She'd see old people sitting in chairs in front yards, more people behind them on the old houses' long wooden porches. Others were in the yards to the side. Some milled; some stood as if watching. Many held weapons. But in one of them, a charcoal grill had been lit, and she'd smelled the scent of meat on the air. There had been light chatter. Civilized. Nothing to fear.

But as they moved farther from the expressway, that almost optimistic mood began to sour. Light bled from the sky, turning it yellow and orange and red, then finally dark blue and purple like a bruise. Neighborhood light seemed to drain. Fewer windows were lit. Many structures were boarded, dark as pits. Trevor suggested breaking into one for the night, seeing as they had nowhere to sleep and even streetlights were scant. The night harbored terrors — or, to humanize the threat — lowered inhibitions about theft and violence. As Meyer had said, they had supplies and were wandering around in a place where people were used to having little.

The idea sounded good (if terrifying) to Lila. She wouldn't be able to sleep in a creepy abandoned house in Chicago's underbelly, but at least they could hide.

But her father shook his head, not even slowing when Trevor indicated a suitable candidate. Breaking in would make noise — drawing more attention, not less. They might find that someone else had already bunkered in, and the resulting territory dispute could erupt like two dogs fighting over a bone. And most importantly, Meyer's tone implied — was the issue of escape should something go wrong. If they broke into a dark house, they'd be boxed in. If anyone entered to see what the travelers had worth stealing, they'd be trapped with no way out.

No, he said. They would only shelter in an abandoned home if they absolutely had to.

So Piper — tentatively, as if suddenly deciding that her place, after the riot, wasn't to ask questions — asked what they would do for the night.

Meyer said, "We'll walk."

After untold hours sneaking through the dark, the moon finally rose. Lila glanced up to see reality like never before. The moon had always been this thing above — a round yellow object that waxed and waned each month. Now she saw it for what it was: a rock floating through space, fathomless emptiness yawning into a lonely eternity. The thought made her cold. Lila found herself imagining the approaching alien ships, picturing them as they'd picture each other, from sphere to sphere: objects by themselves in a vacuum, with no ground nearby to stand upon.

The vacuum's horror seemed to descend like an oppressive weight. Lila felt crippled. If not for the Earth's atmosphere — and the comforting illusion of uniqueness and home it offered her planet — they'd all be floating through cold and empty space as well, prisoners on a giant rock.

Eventually, the air grew cold and strange enough, stirred by threatening noises, that they decided to abandon the road for shelter. The area had dwindled bit by bit into something semisuburban, sprawling away in places to empty expanses and groves of trees. They were edging the outskirts. Gangs might be roving in the neighborhoods to the road's left side. But woods beckoned to the right as the lesser of evils.

They found a small shelter — possibly a fort built by kids. They lay down, huddled against the chill, and said little other than goodnights, knowing a good night was impossible.

Lila wanted to ask her father about his plan for tomorrow. They needed a car, and his obsessive drive toward Colorado meant he hadn't surrendered the idea. But the plan had supposedly been to buy one, and after the riots, Lila couldn't imagine anyone selling something as valuable as a car or fuel. Or not stripping them of all they carried the moment they entered the neighborhood to ask, perhaps raping the women for good measure.

Lila told herself she was being paranoid. There were still good people in the world. Not everyone could have lost their mind — not when so little, other than a threat, had even happened.

Yet.

She closed her eyes, trying to forget the thoughts that swirled behind her eyelids.

The road had grown infinitely harder.

They had no car, no way to travel.

There were over a thousand miles to go, and only two days before the armada of spheres filled the sky.

DAY FOUR

Chapter Twenty-One

DAY FOUR, Early Morning
  Chicago

THEY WOKE TO SCREAMING.

At some point overnight, a critical threshold had passed. Amateur astronomers could now see the alien ships with backyard telescopes. Meyer later learned that this change (and its aftermath) had made the news — but as they slept uneasily in the woods, their only indication was riotous yelling, braying horns, and the crashing of metal on metal. Seeing those ships crystallized the threat, and the world lost its mind.

Lila jerked awake. Meyer was already up, sitting, a hand hovering above his daughter's shoulders, ready to soothe.

"Shh."

"Dad? What is it?"

"Shh. We need to be quiet."

But he wasn't sure that was true. The one thing they

didn't have was the one thing everyone was apparently interested in. The street they'd been walking along had been quiet during the night, and remained still as the others nodded off one by one. But that wasn't true now. They could see cars through the trees, making their way out of the small neighborhoods, honking and tapping bumpers, trying to drive around each other like drowning people huddling to be on top when everyone else's air ran out.

Meyer had stayed awake longer than anyone, and for a while he'd amused himself over his phone's backlit screen. But without the JetVan, there was no signal. Either the networks were down for good, or they were being used nonstop by information and voice hoarders who thought learning more might change reality for the better. He'd tried for much longer than he should have, dialing Heather with a thrumming heart, remembering the horror of her voice cutting off. Had she been able to use her gun? Or was his ex-wife (and best friend; let's tell the truth) gone forever?

Meyer got a connection failure with every try. Even if he could ring out, the cell network near Heather would need to be available to reach her. The obstacles between them (or at least her phone) seemed as insurmountable as the roadblocks between Chicago and Vail.

He'd closed his phone shamefully, looking down at Piper with an unarticulated guilt. Then he'd cabled one of the external batteries to charge his phone, deciding not to let the others know how hard he'd tried to reach Heather, and how badly he'd wanted information his little brick could no longer provide.

They didn't have GPS. If they were going to find a way out of Chicago's urban sprawl, they'd have to do it by gut instinct or find a map. Did gas stations still sell paper maps and atlases? Meyer's grandmother had lived to be ninety-four, and she'd driven almost until the end. Grams hadn't used a cell phone once. She wouldn't complete her medical forms online, either. Meyer offered to do them, but Grams had insisted they send her paper.

The world must still have maps, for stubborn old bitches like Grams.

He'd fallen asleep uneasily. Hours felt tissue thin, giving him the kind of sleep he wasn't sure he even had. Meyer may have laid in semisleep through the night, his mind unwilling to leave their makeshift camp unguarded, his pride unwilling to wake someone else to stand watch in his stead.

How much time had passed?

It was still dark when he'd heard the commotion, but the moon was no longer visible through the canopy. He'd fished his phone to check the time, but was unsure whether it had made the leap to central. It must have, back when they'd still had the JetVan's signal to synchronize it to the satellite? That seemed ages ago.

It read 5:40 a.m.

He'd heard a crack at the edge of his foggy awareness, but thought it might've been the slap of a screen door as someone left a house in the neighborhood past the road. The neighborhood where, in the daylight, he'd been hoping to shop for a car.

But the engines had come alive one at a time. First just a few to break the night's stillness. In the dark, surrounded by trees, it had been easy to believe they were in a forest. But it had only taken fifteen minutes before it was apparent that they were in a spreading panic instead.

Now, with his hand on Lila's shoulder, Meyer looked at Lila, Raj, and Trevor, all of them stirring. Meyer had already sneaked to the tree line and back. He knew the answer to their collective question, had overheard enough to put it together.

Raj said, "Are those car engines?"

Trevor looked at him with the disdain of a teenager woken before he was ready. "So you've heard engines before. Hooray."

Immediately defensive: "Listen to how many there are, you little shit!"

"Don't call me a shit, you shit."

"Shut up, Trevor," Lila snapped.

Piper sat up beside Meyer. She looked toward the headlights illuminating the forest's edge instead of at him, but he looked over at her profile without thinking, taking in her sleep-tousled hair, the strangely confident look in her big, blue eyes. Yesterday's encounter had changed her in some small way. It was as plain as the nose on her less-panicked-than-expected face.

"What's going on?" Piper finally looked over, and for a moment Meyer felt guilty. It didn't make sense. It wasn't his fault alien ships were on their way. But then again, maybe that wasn't why he felt guilty.

"Something happened overnight. I went out there when it started a while ago. I heard one guy arguing with another, saying that he had a good telescope inside and could 'see better than you can.' I think they must be close enough to see."

Confidence bled from Piper's face. It was easy to forget the approaching ships with all the mayhem on the ground. Riots were rational. Aliens were not.

"You mean … ?"

Meyer nodded. "I'm sure they don't look like much with what most people have, but there are plenty of nerds out there with big telescopes who aren't official NASA."

"But we already knew they were coming," Trevor said.

"You know the expression: 'Seeing is believing.'"

"But … why would they all be leaving? Where are they going?"

"Harder to say. I wish we had a TV or a radio. Just from overhearing, though, I think someone might have made some predictions." Meyer looked around the small group. "About landing spots, maybe."

"How could anyone know where they're going to land?" said Trevor.

"They don't have to know. Someone just has to guess, or make a suggestion. Then this happens." He raised his arm toward the growing cacophony. "Once a few people decide they'd better get the hell out of Dodge, everyone else decides the same."

Meyer crept forward. The others stayed behind them, dragging their packs.

"What now, Dad?" said Trevor.

"I wanted to get a car."

"And now?" said Piper.

"I *still* want to get a car."

They reached the wood's edge. It was a poor thicket, really just a handful of unused lots where the trees had yet to get chopped. But it was enough for concealment — especially given that no one seemed to have interest in anything but the road.

It was bumper to bumper, mirroring the riot they'd fled the previous afternoon. The only differences were the number of lanes (the road had two, and both directions were occupied by cars desperate to leave) and the civility. There wasn't any, really. Meyer thought that might be okay. If these people wore fear on their chests and openly panicked, maybe they wouldn't explode into chaos like the expressway had. Alternatively, there might be nothing to halt immediate chaos.

"How are we going to buy a car now, Meyer?" The wooded area was on a slight rise, and Piper was watching the people across the packed street above the hoods of jostling, honking vehicles.

"I said 'get.' Not 'buy.'"

"So, what, you're going to steal one?"

"I'll write them a credit chit if it'll make you feel better. Slip it under the door, and they can cash it later, after they're done murdering each other for food."

He'd been joking, but the comment shut Piper down. Another presence appeared at his side. Meyer looked over and saw Raj beside him.

"You know how to hotwire a car?" he said.

"Not since cars had ignition wires."

Meyer tried to keep the condescension from his stare. The boy was only trying to help.

"No, I don't know how to 'hotwire' a car. But unless you expect to find an '04 Camry in there, that doesn't matter."

Raj had no rebuttal. Meyer sighed.

"Look. We have two choices. I'd love to find an unused vehicle in there somewhere — something that was a second car, and the people who own it took another and left it behind. But that means finding the key fob transponder if we expect to start it, and I don't think it's going to be that simple, even if we break into the house and root around."

"We can't break into someone's house!" Lila said.

Raj put his hand on her arm. "What's the other choice?"

Meyer firmed his jaw. "We take one that someone's already using."

Piper was staring at him. Meyer looked over.

"No," she said.

"We have to get to Vail. We *have* to."

"They have places they need to go." She nodded at the line of cars. "They all do."

"They're running in circles. They don't know where they're even going. They just think one of those ships is going to park over Chicago, and they're looking the things in the eye for the first time. They're not thinking smart, Piper."

"But you are."

"We'll put a vehicle to good use. These people are just panicking."

Piper nodded. "Oh, that's right. Whereas *you're* thinking smart."

"Don't argue with me, Piper."

Something snapped. Her husky, often-sexy, often-demure voice rose, becoming too loud for early morning. Despite the engine noise and shouts of fleeing people below, Meyer thought they might be seen, making themselves into unwitting targets.

"Don't give me your superior bullshit, Meyer! You are not dragging someone out of a car by gunpoint! Just because you think you know something they don't, that doesn't make you …"

"I *do* know something they don't. I have all along." He kept his voice calm, fighting anger fused with frustration. Maybe some fear. If they couldn't get a car, they were stuck. And they couldn't be stuck, no matter what. They had to reach Vail. *They had to get to his Axis Mundi*. Anything else was unthinkable.

"You wouldn't have wanted anyone to take our van."

He flashed back to the teens in New Jersey. The panic had barely begun, and they'd already been ready to rumble. "Didn't stop them from trying."

"Doesn't mean we should do the same."

"How else are we going to get out of here, Piper? *We* actually have somewhere to go! What's really going to happen? We'll strand someone where they should have fucking stayed all along?"

"That's their decision to make," she said.

Meyer looked at the line of vehicles and the gibbering people yelling from their home doorways and car windows. For a few clear seconds, he saw them all as sheep, running in pointless circles fueled by their fear. Clogging the way for shepherds, with places they needed to be.

"Fine," he said. "We'll find another way."

But he had no idea how.

And with a thousand miles left to their haven across packed roads, time was quickly thinning.

Chapter Twenty-Two

Day Four, Morning
   Chicago

ONE SIGNIFICANT ADVANTAGE of this panicky lot versus the rioting expressway, Piper thought as they moved down the berm toward a snaking line of cars and pedestrians: no one seemed to notice them at all.

Everyone here was probably less than a quarter mile from home (the early birds had fled at the front — the Meyer Dempseys of outer Chicago, perhaps), and were therefore properly stocked. They were in their own vehicles, probably fully gassed up, with the kids' electronic games jammed into the back seat to keep them entertained through an apocalyptic family trip. There might come a day when neighbor would turn on neighbor and each would take what the other had. But for now, it seemed that most homes had remained their owners' castles. And most people's parked-in vehicles remained their oases on wheels.

The Dempsey family had no such oasis. But that was the Dempsey family's problem.

Meyer clearly didn't agree with that sentiment; he fumed in silence beside her, holding his pack's straps as if to keep it firmly in line. This was their first end-of-the-world scenario, but Meyer's life had been survival of the fittest. He'd done poorly in school because he never cared about tests, then claimed control of his destiny by starting his own business at age fourteen, selling hilarious fake how-to pamphlets to students right under the administration's nose. He'd partnered with promising idea men and women who'd failed at crowdfunding their dreams, reasoning that if the public didn't want to pay full price, a private investor was justified in spending pennies. Those who didn't like his deals, he beat to market and drove out of business. All fair game, in Meyer's opinion.

Everyone had their shots in life. Not taking them was their own goddamned fault.

But Piper had been raised differently. She hadn't met Meyer until after he'd taken his crowdfunding idea machine further by starting his own platform. His attraction to Piper gave her special treatment. She'd started Quirky Q with Meyer as a fair partner — the way he treated all partners who were reasonable enough to understand that his way was always best. But she'd hidden some of herself as they'd dated then married, because those buried truths were things Meyer, in all his wisdom, would find stupid.

Things like religion. Like belief in a god. Which god, Piper wasn't willing to say. Her parents had believed in the Christian God, but she'd always been more spiritual. She kept it all to herself, though, because of Meyer's overbearing views. He was good to her, but saw belief in "something beyond" as stupid. Ironic, considering all the time he spent tripping with Heather, looking into some great understanding that ordinary folks couldn't see.

Heather. Piper suppressed the thought. No point in ruminating now, considering the situation and Heather's likely death. It was a shame. She'd liked Heather despite her jealousy. Despite her certainty that Meyer had never stopped loving her, even after he'd started loving Piper.

Heather and Meyer, it seemed, had shared everything. Probably still had, right until the end. Piper had only shared a part of herself, and she'd only allowed Meyer to share parts of himself. Which meant it might have been her fault. All of it. All of what continued to happen with Heather, because Piper was too reserved to keep up.

The rules had changed — but not those that mattered.

You didn't take what wasn't yours. You didn't rob someone of what they needed to secure your own survival. No matter whether you were Meyer Fucking Dempsey or some poor slob living on the south side of Chicago.

They walked the line of cars for a while, Meyer apparently reasoning that there was little point in securing a vehicle behind a snarl of traffic. They weren't the only walkers; there were many with packs like theirs and many significantly larger, as if those brave souls planned to head into the hinterlands and live like primitives until this all blew over.

Piper nodded to those she made eye contact with. Meyer stared defiantly ahead. A surprising number nodded back, proving her right: there was at least a little civility left in the world.

Hi, nice to see you.

Wonderful day for an apocalypse, isn't it?

Oh yes. Lovely day for the end of humanity.

They must have ended up heading west because after a few hours, the sky behind them began to purple then warm into reds and oranges. The backpacks began to feel heavy, but despite her grunting rearrangements of shoulder straps, Meyer wouldn't slow. He was pissed. She wondered if he had a *right* to be pissed, flip-flopping on her convictions with every other step.

Wouldn't someone take their vehicle under the right conditions? If so, shouldn't they take someone else's, if they thought they could get away? But no, that would be wrong, because those people would be stranded and unable to flee. Which didn't matter anyway for most of them; Meyer was right about that. Most people weren't going anywhere other than away from Chicago. The Dempseys at least had a destination waiting.

She'd talked to one woman walking alone, hanging far enough back so that Meyer wouldn't hear them. He might snap at her to stop talking to those he saw as the enemy (Meyer had always seen others as an enemy to *some* degree; it's how he built his wealth), and she didn't trust herself not to bite off his head if he did.

She'd learned what they'd suspected: Yes, amateur astronomers had begun circulating their own images of the approaching spheres. Yes, they were now plenty visible as a stubbly rash of miniature BB's in line with Jupiter. And yes, some conspiracy types had begun circulating a growing theory: If there were only so many alien ships to go around, didn't it make sense for them to line up over major population centers to get the most bang for their space bucks? Chicago was the fifty-first largest city in the world, and there were around two hundred ships. The theory had gone viral on the Internet for those who could still access it, and on TV and radio for everyone else. It had the obvious feel of something people should have realized days ago, but now everyone wanted out.

Piper had asked the woman, "Where are you headed?"

"Away from the city," she said.

That, Piper thought, was as legitimate a destination as any other. They were headed to Vail, but maybe this woman would get to somewhere around Naperville. Who were they to say she shouldn't go?

The same was true of every person in every car. They might head into cornfields. Forests. Mountains, if they could make them. It was none of their business.

Still, she could feel Meyer's disapproval. All bets were off, he seemed to feel. And he had that pressing need to reach Vail that, truth be told, Piper didn't entirely understand. Why couldn't *they* go into cornfields? Why couldn't *they* hunker down in the forest? Yes, he was having that whole paranoid compound built in Colorado, and yes, Meyer seemed to see it as some sort of a spiritual "axis" — something that, she thought with irritation, he'd have made fun of her for. And yes, heading there had been a terrific plan before the FAA had grounded flights, back when they'd planned to arrive on the Gulfstream. Or it had been a good plan when they'd still had their van, back when the roads had seemed passable.

But now? Now, wasn't forging bullheadedly along to Vail just … just bullheaded?

She didn't want to ask. He was angry, and was resisting all his natural impulses (say, to take what he wanted in whatever way he could get it) out of a sideways sort of respect for Piper. He thought her way was stupid, for sure. But he also loved and respected her. This was how he'd chosen to show it. But he resented her, too. He resented Piper for what he was doing. He resented her for his own loyalty to her, and his own respect for her wishes.

And he was afraid.

That was the worst part — the part Piper tried to ignore for solid minutes at a time as they made their way alongside the slow line of cars. She tried to focus on Trevor, who kept his distance from her, focusing on the hurt she felt over her stepson's moodiness rather than the worse emotions coming from Meyer. She tried to focus on Lila, who looked green and seemed like she might throw up. She tried to focus on Raj, who kept his hand in Lila's, remembering how she'd once been in relationships that new and sweet. Not with Meyer, certainly, but in her girl-hood, back when she'd been awkward and shy.

Still, her eyes kept returning to Meyer. Seeing his anger for a moment, then seeing the fear below. It was like a visual puzzle: Once she'd seen the solution, she'd never have trouble seeing it again. Or never be able to deliberately *not* see it. She wanted Meyer to be assured. Confident. *Strong*. Feeling his anger at her was so much better than sensing his growing desperation. But the longer they walked, the clearer it became. Meyer was like everyone else beneath his thick skin: terrified down to his bones.

Maybe because he knew what was coming.

Same as he'd known to have emergency supplies on hand. Same as he'd known to keep the Gulfstream prepped, with a pilot always on call. Same as he'd known to build the bunker in Vail — the bunker they were never going to reach.

Piper shook the idea away.

Hours passed. The sky grew lighter by degrees. They kept walking, Piper was too timid to suggest a rest because she was afraid Meyer was near his breaking point. He saw the world as drowning and Vail as a pocket of air. She could have found a place here, but not Meyer. And she was afraid of how he might react if reminded how unlikely it was beginning to seem that they might ever breathe the oxygen he sought.

But she couldn't continue in silence, so after an unknowable amount of time she moved into step beside Meyer, then slipped her small hand into his large one. He gripped it in a way that was probably meant to be reassuring, but to Piper felt like a man clinging to a lifeline.

She looked up. He looked over. She smiled, and he managed to do the same. There was apology in that smile, and a touch of forgiveness, which Piper felt she might have earned.

"I don't want to pressure you," she said.

He nodded.

"And I know I've messed up your plans."

His lips firmed. She'd messed them up *for now*, but the more afraid he grew deep down, the less willing he might be to adhere to Piper's moral code. He was still the family's rudder. When push came to shove, Meyer Dempsey's words were the history written.

"But I don't suppose you have any ideas?"

They were coming to a rise. He nodded downward, toward a lot ahead, as if he'd expected what was on the other side and could answer her question with that single, demonstrative nod.

"I do now."

Chapter Twenty-Three

DAY FOUR, Late Morning
  Chicago

WHEN PIPER TOOK Trevor by his arm to steer him in their new direction, he felt a wash of unwelcome emotion. He'd been avoiding her all day because of last night's dream, and her touch was both pleasant and awkward at once.

Despite the circumstances, he'd fallen asleep almost immediately (he supposed it was sheer mental exhaustion that felled him), and sometime later he'd found himself in a barren, post-apocalyptic battle zone — apparently after the aliens had come and gone. It was just Trevor and Piper. Trevor was holding an enormous weapon like one of the soldiers in the *Death Hunt: Earth* video game, his hands covered in soot and grime. He was wearing a shirt with the sleeves ripped off at the shoulders, and his arms were, thanks to dream magic, rather large and impressive. Piper had been wearing only underwear and a bra. Toward the end of the dream, there had been a scuffle, and the bra had been compromised. For a few glorious minutes before waking, she'd been running around the rubble with her tits out, making suggestive comments about needing some "manly comfort."

Feeling her hand on him now — though much higher on him than he'd want if she weren't his father's wife — warmed Trevor's face. He pulled away, and only after flinching thought how it must look to her. He caught her facial expression, warring with the trio of desire, guilt, and shame he so often felt around Piper lately, but then saw where she'd been leading him and stopped. They all halted, waiting for Meyer to speak.

Lila spoke first. Only, she didn't speak so much as laugh.

"You're kidding," she said.

"Your stepmother wants us to get our car legit, so that's what we're going to do." There was a glance between them, and Trevor saw his father's eyes soften, blunting what might have sounded like an insult into the mere statement it was intended to be.

Ahead was the huge, shiny expanse of a Toyota dealership.

"Nobody's going to be working, you know," said Lila.

"Then we'll take now and pay later."

"How?"

"I'm sure the transponders are in there somewhere. They must have an office, right? Where they go and pretend they're working out a deal, getting special permission from the manager for a can't-beat, low-low price to get you into a brand new Toyota today?"

Piper rolled her eyes. Trevor had been catching their vibes for the entire time they'd been walking beside the slow-moving line of traffic despite trying to move his mind from Piper, and he'd seen how they'd both started hard then softened through the hike. That was how they usually did things. When Piper didn't agree with Meyer (which wasn't often, Trevor had noticed; she naturally avoided conflict), they squared off into silence. Somehow a compromise was reached without a word. They met in the middle, each managing to apologize without ever saying *sorry*. She hadn't wanted to jack a car; he had. Apparently, stealing one from a lot was a fair middle ground.

"Come on," said Meyer, veering away from the road to cut through a field bordering the lot. "They have insurance, and my insurance has been ripping me off for years. I owe them one."

"How do you know it's the same insurance company?" said Lila.

"They're all owned by Satan. Let's go."

The field was unmowed but clean, free of the debris that littered the roadside. They'd made it quite far out of the sprawl and were now mostly suburban, so the lot wasn't the kind they were used to seeing in cities, where kids drank and dug in abandoned basements or homeless people slept below the tall grass. It was gently rolling, coming down and away from the road. The dealership itself was nestled in a miniature valley, down from the road's peak, with its own hills and dales between the subsections of new Toyotas in rows.

They crossed through the line of vehicles, Raj stopping to read the specs. A moment later they were at the lot's front door, which was, of course, locked. But it was also glass.

It took Meyer a while to find something suitable with which to break the doors. The lot had been kept clean, and there were no lead pipes, baseball bats, two-by-fours studded with nails, or any of the other convenient props one would have expected to find on a typical Hollywood back lot. Eventually, he found a chunk of concrete that had broken upward, presumably during a freeze cycle, and tossed it hard through the glass. Then he reached in and unlocked the door. Meyer was flicking on the lights when there was a click in the empty lobby, filled with desks and abandoned paperwork.

Trevor almost didn't see the reason for his father's raised hands until it was too late. He was striding toward a water cooler when there was a shout.

"Stay where you are!"

Trevor looked up to see a man holding a rifle pointed directly at his chest. He was mostly behind a desk, apparently kneeling. The rifle had a scope, and the man was peering directly through it as if hunting Trevor like a deer — probably what the rifle had been intended for, before it had become a weapon of preservation.

"Get down on your knees, both of you!" He looked up at Raj, Piper, and Lila, who were a few steps back and added, "*All* of you!" He waved the gun with a jitter, jerking the long barrel side to side in staccato movements, meeting each target in turn.

"Easy," said Meyer. "We didn't know you were in here."

"Well I fucking am! And now you can just get the fuck out!"

Meyer looked over at Trevor, nodding toward the floor: *Kneel as he says.* He was doing the same himself, glancing back at the others to follow.

"I'm just kneeling like you said. But if you want us to go, we will."

"Kneel!"

"I'm kneeling. It's fine." Meyer's voice was a glassy lake. Trevor felt like he might pass out, and Lila looked seconds from doing the same, breathing through her mouth as if unable to catch her breath.

"I said kneel!"

He already was kneeling. The man sounded hysterical, almost out of his mind. He appeared to be in his early forties, bald on top with a ring of brown hair in a halo from ear to ear. He was wearing a long-sleeve white shirt and a brightly colored tie, as if ready to work. Only his armpits seemed yellowed with sweat, and everything was rumpled, as if he'd slept in it.

"It's fine. No problem."

"What are you doing here?"

"We came for a car. But we'll leave. No big deal." Trevor flexed to rise, but his father stared him back into place.

"This is my place!" the man shouted. His voice was tremulous, cracked.

"Of course. It's your place."

"Don't you fucking humor me!"

"I'm not. We'll move on. Can I stand?"

The man raised the gun higher, refirming its butt against his shoulder. "You think I won't shoot you? I shot the others! You hear me? I'm not soft! This is my place!"

The statement made Trevor feel cold: *I shot the others.* A thousand movie scenes raced through his mind. Loud action where one fighter battled for what was his. Creeping dread, where one person did what he had to survive, even if it meant killing sick friends, or competing for resources.

"No problem. I'm just going to stand."

"Don't you fucking move!"

"Listen," said Meyer. "What's your name?"

"None of your fucking business."

With his hands still raised, Meyer's eyes narrowed.

After a moment, Trevor saw what he was peering at: the brass-colored plate on the desk he was crouching behind.

"Frank," he said, reading the plate. "Can I call you Frank?"

"Isaiah!" the man blurted.

Trevor watched his father nod. He'd known his name wasn't Frank, but getting people to do things they thought had been their own idea was one of his specialties.

"Isaiah," Meyer said evenly. "I'm going to stand. My son over there is going to stand, then the rest of my family behind me. Please. One father to another, I'll ask you: keep the gun on me."

Something registered in the former car salesman's face. The rifle lowered a fraction of an inch. Apparently, the man did have a family. Then Trevor saw a different desk with another nameplate, right where his father's eyes had been while Isaiah looked at the others. The plate on that desk said *Isaiah Schwartz*, and there were several photos beside it in frames, of children with brown hair.

Isaiah didn't ask Meyer how he knew what he'd known, but he did allow Meyer to stand. Slowly, Trevor and the others did the same.

"We're just going to walk out. Okay? Keep your gun on me."

Meyer stepped backward. Piper, Raj, and Lila were already out of sight. Trevor watched his father's eyes beckon. Trevor had gone the farthest in, but Meyer wanted him behind. The man probably wouldn't shoot, because Meyer's voice had a way of soothing the savage beast. He'd once told Trevor he used anger and indignation as a negotiating tactic — not in himself, but in others. If he could get the other party ranting and raving before he calmed them, they always felt stupid and somewhat conciliatory. Once they blew their energy being pissed off, they lost their

advantage unless they could maintain their anger —
which, thanks to Meyer Dempsey's considerable charisma,
they never could.

Trevor walked behind his father, then watched his slow
retreat. There was something different in the way he was
moving. He wasn't like himself. He had a slight waddle, just
as he'd had a slight affect in his voice a moment ago that
wasn't usually there. It was subtle. But once you knew what
he was doing — once you realized he was matching Isaiah
Schwartz's vocal patterns and walk as he came forward —
it was obvious.

People like people they're like, Trevor's father had once told
him. It was amazing what people would agree to if you
spoke like them and copied a few of their mannerisms. Just
like how Isaiah, now that he'd risen from behind the desk
to march them out, kept tilting his head to the side as if to
crack or stretch his neck. Just like how Meyer, backing out
of the car dealership, was doing exactly the same thing.
You'd think people would notice being copied. But that
was another thing Meyer had told his son: *most people are so
far up their own asses, they barely notice there are other people in the
world.*

"Don't come back. And if you tell anyone I'm here …"
said the salesman, still walking forward.

"We won't." Meyer tilted his head. *Crack.*

"Don't you hide on my lot, either. You go up there. To
the road."

Meyer stepped backward, barely looking down to
watch the stairs. He effortlessly descended heels first,
bringing himself below the salesman's eye line. It would
make the man feel superior — elevated in status because
he was literally higher up. Trevor knew that trick, too. He
fumbled down slightly faster, less graceful than his father,
and looked up doe eyed. Just another helpless animal of

prey, like those he probably used to shoot on the weekends, using the rifle he kept in his trunk.

Meyer was now halfway across the apron of driveway in front of the building's doors, his hands still obediently raised. He waited for the man to lower his weapon or definitively allow them to go, but instead he stood on raised steps, the rifle's barrel slowly lowering.

"They left without me," he said, his voice suddenly small.

Trevor looked at his father, seeing if he wanted to parlay this moment of weakness into a new advantage.

Who left? His friends? His co-workers? Or most coldly: his family?

Trevor never found out. Raj stepped out from behind the alcove behind the door and hit Mr. Schwartz hard with a large cigarette Butt Depot that had been set in the designated smoking area around the corner.

The salesman hit the ground. Lila, behind Raj, looked aghast and as if she'd been trying to stop her man from acting. Piper snatched the rifle, taking too long to free the strap from the man's unconscious body.

"Stupid, Raj," said Meyer, shaking his head, clearly surprised. "But good job."

Chapter Twenty-Four

Day Four, Early Afternoon
Chicago, Rural Illinois

According to Lila's phone, it was just after noon by the time they located the transponders, then figured out the dealership's system for matching key fobs on hooks to vehicles on the lot. Her father wanted a Land Cruiser — and, given the vast selection they finally found themselves able to take advantage of, would settle for nothing less. Now that Toyota offered a Land Cruiser hybrid, there were tons of upsides with almost no real downside.

The tanks were massive, and the new hybrid engines averaged 32 mpg on the highway when running on full auto. A driver, if they needed to go manual, would lower the efficiency, but they could still expect to hit thirty or more once they found open roads. With luck, they might be able to get all the way to Vail, stopping just four times for gas — more if they could fill tanks to carry as they had in the JetVan. The Land Cruiser was also heavy enough to crush through smaller obstacles and push lesser vehicles out of the way if it had to. And it would run off road, which meant they could cruise up the medians if they found open grass.

They didn't tie the salesman, at Piper's insistence. He'd need his freedom to survive. They needed to get away before he woke (taking his rifle; Piper was foofy but hardly naive), but he wasn't a threat if they left him inside the building, on his side in case he vomited in his sleep.

The dealership also had a wide variety of paper maps — something Lila hadn't considered but that her father took as a great relief. They didn't have atlases, but they had Chicago and the outlying areas, and a wide-view Midwest map that showed a good chunk of their forthcoming trip from far up. Lila wasn't used to navigating without a GPS, but her father had spent a childhood with parents who were always behind the times, and hence knew the basics of following a line on paper. And beyond that, she suspected he'd boned up on map reading as part of his crazy survivalist fetish — no longer so crazy.

Before leaving, Meyer tried the dealership's hardline phones to reach her mother. He had no luck, but kept at it for long after Piper had begun waving frantically that they needed to go. They'd hit the road, and he'd resumed trying on his cell. There was still no data coverage and intermittent voice. Their devices were quickly becoming useless, not much more valuable than rocks they might throw to defend themselves.

The Land Cruiser was as good as its name, and Meyer wasted no time heading out in the grass bordering the highways. Seeing this, several cars in the slower lanes on concrete followed, zagging out of line and into the faster way paved by the oversized vehicle. Most made it just off the road, then stuck in what was essentially a large drainage culvert. A few made it onto the grass and rattled bumpily along for a few miles behind them before sticking. Only the toughest, most off-road-ready trucks and SUVs kept up, forming an impromptu express lane beside the road.

Eventually, traffic thinned enough to jockey back onto the highway. Meyer kept going, always staying in the right lane and keeping an eye on the berm to keep a lane of escape available. But luck stuck to them, and once past the outermost of Chicago's sprawl, roads became rural. Lila's father handed the paper maps to Piper, who proved an adept navigator. She led them onto forgotten roads, reasoning that the more they avoided people, the better. The gas gauge was the only barometer in need of watching, and until it started to creep down near a quarter, they'd stay out in the backwoods, pretending humanity was already gone.

They followed signs for Davenport and Moline, then skirted the cities by a wide berth on approach. "We don't want another Chicago," her father said from the front seat. No one disagreed.

The way was smooth and predictable enough that once Meyer was through watching the berm in case he needed to go off roading again, he turned on the autodrive and they rode like normal people on a regular trip. The car's GPS wasn't working any better than their phones', but the maps programmed into memory did a fair job working with the odometer to keep an eye on their rough position. Proximity detectors worked fine without a connection, and when they approached other, slower vehicles (decreasingly often), the car corrected easily, passing with everything but a wave.

Lila tried to stay calm. She didn't want to raise her father's ire (or hopes), so when he was turned from the car's middle, watching the sun-washed flat land ahead, she tried to call her mom. She knew the phones didn't work and that she was foolishly wasting battery power (though Lila supposed she could rummage for the charge cord), but still, each time she heard the out-of-service message her heart dropped a little. She tried not to think of Mom, of the way she'd been cut off when Dad's phone had failed. But it was hard not to think of something — like her mother probably raped, murdered, and left in the burning desert.

She looked at Raj. He smiled. She smiled back, supposing she owed him some adoration. She'd protested when he'd gone for that smoker's station to clock the man with the gun, but it had been a catch-22: if she protested too loudly, the man would turn, see Raj, then shoot him. Still, whether she'd thought him an idiot or not, it was thanks to Raj that they had the Cruiser and were on their way to Vail.

She gave his arm an affectionate squeeze, then looked at the passing scenery. Close to the wheels, grass and wire fences whipped by. Farther out, pastures and even a few grazing cows seemed almost stationary, creeping by as if on a conveyor. Little by little, they were moving west. Little by little, they were going to make it.

They'd have their shelter for whatever came.

They'd have food, water, and (if her father's preparation was as thorough as she suspected) an impervious wall between them and anyone who might want in. The bunker itself was under a sprawling estate, and while her father had said it was finished and stocked, the house itself was only at about three-quarters. The bunker's entrance from the house would be concealable. Vagrants and opportunists might camp upstairs, but nobody would even know the underground refuge was there, if they were lucky. And so far, they were getting quite lucky indeed.

They'd have soft beds.

They'd have pillows, too, which was good because Lila remembered the way Piper's friend, Willow, had gone on and on about her huge body pillow while pregnant. Lila even seemed to remember her mother having an enormous pillow when she'd been about to have Trevor, though those might have been false memories because she would only have been two years old. But either way, pregnant women needed their pillows. And Lila would have hers.

But she wouldn't have a doctor. Not for the delivery if they had to stay underground, and not for the checkups. How would she know how the baby was developing? Who would she ask her medical questions? If Mom arrived, she could ask her, but Piper had never been pregnant. How would she know if she was gaining enough weight, too much weight, or if something was wrong? What if the baby's umbilical cord was wrapped around its neck during the delivery? What if it was breech?

Oh, shit — what if she needed a C-section?

Lila told herself to relax. As her father had pointed out many times already, nothing had even happened yet. Wasn't it possible that the aliens would be friendly? Wasn't it possible that there *were* no aliens, and that the spheres were just probes or something? Wasn't it possible that they were, indeed, alien ships ... but that they were bound for somewhere beyond Earth, maybe on their way to the sun?

And besides — women had been having babies forever. Since way before modern medicine. It's the reason humanity still existed. Even Eve had managed it, and she'd had the world's first vagina. And it's not like Adam had been prepared to be an obstetrician, amateur gynecologist though he'd undoubtedly been.

And hey, throughout history, only, like, half of women died in childbirth.

She was pulled from her reverie as the car slowed, shocked to realize hours had passed into dark. They'd found a gas station at the crossroads of nothing and nowhere, and its lights were on — obvious now that the light had mostly drained from the day. It was fully automated, like a real civilized station in the city. There didn't need to be an attendant — and there was, therefore, nobody around.

At least that's what they thought before they knew they were wrong.

Chapter Twenty-Five

DAY FOUR, Early Evening
  Rural Iowa

PIPER DIDN'T WANT to breathe a word, but she knew something was wrong, or about to be.

They'd been too lucky. Things had gone entirely too well. They'd found themselves stuck in a highway riot, in the middle of an apparent alien invasion, and they were still alive and together. They were still on their way. They still had a fair amount of supplies, including not-terrible food and clean water. They'd managed to steal a good car without so much as getting shot, and were only a dozen or so hours away from living out the coming apocalypse in opulence.

It bothered Piper that they were cut off from the world. The Internet had still been up and running as of twenty-four hours ago, but they hadn't been able to access it since. The JetVan had a private network fed from the satellite, but without the van they were subject to the whims and traffic limits of ground-based towers like everyone else. That meant no service, no access, and no news beyond what local radio (not even the satellite network, which didn't have an active subscription in the Land Cruiser) provided.

The same was true of voice coverage on the phones. She and Meyer both kept turning their seats around, to check on the kids' mood and to pass the time with conversation. Several times, she'd seen Trevor and Lila listening to their phones like kids hoping to hear the ocean in a conch shell. They'd dropped the phones guiltily into their laps as soon as Piper looked back — and Piper, sensing she should allow them their dignity, hope, or both, allowed them to think she'd seen nothing.

But she knew what they were doing: trying to contact their mother. Trying to call Raj's parents. Trying to call friends they'd had back when the world was still a more innocent place.

Not that the adults were immune to hope. She'd tried her parents several times, and she kept seeing Meyer listen to his phone from the corner of her eye. Sometimes she let him have his privacy and sometimes she raised an eyebrow as he hung up, silently asking if he'd had any luck. But of course he hadn't, same as her. No one could answer without a connection.

Trevor and Lila's mother might be dead. They might never know for sure, but privately Piper thought it was a safe bet, given the last they'd heard of her.

Raj's parents might be dead too. That one seemed less likely as an isolated event, but it raised a troubling uncertainty for Piper: the fate of New York as a whole. Piper was just twenty-nine, and felt herself still just a child these past few days. She'd grown up in a connected world, where you could learn just about anything about anywhere at any time. Having no news of New York — or anywhere — for long stretches of time unsettled her to the core.

They'd been sticking to back roads, with Meyer always watching the map for a way out in case they ran into another traffic jam. There was always a way around, but that precaution meant sticking to farm roads big enough to be on the map but not large enough to risk congestion. It meant a lot of driving through nothingness, and sometimes all that prickled the radio dial were low-wattage religious broadcasts: preachers who thought the aliens were Jesus coming home, or that they carried the wrath of God in their round ships' bellies.

When they could get news, it felt to Piper like surfacing for air in a vast expanse of water. Each time she heard a broadcast, it felt like Genesis, with the world created anew rather than simply reported upon.

Chicago was back! It hadn't been destroyed!

New York was back! Nobody had burned it to the ground!

But between strong signals, both cities might have perished. Anything could have happened. Nobody could contact anyone, and no responsible souls had taken to available airways to trumpet the good news of America's survival.

Piper found herself pondering the sky's edge as dusk slowly turned it from dim to dark. How far away was the horizon in flat land? She had no idea — and, being a child of the Internet, felt helpless with no way to Google the answer. Maybe fifty miles? Maybe less?

It meant she knew that for fifty miles (maybe less) in every direction, the world still existed.

Beyond that was anyone's guess.

The thought made Piper feel cold and lonely, so she unlocked the seat and slid it closer to Meyer's, then lay down with her head in his lap. He looked down, brushed dark bangs from her eyes, and smiled. Piper suspected he knew what she was thinking — at least her thoughts' vague color. He always did. Meyer seemed to know everything in advance, same as he'd known to build a bunker and make plans bent on getting them to it. Same as he claimed, through visions brought by the drug Piper feared and didn't understand (and partaken with Heather, her mind added bitterly), that Meyer knew they'd better be in their shelter when the clock ran out.

She'd asked him, in a whisper, what he suspected.

What will happen, Meyer? What will happen when those ships arrive?

But he wouldn't even answer. He'd shaken his head as if he didn't know, and maybe at the top level of his mind, he didn't. But *something* in Meyer knew. *Something* had them running scared, thankful that they were a night's drive from Vail, afraid that something might yet stand in their way.

Now she lay with her head in his lap, his reassuring fingers stroking her hair as if she were a pet. Just another child for him to shepherd, another mouth to feed.

She must have fallen asleep, because by the time Piper looked up again, she saw a dark pall behind Meyer's head, the cut of his strong jawline above.

She straightened.

"Where are we?" she asked.

"Outside Des Moines."

She looked around. By their new definitions, being "outside" a city meant a horizon at least. She was reminded of her earlier solipsistic thoughts and considered asking Meyer how he could be sure Des Moines was even still there. But it was a silly thought by a silly, frightened little girl. She let it go.

"What time is it?"

He apparently didn't know, because he looked at the dash before answering.

"Almost eight."

"From Chicago. Is that good time?"

Meyer shrugged. He was fourteen years older than her, but no less used to GPS and the Internet. They could unfold the map and see if it looked like good time, but it hardly mattered. They were where they were, and they had to go where they needed to go.

She looked through the windshield, feeling the car slow around her. A gas station was ahead, in the middle of a dark crossroads spotted only by a few yellowish streetlights. There were houses in the distance, but they were mute, with only scant illumination in the windows. She looked back at the kids to gauge the vehicle's mood (or to assure herself that there were still people in the world, seeing as she couldn't count on more than fifty miles of America), and found Lila looking uneasy. She was about to ask what was troubling her, but Meyer nodded at the station and spoke first.

"I want to stop here. It looks automated, so the pumps might still be unlocked."

"Do we need gas?"

"We always kind of need gas. Maybe they'll have cans."

Maybe. But they'd passed a few stations along the way so far, always on these quiet back roads where it seemed that only horses and buggies truly belonged (not really, of course, but Piper had grown used to the hurly burly of a city), and this was the first in a while that still seemed operational. Just one more thing for Piper to worry about. Had the other stations been down because the attendants had shuttered them up before running home to hide? Or had the grid finally failed? But even the dead stations had been devoid of gas cans, just as they'd been stripped of food and water. There wasn't much out here in the boonies, and the locals seemed to have divvied it up well before the city mice showed up.

"Sure," Piper said. But she wasn't sure at all. That creeping feeling of luck running thin was like a splinter in her spine. She wouldn't say anything to Meyer because he'd only laugh, but Piper felt it just the same. They'd taken this trip on Meyer's hunches and foreknowledge, but still she felt her own wasn't worth saying. She was being chicken. Immature. A fool, with her head in the clouds.

But Meyer was studying her. The roads had been plenty clear for autodrive using the banked (but apparently undisplayable) maps, and he only took over manually when he wanted to stop. So far, he'd just told it to slow. He'd take the wheel soon, but for now he still had his eyes free. And you couldn't hide much from Meyer Dempsey's careful gaze when he decided to look.

"What is it?"

"Nothing."

"Piper." More earnest, more firm. "Tell me what's bothering you."

She laughed, and the sound was too loud. She should have left the radio on. They should be able to get to Des Moines by now, and probably had been able to for a while. If it was still there, of course.

"I'm just a little freaked out. I know it's ridiculous."

He gave her a small, bittersweet smile. "It's not ridiculous to be freaked out right now. Not even a little."

"I'm sorry."

"Don't be sorry."

That was sensible advice, but Piper kept thinking of all she didn't know.

Were the ships closer to Earth?

Had they sped up or slowed down?

Had they annihilated Shanghai?

Was the president promising a quick response or urging a nation-wide evacuation?

Strictly speaking, they should have kept the radio on at all times, scanning for new information. But they could only take so much, even when the signal was strong.

She reached for the radio, but Meyer held up a hand to stop her.

"I want to be able to listen," he said.

"Why?"

"It just ..." He looked like he'd said too much. His eyes flicked to the kids as he turned the Cruiser to manual and settled his foot on the pedal. "It pays to know what's going on around you."

Piper looked at the approaching gas station. She was suddenly very, very sure that stopping was an awful idea. They were in the middle of nowhere. The station was deserted, but that wasn't necessarily a good thing. There wouldn't be witnesses if something went wrong.

"You don't really want to stop," she said, watching him.

"We have to. We're down to a third of a tank, and this is the first station we've seen with lights on. Probably all computerized. Might be our last chance for gas."

They were coming closer. The parking lot was empty, the pumps lit but quiet. There was nothing wrong with the place, and yet something seemed off just the same. Something Piper could *feel* rather than see.

"Let's keep going. A third of a tank? That's plenty."

He looked over.

"Let's wait until it's light."

His look turned almost pitying. It was exactly what she'd been afraid of — both for his reaction and her worry.

Was it the dark that bothered her? Why not stand on a chair and squeal for the big, strong man to save her? Piper hated herself a little, but couldn't ignore the press of fear.

"We can't drive until light."

"Then let's stop and rest."

He shook his head. "We drive through the night."

"Meyer …"

He gave her arm a pat. Piper wanted to shake the gesture away, insulted. The pumps were closer. The Cruiser was slowing. He stopped it short of the drive, paused in the middle of the street.

"We don't know if we'll find another station, Piper. Not one with working pumps, and I don't really want to break into a Walmart for a generator and a sump pump. You heard about the blackouts."

Piper said nothing. No, she hadn't heard that; he must have turned on the radio while she'd been sleeping.

"Look," he said. "I figure it's somewhere between another seven, eight hundred miles. We might be able to get that far on a tank if we don't stop and start a lot and if I let it autodrive. Look, there in the window: insurance."

She looked and saw several big red plastic gas tanks just inside the station, a row of five-gallon cans.

"We fill the gas tank. We fill two or three of those and carry them with us."

"In the back seat?" said Trevor. "They'll stink!"

Meyer ignored him and continued talking to Piper. "That might be enough, and we won't have to stop again." He flashed a smile. "Besides — I have to go to the bathroom."

"Me too," said Lila. Piper had noticed that Lila had to go a lot recently. Maybe she had a nervous bladder. Maybe she was developing diabetes.

"You can pee at the side of the road," Piper said.

Meyer put his hand on Piper's arm, then steered the car forward again with one hand on the wheel. The thing wouldn't stop on auto without the GPS, but Meyer actually liked to drive. Probably because he liked the control.

"We need new maps anyway," he told her.

Piper felt her heart flutter, then pushed the feeling down. She tried on a smile, knowing she was being stupid, and managed to hold it until the engine was off and Meyer had entered the unlocked store to retrieve the gas cans.

He realized the tanks were empty a moment before the locals arrived.

Chapter Twenty-Six

Day Four, Evening
Rural Iowa

TREVOR WAS REMINDED of *The Children of the Corn*.

He'd never seen the movie nor read the story, but his father had told him the basic storyline the same as he'd given him the gist of the other classics he suspected modern kids were too cool to know. There were just some things that were part of culture, Trevor's father seemed to think — references that had become vernacular even to those who didn't know their source. Things like "using the Force," "entering the Matrix," or (and this one was particularly apt), "Beam me up, Scotty."

All Trevor knew about *The Children of the Corn* was that it was somehow about farmlands and cults. Old gods and sacrifice. But most of all, creepy country people who surrounded outsiders like zombies.

They'd come out of houses. Out from behind the gas station. From a leaning shack that might have been a post office or another government building. They were in the middle of the streets.

Men. Women. Even — and yes, there was that old cinematic reference again — children.

It was dark. Trevor tried to remind himself that he wasn't used to such darkness, having been raised in New York City. He wasn't used to quiet or the sough of the wind through wheat and corn. He wasn't used to the peculiar subaural echo that lived between buildings in the open air when nobody was speaking and no engines were running. It was a kind of hum, too low to be heard and more there to be felt — or sensed.

To Trevor, fifteen years old and unused to the country, simply being here was creepy no matter what happened. There might be nothing wrong. Nothing unusual. No reason to fear.

But clearly, his father felt something was amiss as well. Trevor could see it in the way he carefully racked the pump, now finished swearing over its spitting and gurgles. He'd seen it in Piper before they'd stopped, and in the way she hadn't even wanted to stop in the first place.

It wasn't just Trevor. Something was wrong.

"Hi there," said Meyer, nodding toward the man in the lead as he approached from the front. He seemed to be trying hard not to look around. This was all very normal. Just a welcoming party of two dozen people who'd chosen to slowly approach from all sides at once.

This is how we say hello 'round these parts. Jest have a sit, and we'll talk about the crops and the weather.

The man was wearing a green hat with a brim entirely too stiff for something so filthy and battered. He nodded and gave it a tug.

"Howdy," he said.

"Looks like your station is out of gas." Meyer tried to

affect a laugh, but the sound came out hollow. Several eyes moved to Piper, Trevor, Lila, and Raj. More hollow laughs abounded in the quiet darkness.

"Ayuh, we noticed the same." The man stopped walking. Now they were in a rough circle around the Land Cruiser, maybe thirty paces out. The feeling of being in a creepy movie he'd never seen reasserted itself on Trevor, and he felt his pulse quicken.

"I'm Meyer Dempsey, and this is my family. Piper, Trevor, Lila, and her boyfriend, Raj." He looked back, his voice too even to be natural. "Say hi, everyone."

Muttered hellos.

"Hey, I know you," said a woman behind the man. "You're that movie guy."

The man beside her — slightly rotund, balding, with three days' stubble — cocked his head. To the woman, he said, "He's in movies?"

"No, he's a movie maker. I seen him on the web before. And on TV, too."

"That right, friend?" said the man with the green cap. He was probably in his late forties with slightly saggy jowls and tired eyes, like an old hound dog's. "You in Hollywood?"

"His wife's that comedian," said the woman. "Heather Hawthorne." She looked pleased at having remembered.

"I know her," said the man. "She does that filthy show. About panties or whatnot."

Trevor felt himself tense. The man didn't sound approving. Trevor didn't want to stereotype, but it seemed that Midwestern values may have trumped his mother's rather outrageous West Coast comedy routine. He'd only been allowed to see his mother's act this past year, and even then the most colorful bits had been censored. He'd had to watch the rest online, off a pirate site.

"I heard she's with that other comedian," said the woman. "It was in *People*."

This seemed to be the final word. The woman seemed to be waiting for Meyer to elaborate, and the others were following her lead. Trevor found himself inching back to touch the Land Cruiser's cool security. He didn't like this at all.

They're just making conversation about your mom and dad and the tabloids. And Sam Blackwell, whom they love to rub in Dad's face. No big deal. Just having a chat. At night. In the middle of the street. Surrounding us in a circle, slack-jawed and vacant, like the people of the corn.

"We're not together anymore," Meyer said.

The woman nodded. She looked at the fat man. "See? Toldja." She looked at Meyer. "I knew a couple got a divorce once."

Meyer didn't seem to know what to say to that. So he stepped away from the pump and put his hand on the door handle. "Well. We'll just be on our way, then."

"Why don'tcha stay a bit?" said the man. The others were silent, standing and waiting. One woman held a baby, but even the baby was still — *or*, Trevor thought darkly, *dead*. "No rush to head out."

Meyer forced a new smile. "We have to be going."

He opened the door.

The man moved forward again, causing the others to do the same. The circle tightened, now just twenty or fifteen paces out. He held up a hand.

"Now, hang on a bit. You just picked up them gas cans from the station, and I know the payments aren't working inside. How were you planning on paying?"

"Oh, I …"

"Maybe you can pay with your gas."

"That's what I was planning. But there's no gas, so I can't pay for the cans when I pay for the gas, so …"

"Ayuh," the man repeated. "Gas ran out last night. Whole huge caravan of people came through in a line from the west, but no refill truck. Whole pack of cars, one after another."

"Out-of-towners," said a new woman. "People like you."

"Funny thing is," green cap continued, "few of us wanted to head out to see family and whatnot, and few of us did, just this morning, early, before light. But you know what they did before they went, those people who headed away?"

Meyer looked around, assessing. Green cap stepped forward again.

"Took the gas right outta our cars. Overnight. Took hoses and sucked it out in the dark. Like thieves."

Meyer gritted his teeth in a humorless grin. "That's a shame."

"Sure is," said the woman who'd recognized him. "Seeing as this is the only station around."

"So I was wondering," said the man with the hat. "Maybe I can borrow your car to head up the road."

Meyer looked at Piper. "Maybe I could run out for you." Trevor wondered if his father was serious. Meyer Dempsey was many things, and sometimes generous was one. But he didn't think this was one of those times. They had to hurry. Everyone in the world had to hurry, and there wasn't enough room or time for them to all have their way.

"Maybe I could do it," said the man, now holding his hand out. "If'n you'll just give me the keychain there."

"I'd rather not."

Mumbles of protest.

"Tell me," said the man. "Why is it that all those people should be able to come through and suck our station dry and leave us stuck here, and you won't help us?"

"Your problem is with the people who siphoned your tanks. Not with me."

"We're just as stranded, mister." The man nodded toward the Land Cruiser. "And I'd bet you still have enough gas left in there to be worth taking, should a man be sufficiently motivated."

"One of you must have a gas can. Something your people missed. There must be one gas can in a shed. Something for a tractor or a log splitter."

"Tractors," said the fat man. "Yep, we must know nothing but tractors, being poor country folk."

"We don't have any quarrel with you." Meyer was now half in the cabin. Through the open door, Trevor saw him reaching into the cab, his hand searching without looking.

"Maybe we have a quarrel with you," said the man.

"We're going to go now."

"And bring us back some gas, right?" said the man in the cap.

"He ain't coming back," said the woman.

"I'll bring you gas." Trevor could hear the lie in his father's voice.

"Maybe," said green hat, "we want the whole car, and whatever else you might got inside."

Meyer found what he was looking for. He whipped his hand out and waved the pistol.

The man wasn't a zombie after all, it seemed. His hands went up, and he fell a step back. But others were eyeing him, waiting at the flanks. They only slunk back after Meyer waved the gun at them, too.

"You're making a mistake, friend," said the man. "End times are coming, and you're apt to be on the wrong side."

Meyer tossed his head at Trevor and the others: the universal gesture for *Get the fuck in the car right now, before we get butt-raped.* Then he slid into the Cruiser's front seat, now pointing the pistol through the open window.

"I'll tell Jesus you said hi the second I can get cell reception," he told the man.

Meyer fired the engine and sped away, not seeming to care if the people in the circle jumped out of the way or if he ran them into the dust.

Chapter Twenty-Seven

Day Four, Evening
  Western Iowa

"Where are we?" Piper asked.

Meyer's eyes were on the road. He'd driven fifty hard miles and still hadn't returned the car to autodrive. They were burning an already low fuel tank and they'd driven off their last map's edge. They seemed to be driving west, and he figured that as long as they didn't start seeing Kansas City or Wichita to the south or cross I-80 to the north, they were roughly on target. They could course correct the minute they had a new map, and keep themselves from running dry the minute they found a gas station where they could again try their luck, though Meyer felt gun-shy, surely like everyone else.

"Doesn't matter."

"Sure it matters. We're …"

"Doesn't matter, Piper. We were south of Des Moines, and now we're headed west. Vail is west, more or less."

Heather would have repeated his last words with heavy sarcasm, beating on him until he clarified just what the hell "more or less" meant. She might remind him that if the geeks' estimates were right, tomorrow would be the last full day Earth would spend before meeting ET. It might be the last full day Earth and its inhabitants had to *live*, for all anyone knew. Heather wouldn't take his pat answers or tolerate his bullying insistence on having his way while everyone fell in line.

But Piper wasn't Heather. She was sweeter. More innocent and malleable. Younger than his ex by a decade. And much, *much* better for him than Heather, as much as he still loved them both.

Piper sat facing forward, small lines of anger on her pretty face. Even the lines were new. This trip was hardening her, just as the riot outside Chicago had hardened her. He'd told her not to hesitate in the future, and she was barely hesitating now, just a day and a half later.

"We're almost out of gas," she said, her arms crossed.

"Yes."

That was the elephant in the Cruiser's roomy interior — the one thing they all knew but seemed intent to ignore as if it might go away. Without a new map or GPS, they couldn't be sure where they were. Without knowing their whereabouts, they couldn't anticipate the small burgs ahead. Large towns might be overrun and panicky, having surrendered to the strange critical mass that happened when too many people were stupid in close proximity. Small towns might have only operator-run stations or might have lost power — something they'd already seen in entire rows of homes and businesses just these past fifty miles. They needed fuel, but this was a Goldilocks mission; they had to find something just right.

Until then, there was no way to tell where they should

stop. They couldn't find their starting point until they found their stopping point, and without that, where to begin was anyone's guess.

It was an endless loop — a snake eating its tail.

They were tacitly lost. Definitely low on fuel.

They drove on as minutes stretched into hours.

THE GAS NEEDLE had edged below the thick red "E" line by the time they pulled into a gas station in a one-stoplight town somewhere in Iowa. Meyer had no idea *where* in Iowa. He only knew that they hadn't passed I-80 to the north, and that probably meant they were still headed west. When the sun rose, he'd know for sure, but for now could only guess. Meyer also knew that unless he'd missed a sign, they hadn't yet entered Nebraska. So Iowa it was. And good riddance it would be.

When the gas began to flow and no angry villagers arrived, Piper's demeanor thawed. It was nearly eleven o'clock, and they were all exhausted, but no one had slept. Sleeping, said an unspoken agreement inside the Cruiser, was merely spinning wheels. Until they solved the fuel problem, they were only in abeyance, not at all settled. They were in driver's purgatory, and only time would tell if they found combustible salvation or were left stranded, their only choice to hoof it until morning dawned — at which point, if they feared discovery, they could always sleep in rows of roadside corn.

Piper came around to the vehicle's side while the kids milled. Neither Meyer nor Piper had told them to stay close (they were fifteen and seventeen, both beyond being told much), but after the encounter near Des Moines, nobody wanted to wander beyond the station's lights. Or even enter the station unarmed — something Meyer had already done. He'd returned bearing extra gas cans to replace those they'd left on the concrete the last time. He'd discovered a Comstock Lode of supplies, nervous purely by how excited he was to find them. Water, candy bars, and potato chips. The kids looked almost happy.

"Hey," Piper said.

"Almost done." Meyer nodded at the pump.

"I'm not asking you to hurry."

They were in an odd apologetic standoff. She wanted to apologize for being cold, and he wanted to apologize for being dismissive and distant. They wanted it so badly that neither would actually say anything because it was so intensely implied.

"I know. But it's still almost done."

"You already filled the gas cans?"

"No. I figured I wanted to get it into the tank first, just in case we met more friendly locals."

Piper reached into the Cruiser. She came out with the hunting rifle they'd taken from the man at the dealership. She held it up to her eye and pointed into the darkness. Despite being dim, the streets were obviously empty. If anyone came to challenge them, they'd have plenty of time to duck and run.

"I'll take them out if they come," she said, peering into the scope.

"You're looking through that with the wrong eye."

Instead of switching eyes, she turned them both to him. They were the same huge blue eyes they'd always been, but seemed ten years older. Apparently, his wives weren't that disparate in maturity after all. It had merely taken the threat of armageddon to equalize them.

"Maybe I'm left-handed," she said. "Or left-eyed, or whatever it would be."

"You're not."

"Maybe I'm a better shot than you think I am, no matter which eye I use."

"You look sexy with a gun," he said.

"Yeah, yeah. All the guys tell me that."

Trevor came around the Land Cruiser's side, took one look at the rifle, then scanned the lot. Only after assuring himself that his stepmother was merely playing with firearms in clear defiance of everything everyone has ever been told by the NRA did he finally exhale.

"Almost done, Trev," said Meyer. "Get your sister."

"She's being a bitch," he replied.

"Get her anyway."

Trevor did. They packed up and moved on.

Hours passed. Meyer surrendered the left seat to Piper in case manual driving was required, then tried to sleep.

He woke intermittently, always glancing at Piper before checking the clock. He found her reading two times out of three, her feet kicked up on the dashboard, her Vellum reader unfolded. It was good, seeing her doing something so normal. Piper read all the time at home. Once, he'd grown curious about what she always had her nose buried in — and, knowing it was a huge violation of her privacy, peeked through the Vellum's directory while she was away. She read all sorts of genres, but erotica was the largest. The discovery had surprised him so much, they'd made love twice that night, Meyer immensely excited by the depth and breadth of his pretty wife's secret sex life. He wouldn't tell her what he knew, but it thrilled him to see her read now, wondering what fantasies may or may not be capering inside her mind and prickling between her legs.

Then he looked at the clock on the dashboard.

12:47.

2:13.

3:23.

He wasn't sure if the hours passed between glances were even spent sleeping. He drifted in and out of a semi-haze, sometimes seeming to dream in a way that was as real as anything. He walked with Heather. He watched the spheres arrive from above with a feeling of nonspecific knowing. He returned to Peru, this time without consulting his shaman. He even dreamed of the Land Cruiser itself, his brain turned off enough to filter his dreams through boring nighttime reality. The doubling was a dream of a dream — visions of himself asleep in the leather seat, his head lolled to the side.

4:14 a.m.

5:02.

Still, the roads stayed mostly empty. He'd have to ask Piper, but from what he'd seen (and the progress they were making; he was quite sure he'd been awake to see the Colorado welcome signs), the way had been smooth. Piper showed no signs of tiring. The children slept, Trevor snoring and drooling. Raj and Lila leaned together in a two-person huddle, Raj's hand too close to Lila's breast. But everyone had to take comfort where they could find it, and the game had changed. He could be an irate, overprotective father later.

It would almost be a relief to do something so normal.

"MEYER. MEYER, WAKE UP."

He shook his head, then blinked. He'd fallen asleep again.

He didn't remember doing it and hadn't intended to. They'd watched the sun rise together through the back window, seeing it turn the sleeping children to silhouettes.

The morning had been quiet, and Meyer had repressed his need to take a leak so that the others could get much-needed rest. He'd asked Piper if she wanted to sleep, but she'd been as bright and cheery as a pixie, as if she stayed up all night often. She didn't even seem to need coffee, which was good because they wouldn't be pulling into a Dunkin Donuts any time soon. They'd been living on Lays, Luna bars, and water. What he wouldn't have given for a propane travel stove and some Folgers crystals, and damn the threat of asphyxiation, or the flammability and fumes wafting from the gas cans in the back. They'd been in Colorado by then, closing on Denver, and the tank still had plenty. They were going to make it just fine.

But sometime after sunrise, Meyer must have nodded off again. He looked back, trying to gauge the sun's height. But it was too high, out of view. It was late morning.

"What time is it?" he asked, fighting cobwebs.

Piper didn't point to the clock, and he didn't even twitch his head to look for himself. He was too drawn by the look on her face.

"Shit," he said.

She'd put the car in manual. Both hands were on the wheel, and her right foot was on the gas pedal. "What do I do?"

A semitrailer lay on its side up ahead, fully blocking the road. Vail had to be close; he could feel the altitude pressing against his eardrums. They were well above sea level, still on back roads plotted by Piper while he dozed. But in the mountains, cars could only travel to so many places, and around the touristy ski area, options were limited. Like now: they had no way around the trailer. To one side was a gully, to the other an escarpment. How the semi had ever managed its position was a mystery.

"We'll have to go back," he told her.

"Shit. Shit-shit-shit ..."

"Piper, what? It's no big deal. Just back up there and turn around and ..."

But she'd been awake for more than Meyer's thirty seconds. Maybe she'd seen signs but chose to ignore them. Maybe she'd already noticed that the semitrailer had no cab attached, begging the question of how it had ended up where it was without someone doing it deliberately. Or maybe she'd just felt the air change as she had back near Des Moines, when he should've listened but chose to ignore her.

Something struck the Land Cruiser from behind: a large Jeep, with bars welded across its absent windshield.

Men crawled over the sideways tractor trailer ahead, each holding a weapon.

Meyer reached for the Land Cruiser's center console, but there was a knock on the window before he got there. He looked up to see a man tapping the glass with the barrel of a pistol. On the other side, beyond Piper, a second man was doing the same.

Meyer's visitor motioned for him to roll down the window, which Piper did for him.

"Best not reach for your weapon, mate," said the man. "Leave it where it is."

Meyer's hand retracted. The man reached across to open the console and fish out the handgun. Meyer tried to remember where Piper had set the rifle, but it hardly mattered. Their chances of turning a hunting rifle on assailants in close quarters were somewhere between slim and nil.

"Come on out now," he said, his voice eminently polite.

Meyer was still thinking of the rifle, still looking

around. The man watched him, then tipped his head at Meyer as if he could read his thoughts.

"Open the door, and let it go, mate," he said. "Be a good sport, and you can keep your lives. But dead or alive, we'll be taking your vehicle."

DAY FIVE

Chapter Twenty-Eight

DAY FIVE, Morning
  Colorado

IT WAS hard to call the people who stole the Land Cruiser bandits. They worked with an efficiency that Meyer couldn't help but admire: no drama, no bloodshed, no unnecessary emotional entanglement aside from the obvious implied threat.

Their compliance wasn't a question. There were at least as many of them as there had been hicks in Iowa, but this crew was entirely armed. They'd blockaded the road, boxed them in, then waltzed up to the window with weapons capable of killing them all. Maybe the Dempsey family could have fought, but they'd never have fled without a fatality, and Meyer wasn't willing to spend one. Even Raj.

Once they stepped out of the car, one of the men climbed inside as dispassionately as a mechanic driving a car into the garage for service. The only difference was that instead of driving the Cruiser into a garage, the man drove it around the Jeep and back in the opposite direction.

Meyer shouldered his backpack and nodded silently at his party to do the same. The highwaymen said nothing. They didn't want food and water. Only the car, and perhaps the fuel in its tank.

After being relieved of their vehicle, the outlaw waved them around the semitrailer and suggested they start walking. Meyer looked back a minute down the road; no one was following. The trailer seemed to be deserted and maybe it was: a one-time carjacking, and then everyone retired. It was a mystery Meyer didn't suppose he'd ever solve, but it hardly mattered. Yet again, they had no car. Ten minutes later, he insisted on circling back alone to ambush the bandits, intent on recovering their vehicle (or any other), but found them all gone. Only the trailer remained.

They were alone in the mountains. The surrounding resorts all seemed deserted, waiting for a winter ski season that would never come.

The going was tough, and their lungs were unaccustomed to the thin air. After a half hour of walking, Lila sat on a rock by the roadside and stared up at her father, refusing to move like a stubborn dog.

"Come on, Lila."

"What, Dad? We don't have a car. It's not like we can hitch a ride."

Meyer looked around. They'd left what passed for a main road a while back, beginning the long and winding trek to the compound. He'd picked the spot because it was isolated, hours away on tiny roads, so hidden that even Meyer sometimes got lost trying to reach it when checking construction.

"We can walk."

"How far is it?"

Meyer shrugged. He thought he knew exactly how far it was, but telling Lila wouldn't do anyone any good. If anything, it would make the others refuse to budge.

"How far, Dad?" she repeated.

"Considering how far we've come? We're almost there."

"How about if you *don't* consider how far we've come? *Then* how far is it? You know, in real-person miles. The way someone normal would measure it."

"I'm not sure. But it's that way." He pointed.

Lila stared at him. He had a strange urge to grab her arm and drag.

"It's outside Vail. This is basically Vail."

"How far outside?"

"Lila, get up."

Instead of Lila standing, Raj sat. Trevor followed a second behind. Piper, standing across from him, looked very much like she wanted to do the same, but this seemed to be a show of support. She could collapse later. Right now she had to stand with her obsessive husband against the will of her reasonable stepchildren who were, despite their father's wishes, talking sense.

"We only have a day." Meyer looked up. It had to be 9 a.m. or later. He looked over at Piper. "Right? Just a day still?"

"Why are you asking me?"

"Did you listen to the radio last night, while I was asleep?"

"A bit. As much as I could stand, anyway."

"And?"

"And what, Meyer?"

"Well, what are they saying?"

"Riots, looting, people doing stupid shit like stealing cars." She looked back toward the ambush. "Although I'm not sure if the stupid shit is them taking the car, or us taking it a few days earlier."

Lila was smiling broadly behind the hand clapped to her mouth. Piper never swore unless she was being playful in bed. To Lila, right now, at this hideous moment, hearing Piper break her usual unspoken rule to say "shit" (twice) was a bizarre kind of Christmas.

"What about the ships?"

"Oh, I don't know, Meyer. It's hard to tell the real reports from the crazy ones. Remember what your dad was saying about 9/11? How it got all 'foggy' and nobody knew what terrible things were actually happening and what wasn't true? That's the whole world, right now."

Meyer decided not to push. He'd made his living negotiating one thing or another, and a forgotten key to success was knowing when not to play the game. He wouldn't make Piper say what he wanted, but she hadn't denied it. They had a day, maybe thirty-six hours. They could walk it in that time if they'd toughen up.

"Look," he said. "It's stupid to give up now. I know you're tired. I'm tired too. But we have to do it. We can rest at the house."

Raj lay back on the gravel. "Let's rest here."

Lila lay back beside him. "I agree."

"Get up, Lila."

Piper perched on the guardrail. Why not? Nobody would be traveling these roads anytime soon. They could sleep in the middle of the road if they wanted to.

"Get *up*, Lila," he repeated.

"I'm tired, Dad. And I feel like I'm going to throw up again. Maybe you should show some mercy, considering …"

"Considering what?"

She rolled her eyes. "Nothing."

"We have to go," he said. "We can rest for a while, but then we walk. A bit at a time is fine, but we have to keep moving."

"Let's just find a nice barn to shack in," said Piper. "Like I suggested back in Pennsylvania."

Meyer straightened. Then he took Piper by the hand and practically picked her upright. Something in his manner must have registered with Trevor, because he stood too. Even Lila and Raj sat up, but showed no sign — yet — of coming along.

"What?" said Piper.

"You gave me an idea."

"About a barn. So we can do that. Shelter in a barn. Maybe steal some guy's car later on so we can make a run."

"Not the barn." Meyer shook his head. "What's in the barn."

"A tractor." Lila looked at Raj. "I am *not* driving down the road on a tractor."

"Horses," Meyer replied.

Chapter Twenty-Nine

DAY FIVE, Afternoon
 Colorado

LILA DIDN'T KNOW that Colorado — this part, anyway — was horse country. But it clearly was, and once they started walking and knew what they were looking for, they found a farm almost immediately. But there were people visible, milling in the house and walking back and forth to the barns. For a moment as they walked past on their way to the next one (not so close as to be obvious), Lila thought of who those people might be and what they might be thinking. Were they a family, like the Dempseys? Were they highwaymen who'd left the road to occupy a ranch? It was impossible to tell from a distance. Good men and bad men looked the same from the road, especially considering how thin the line between them had become.

Lila forgot her pregnancy for hours at a time. It was still important (vital, really), but so many matters of consequence had surfaced in the past four days. There were the alien ships; there was the riot and fear of death; there were two ambushes resulting in one grand theft auto. Only during the slow times — like now, as they walked — did she stop to be a seventeen-year-old girl again. There would come a time when Lila grew large and another time when she'd have to discuss what had happened with her father. It hurt to think of; she'd always been such a daddy's girl. Admitting to a baby would be admitting, in an irrevocable way, that she was no longer her father's. She'd had at least one deeper relationship with a man her age. And she'd soon be a full-grown woman in nature's most obvious way.

Thinking about the baby made Lila think of her mother. Mom had, despite her caustic comedy act and her reputation for outrageousness, been an excellent mother. She'd only given Meyer custody because his life (with far less travel and fewer late nights) was more stable. It had crushed her to give them up, and she still doted on Lila and Trevor whenever she saw them. She stopped being irreverent Heather Hawthorne and became Mom again.

Lila watched the first horse farm vanish behind a rise. Who were those people? Did they own the ranch and had simply never left? Was this all business as usual for them? Were they tending to chores as if the world wasn't about to change forever — feeding horses who had no idea, no fear that Earth might be seeing its final days? Supposedly, animals could sense threats like storms and fires well before they were upon them. There was a hardwired, inborn fear that told them when running was worthwhile. What would it mean if, when they eventually found some horses, the animals were as calm as those people appeared from a distance? Would it mean there was nothing to fret about after all, and that their human fear of change was manufacturing the panic — all this chaos and lawlessness?

What did it mean, when they found those horses, that they themselves would resort to theft … *again*?

It was okay to commit crimes if it was for your own good, it seemed.

It was okay to steal if it meant getting away from people who wanted to steal from you.

It was okay to beat people up and make your own rules if it would get you to your hole in the ground, where you could hide while everyone else either died or tore themselves apart.

Maybe the Dempseys weren't anything special. Maybe they were just five average people, marching toward judgment like all the rest.

TEN MINUTES LATER, they came to a large horse farm just as nice as the first. It was either deserted, or the owners were hiding. Either way, the horses whinnied loudly when they entered, clearly hungry, their stalls overfull of manure and in need of cleaning. Meyer and Piper strapped saddles on five of the horses while Lila closed an access gate and opened the seven remaining stalls to let the horses run free in a large indoor arena. Then she opened a gate at the other end, giving the animals access to stacked hay and a few unopened piles of feedbags in a storage area.

Trevor was behind her, watching with ambivalence. "I think horses just eat and eat until they explode if you don't ration their food."

"You're thinking of goldfish," she said.

"So you're saying they'll stop when they're full."

Lila shrugged. There was only so much she could do. If nobody had come back, they'd have starved in their stalls. If nobody came back even now, they'd run out of food and starve in the arena. Maybe they'd eat themselves to death. Maybe she was choosing their doom, same as she was choosing her own.

Raj closed the gate to the storage area, and proceeded to toss several hay bales inside, followed by three cracked-open bags of feed. Then he vaulted the gate, walked to the arena's far end, and opened the outside door. They were in the mountains, a wild area, with barely any traffic. Horses were animals. They'd adapt.

"Split the difference," he said.

TIME PASSED DIFFERENTLY ONCE they were riding. Lila hadn't fully realized her exhaustion until she was back to traveling without using her legs.

Something in her mind had shut off a lot of what was happening in her body — perhaps trying to keep her feet moving despite pain and fear and fatigue, obeying a primitive sense of self-preservation. But now that her only job was to balance atop the horse, Lila found her mind had returned to wandering. She wondered if she was in shock.

What was shock like? Yet another condition she couldn't look up. When she felt dizzy thinking of their destination, was that morning sickness, shock, or cowardice? Did Trevor and Raj feel the same? Did Piper?

A few days was all it had taken to affect a change in Piper. She was still Lila's quirky, vaguely New-Age stepmother. She was still cool; she still shared a surprising amount of Lila's tastes in music — and of course in clothing, seeing as she was the brain behind Quirky Q. Lila's friends had been over the moon when Lila's father had married Piper Fucking Dempsey — but to Lila, it had all been so obvious. Yes, Piper was amazing. But her father had married her when she'd been Piper Fucking Quincy, a nobody known by no one. Piper Quincy had put the Q in

Quirky Q, but the world only knew her after she'd married the mogul who funded her business to make it what it was now. To put the Fucking in Piper Fucking Dempsey, as it were.

But now, in addition to being all those cool things — more an older sister than a mother figure — Piper had grown an edge. She rode beside Lila's father rather than behind him as she would have in the past. She'd taken the driver's seat several times when they'd still had a car — not just when Meyer needed rest, but sometimes because she liked her hands on the wheel.

"Hey," said Raj.

He'd ridden up alongside her, same as Piper had ridden up to her father. She looked over, trying to see him anew. He'd proven himself during this trip, even though he technically shouldn't even be on it. He'd been forced into the family as if by a crowbar, and seemed to fit. He'd been noble and stupid enough to run after the woman in trouble when the freeway riot began, then smart enough to cut his losses and drag Lila back out. He'd handled the car salesman with the gun. He'd stood up to her father, even though he'd lost. She could hardly count that against him. Everyone lost to Meyer Dempsey.

"Hey."

"How are you? I mean …" He looked ahead, past Trevor, to the adults at the front of their five-horse caravan on the road's side. He patted his own stomach and lowered his voice. "You know. With the … ?"

She forced a smile. "I feel okay. For now."

"Not sick?"

Lila looked up at the bright-blue sky, hemmed in by hills and trees. Being up in these mountains was almost like being in a valley, but the feeling was secure rather than claustrophobic. It was almost possible to believe they might escape the spheres. The sun was high though the air held a chill.

"Only in the mornings. I don't feel like throwing up once it gets past noon, like clockwork." She pointed at the high sun, establishing the time without digging for her phone.

"You didn't seem like you wanted to throw up this morning."

"I barfed in one of the stalls."

"Oh."

"But I don't know if that's morning sickness. I might just be convinced it *should* be morning sickness."

"How would that work?"

Lila let it go. Her own mind could manufacture all sorts of illnesses if it thought it was supposed to, but Raj was cut and dry. He'd make a good doctor. Maybe even a good dad.

"Never mind."

"Piper said she heard on the news that the ships are slowing down."

Lila looked over. Why did he have to say that? She'd managed to feel human and normal for a few minutes. They had a sunny day with long shadows and crisp mountain air. It was almost possible to imagine all the skiers arriving a few months from now, parking their expensive vehicles and walking toward lodges with their overpriced skis. That was a world where people had nothing better to do than reach the top of a big hill and slide back down on boards. A world that she suspected might never return.

Lila recovered anyway. Denial wouldn't help. If things were coming, she might as well force herself to get used to it.

"I thought they were already slowing down."

"Well, sure. But now they're, you know, braking."

"Like breaking into pieces?"

"No. *Braking*. Like, 'whoa.'" He pulled the reins back to demonstrate, and the horse dutifully stopped. Lila laughed as he nudged his mount's sides to catch up.

"What does that mean?"

"That they don't want to ram us."

She'd forgotten the idea that the ships might simply ram Earth to begin with. Raj's bringing up the threat then dismissing it immediately didn't feel like good news. It felt like a wash.

Lila looked up, wondering how long it would be before people could see the ships with the naked eye. Maybe some people already could. The thought gave her a chill, but she stuffed it down.

"Oh. Well, that's good."

"Sure." Silence, then, "What do you think they want?"

Lila shrugged, trying to hide her dread.

"What do you think they're *like?*" he said.

Lila didn't like the images *that* brought up, either. She wondered at herself, watching her own reactions as if from the outside. Had she been thinking they might be giant marbles that would show up, hang out, then leave without doing anything? Because based on her reactions to Raj's perfectly sensible inquiries, it sure seemed she had.

"I have no idea." She decided to rip off the Band-Aid. "I just hope they're not those gray things with the giant, black, almond-shaped eyes."

Raj studied Lila.

"You have *big, brown,* almond-shaped eyes. Maybe they'll like you."

Lila wondered if she should be insulted, but he clearly meant it as a cutesy compliment. And besides, it was true. She did have big, brown, almond-shaped eyes.

"Maybe."

"I get a little ashy sometimes," he said. "Do you think our baby might be able to pass for one of them, if they take over the planet and enslave us all?"

Now he'd taken it too far.

"Raj, that's not …"

But her horse — with autodrive as good as either of their two cars on this long trip — had stopped to keep from rear-ending Trevor's. His horse, in turn, had stopped behind the leads.

They'd been on a long, packed-dirt road that Lila now realized was her own new driveway. She'd never been to the under-construction compound, but if they were really the only house on what she'd taken for this long road, it was isolated indeed.

The house peeking between the trees looked finished to Lila, though there was a stack of lumber and shingles to one side and a port-a-potty standing on the unfinished dirt lawn. It must just be final details that needed doing up top, but her father had been clear: the bunker, which mattered most, was finished, full, and downright bombproof.

"Wow, Dad," said Trevor. "It's awesome."

Meyer said nothing.

"Dad?"

Piper reached out slowly as if she wanted to touch him. But her hand seemed to decide it had been foolish and settled back on her leg, twitching as if unsure where to go.

Lila looked from one to the other. In front of her, Trevor turned back, puzzled.

"What's wrong, Dad? Why did we stop?"

"That strikes me as off." He pointed toward an out-jut that was, seen from the side, probably a garage. Beside it was a blue PriusX, its bumper half-off and resting on the concrete.

224

"Is that ... ?" Lila began. But it almost had to be. "That's Mom's car!"

Trevor's head whipped around. Lila and her brother stirred, their horses sensing their desire to move forward.

Meyer held out a pacifying hand, palm back, to stop them. "Hang on."

Lila waited for him to elaborate, then saw silhouettes moving in the window, behind a pair of pickups parked at the end of fresh ruts — two vehicles that had no business being here.

The silhouettes were holding long things that could only be shotguns.

"We're not quite home yet," he said.

Chapter Thirty

DAY FIVE, Early Evening
  Axis Mundi

HEATHER WONDERED if it meant anything that all three of the men who'd taken over Meyer's house had facial hair.

She wasn't tied to a chair like a movie damsel, and she wasn't gagged, but the three men had mustaches appropriate to binding and gagging damsels just the same. They kept threatening to rectify the gag situation if she didn't shut the hell up.

As far as Heather could tell, they didn't recognize her. That was probably good because they wouldn't see her as having any special value (as if the world, right now, cared about C-list celebrity), and it was similarly good because it meant she'd just be a loudmouth fortysomething Jew rather than a famous girl worth raping, if for no other reason than bragging rights.

Or a rousing game of I Never.

I never fucked a famous comedienne. And then these three assholes would have to drink.

But she hadn't been raped outside of Vegas, she hadn't been raped after those onlookers had responded to the gunshots she'd managed to squeeze from the pistol despite her revulsion, and she hadn't been raped the nights she'd had to stop her car after the GPS had failed and her Prius — not the most advanced vehicle — lost its ability to navigate without her.

Heather wondered if she should be offended that so few people had tried to rape her. She was still smoking hot. All the tabloids said so.

It was the kind of wry, inappropriate, that's-just-wrong joke she'd make in one of her shows. Nobody would even flinch, probably. After all the shit that had made her famous onstage? She was immune. The infamous Hitler jokes assured that. Now, nothing from her mouth could shock an audience. And besides, the minute people started laughing at her wrong jokes — which they always did, and rather breathlessly — they were culpable. If someone had a problem with her jokes about wet panties and Hitler (note to self: need jokes about *Hitler's* wet panties), that accusing finger would have to turn on everyone who'd ever thought they were funny, too.

Heather stood, sat, stood again. They'd locked her in the second pantry, apparently agreeing that binding her to a chair was a bit too tried and true. The pantry wasn't stocked yet, but for some reason only Meyer understood it had a mesh door that the assholes in her house had locked via two screwdrivers hammered into the jamb. They had a lot of screwdrivers. For a while, the leader (the one with the best, most Snidely Whiplash mustache; the others were closer to simply unshaven) had forgotten about his tool belt, as if this were just another day on the Vail house job. He'd taken it off after Heather mocked him about it through the grate, and for a while he'd stared at her with hatred. She was sure a revenge-raping was on the table. But then he'd pussied out, like all tough guys did. Heather should know, as a woman in an industry dominated by men. They'd all tried to push her around for a while when she'd been new, but then she'd crossed every line that anyone could possibly imagine, including that of her father's secret alcoholism and discovering her mother's vibrator and how it had been clumped with disgusting goo. Then the boys had left her alone. It was like fistfighting with a crazy person. You never knew what stupid shit they might do, seeing as they were out of their minds, so those with no stones just stayed in the corner.

These guys were like that. But there was a fine line, and it wasn't lost on Heather that they'd thus far kept her 1) alive and 2) unraped. It might mean they were saving her as a bargaining chip, should the home's owner appear with guns blazing. Or it might mean she'd so far been lucky, and could be shot through the bars at any time.

She couldn't decide. On one hand, the trio's leader, Garth (he of the black Snidely Whiplash mustache) had served Meyer loyally until just a few days ago. Heather had even greeted him warmly when he'd arrived, just twelve hours after her. She didn't really know him, but had seen him once when she and Meyer had taken the Gulfstream from LA on one of his "business trips," intent on spending the day checking progress and the night with Juha, Meyer's shaman. Garth had seemed a competent foreman at the time. And she'd decided he did an excellent job once she was high — while she was seeing colors and Meyer was off in the spirit realm … or whatever the fuck he felt after he'd drunk and purged.

But on the other hand, Garth had that mustache.

Ultimately, the decision about whether Garth was a solid employee or a fucker was decided when he'd grabbed her wrist that first night, made her scream, then shouted for the two buddies he'd brought with him. Into the pantry she'd gone. And now the only thing keeping them from gagging her was the effort of removing the screwdrivers holding her in.

Heather wondered if she should pace her cell, bounce a rubber ball off the walls, do pull-ups and push-ups, or wistfully play the harmonica.

But ultimately, she decided most of the time to stay mute (against her instincts; it wasn't easy) and to sit on the floor, pretending she didn't exist. They'd tossed her a few boxes of crackers yesterday, and it would be a while before she'd have to ask for more. For now, if she lay low, maybe they'd let her be.

Then she could bide her time and wait for Meyer.

Heather really had no doubt that he would, indeed, arrive. The man was relentless. She'd joked about Meyer onstage too, but with decidedly more unspoken affection. His will (like his cock) was a battering ram. He'd be here. Somehow, he'd be here, and get her out.

A small, hidden part of Heather wondered at that, though, and the larger, louder Heather spent every moment trying to crush her quiet doubts.

In truth, she didn't feel quite as obnoxious and brash as she sounded.

In truth, she was a little afraid of Garth, Remy, and that fucking wildcard kid Wade. Wade was as crazy as Heather pretended to be, but she was pretty sure his craziness was greased by speed and PCP. He had an idiot's mania and, despite his wiry frame, the strength of a person who literally has no idea how hard he can hit. He'd already buckled a joist after Garth had yelled at him. And, probably, broken every bone in his arm and hand.

In truth, Heather wondered if Meyer really *was* coming, despite what she kept telling herself. He was strong and smart, bullheaded. Behind the sarcasm, she loved him very much. But she'd seen Vegas burn, and she'd heard enough panic on the increasingly intermittent news to know that anything could happen out there. He might have been shot and killed, as she nearly had been. Or ripped off and stranded, unable to reach his destination in time.

And the kids?

Heather suppressed a shudder, then doubled the effort to force reality away and reinforce her sarcastic wall. She wouldn't even consider what might have happened to … to whatever it was that she'd already forgotten to think about.

Outside the pantry, Remy (pathetic- and confused-looking, light-blue eyes, around her own age) was eating a snack-size bag of Cheetos. Predictably, crumbs were lodging in his sad little mustache. He brushed at the thing, but a rather large chunk remained.

"I see you're saving some for later," Heather observed.

Remy trained his pale-blue eyes on her, gripped the gun butt at his side, and said nothing.

Chapter Thirty-One

KICKING the door in and charging whoever had occupied the ranch — as Trevor and Raj had suggested — would have been a terrible idea. Chances were good that someone would get shot. But they shouldn't make it easy.

Meyer rolled the thought in his calculating mind, weighing it, trying to decide if he could live with the odds. Given the near-certainty of getting shot, he didn't want Piper or Lila putting themselves at risk. Yes, it was sexist. Meyer didn't care. It would also keep them out of the way, and safe from the bullets.

If they listened to his instructions, they wouldn't even approach the house. They'd stay at the tree line, and if Meyer, Raj, and Trevor failed, the bandits would never know they were there. Plan B was for the men to fall on the blade (metaphorically, Meyer hoped) and for the girls to go somewhere else — anywhere that seemed to offer unconventional shelter rather than predictable homes and barns. And if the men in the house killed them and came after Lila and Piper, they had a plan for *that*, too. They were on horseback, and trucks couldn't fit between the trees. So if the bandits gave chase, they needed only to take the wooded path.

Meyer was crouched behind the first truck. Raj was behind the other. Trevor was in the least responsible and safest position, present only because Meyer had encouraged him to stand up for himself in the past and denying him now felt hypocritical. Besides, they needed a lookout — someone on the other side of the house looking through windows, able to shout locations if they swarmed at Meyer and Raj. Sure, it was cowardly. But it was also insulting to tell the women they shouldn't fight, and right now social rules didn't matter much to Meyer. All that mattered was winning his Axis Mundi back — and if he had to be an asshole and fight dirty, so be it.

Life wasn't like the movies — not even quality movies made by his studio. In non-close-quarters gunfights, people tended to aim poorly and rarely got shot. But things changed when one party wasn't willing to back off, determined to keep coming no matter what. Meyer wasn't willing to come so far only to turn away. He'd keep coming, and someone might be killed. He was okay with it being him if that meant victory, and truth be told he was mostly okay with it being Raj. If that made him a bastard, oh well.

Right now, his family was all that mattered.

Meyer had learned a thing or two about gunfights as he'd trained for history's inevitable shift. But he didn't need training to know that gunfights were harder and a lot more dangerous when you didn't have any guns.

Raj looked over. Meyer motioned for him to wait.

Maybe it was stupid to even try and get in, past the men with shotguns.

Probably it was stupid.

But even though they'd lost their weapons with the Land Cruiser, they had to try. Meyer knew it. He knew it in the way he'd seen this all coming.

When the ships arrived, they needed to be here, in Vail, inside this bunker. It was all over if they weren't. Piper and Lila might be able to survive out there somewhere if this all went south, but even that scared him. He had to get them all safe, including Heather, who was probably inside, having apparently rolled out of the Vegas fat and into the Vail fire.

Get inside or die.

Or: *Die trying to get inside.*

Raj was pointing at the truck in front of him. He was behind the tailgate, but gesturing toward the cab. Meyer watched him mouth, *Gun.*

Meyer shrugged.

Gun in truck? Then a shrug, as if asking a question.

He was saying there might be weapons in the trucks. Meyer doubted it. Only a stupid criminal would invade a home, then leave firearms outside for the cops to use on arrival. Only, this wasn't the usual home invasion, and the police wouldn't be coming. It was a mystery how anyone had even found the place. In the end, only two things mattered.

Heather might need help.

And they had to get inside.

Both problems pointed to one solution: they had to reach the bunker, below the house.

The invaders wouldn't even know it was there. Its entrance, like that of any respectable panic room, was concealed behind the back of a mop closet off the kitchen. You slid aside a panel, you entered a code, and then the back of the closet would swing forward like a secret passage in an old haunted mansion. Behind that wall was a tiny space, too small to be noticed from the outside by all but the most observant architect. A tight spiral staircase wound downward, set in concrete. You could retract both stairs and central spindle to lower supplies down on a dumbwaiter, but the largest items were added before the construction crew had laid the steel and concrete floor to seal it in. Tough cookies if they wanted a new couch for the apocalypse.

But there were guns in the bunker. Plenty. If they could get downstairs quietly, they could arm up. Then they could come up blazing. Meyer could even handle that bit of unpleasantness himself. He had body armor and riot helmets. He'd even spent a fortune on an Uzi, thus ensuring aim as an afterthought.

Then they could find Heather.

Then they could head out, give the all-clear to Lila and Piper, and bring them inside.

Get to the kitchen. Get into the bunker. Get armed, then get lethal. The plan was reliant on stealth. Their current lack of weapons barely mattered.

Raj was still looking at Meyer, waiting for an answer.

Meyer shrugged as if to say, *What the hell.*

Raj, staying low, crept forward. He peeked into the cab, then eased the door open and stuck his torso inside, making himself a rather obvious target. Meyer held his breath, knowing he couldn't shout at Raj to stop. Finally he came out and showed his empty hands.

Of course.

Movement caught Meyer's eye, now around the side of

the garage. Trevor held up two fingers, the index and middle. He touched the index and mouthed, *Living room*, then touched the middle and silently added, *Dining room*.

Meyer nodded.

Trevor seemed to be saying more. He was pantomiming, touching fingers, making gestures. Then he bent into a squat as if preparing to take a shit right there outside the garage. Like a cat expressing its distaste of the general situation.

Meyer scrunched his eyebrows: *What?*

Trevor squatted. Touched both raised fingers at once.

Meyer shook his head. He looked at Raj, who shrugged.

Trevor ducked low, looked both ways like a child crossing the street, and ran to stoop behind his father. Meyer didn't even have time to raise his hands to tell him not to. The kid was slightly reckless.

But no gunfire erupted. Trevor was breathing hard, flushed, but admirably coherent. Like a cocky teenager who thinks he's going to live forever.

"I told you to stay put," Meyer said, his voice half hiss, angry and scared at once.

"I told you. They're not on this side. Living room and dining room."

"There could be more."

Trevor shook his head. "I looked everywhere. In every window, including both ends. It's not like I needed to check upstairs or downstairs."

Meyer looked at the house. It was large and sprawling, but only one story. Given the price and isolation, anyone else would probably have stacked another floor on the place, but Meyer hadn't wanted a vacation home. He'd wanted a shelter, and that meant that the most important parts had been safely concealed below ground months ago.

"Still stupid, Trevor." But he patted his son on the back, pleased despite the boy being foolhardy. "What was with the squatting?"

"Oh. They're sitting down. One is watching TV. The TV's still working. Can you believe it?"

Meyer could. As long as TV existed, the ranch would get it. It ran on a generator with several large, underground fuel tanks when it wasn't collecting solar from the roof, and a surprising amount of wind power from two huge turbines a mile higher up the hill. The signal came from a satellite, same as the Internet. Meyer had already considered connecting his phone to the wireless, hoping for an update before they charged to their possible deaths, but he didn't remember the password by heart and would need to get into the office to find it.

"And the other?"

"Dining room table. Looking through papers or something. They look pretty involved."

Meyer looked to the right, to the home's far end, toward the kitchen and the bunker's hidden entrance.

"Okay," said Meyer. "Let's go."

They stayed low, well beneath line of sight out the windows. But as they approached the glass, Meyer found he could easily hear the television blaring. He recognized the show. It was *The Beam*. A show he hoped he could catch up on later, and was loaded in the juke already.

Still, he peeked up, trying to get a look inside. Raj yanked at his shirt, and Meyer resisted an urge to push him away. This was his house, his errand, his preparations, his plan. He could look through his own windows if he wanted to.

He came back down.

"Motherfucker."

Trevor shook his head.

"That's Garth in there."

"Who's Garth?"

"Construction foreman. His crew built this place. I guess that explains how he knew it was here, and what it was built for."

"So he knows about the bunker?" Raj sounded nervous, as if all bets were off.

"Yeah. But they finished the bunker a while ago, and last time I was here, I stocked it up and changed the code."

"He can't get in, then."

"No. But he knows where it is." Meyer looked at Trevor. "Did you check the kitchen?"

Trevor nodded.

"The bay window. The big one, overlooking the lake."

Trevor nodded again. "Yeah. Nobody in there."

"Could you see the broom closet?" He turned, miming facing the home from the other direction as Trevor would have, and pointed to his left. "Over here. Past the ... shit ... I guess there's an oven there?"

"The oven is in the middle, Dad."

"Right. I forgot. They were putting the fume hood in when I was here last time. But it's here, and ..."

"I saw it, Dad."

"You're sure?"

"The door was open. I could see brooms and stuff. All over the floor, too."

That made sense. They'd tried to access the bunker. That was *why* they were here. It might even mean Heather was safe. Maybe they thought she knew the code.

"But just an outer door. There was no inner door open?"

"You mean inside the closet?"

Meyer nodded impatiently. "Like there's another room at the back of it."

"Is that where the bunker is? Behind the closet?"

"Yes, and …"

"Oh, that's *awesome.*" Trevor was grinning, despite the situation. Raj too. Meyer wanted to punch them both back to reality.

"Was there another door open, Trevor?"

"Oh. No. Just a closet."

"And you looked around the kitchen. All around it. Including the door to the porch. The windows."

"As much as I could see."

"How much could you see?"

"Unless someone was crouching behind the island, playing hide and seek …"

"Fine." He looked up again, peering in on Garth. He'd wondered about Garth from the beginning. Garth was greedy and very win-lose. He didn't seem to believe in mutual benefit and kept wanting more from Meyer's contract. It made sense that he'd come back to take what wasn't his. It made sense that he'd brought a friend, but it made even more sense that the friend would eventually find a knife stuck in his own back, figuratively if not literally.

Garth was still watching TV, kicked back, his black mustache tenting as he laughed at something funny. Must be a commercial. *The Beam* wasn't exactly a laff riot.

"Raj. Run up, and check the living room."

Raj scampered low. Peeked up carefully. Then nodded.

Meyer and Trevor crept forward. He checked for himself, poking his head up to find a blond man in his forties shuffling papers, looking as comfortable as Garth, equally unlikely to get up and head for the kitchen in the next two minutes.

"Okay," said Meyer, swallowing then affecting a certainty he didn't feel. "Stay low, and follow me. Let's see if we can get past them."

Chapter Thirty-Two

DAY FIVE, Evening
Axis Mundi

TREVOR LOOKED BACK at his sister, mounted on her horse near the tree line, mostly concealed unless you were looking directly at her. Piper was on her own horse beside Lila. For the first time in a long while, Trevor wanted to attract Lila's eye more than Piper's. In theory, he was about to be a hero and come out like the hunk on the cover of a bodice-ripper romance. That should impress Piper, if the world were a fair place. But instead of thinking along those lines, he looked to Lila. His sister, who'd been his best friend in the world for so long.

They had to be fifty or seventy yards away, and still Trevor thought he could see the reassuring, concerned look in Lila's eye — meant for him this time, not Raj.

You'll be fine, she seemed to say.

I'm scared, Lila.

But of course she'd said nothing back, psychically, to

try and reassure him, and of course she couldn't see what he was trying to say in the first place. She'd probably been drooling over Raj as usual when Trevor thought she was looking at him.

There was a moment of resentment, and the fear reclaimed him. Trevor had never been so afraid. It was different from normal fright. This was fear mixed with adrenaline. The closest thing Trevor had ever felt was the time he'd played paintball, only once, in a warehouse battlefield outside the city. They'd given him a helmet, and even though the guns didn't fire bullets and the danger wasn't real, he'd fogged the helmet beyond his ability to see, wanting to rip it off and risk losing an eye. His chest had pressed into his three thick shirts until they constricted like armor. He'd run from obstacle to obstacle, firing until his gun ran dry, and wasn't disappointed when the game was over. Because he'd barely been able to breathe, and could only imagine what real battle must feel like.

Like this. It's like this.

But that wasn't true; nobody even knew they were there. This was just waiting. This was creeping along, exposed and indefensible, knowing that being seen meant death. When they got the guns from the bunker and came back up? *That* would be battle.

His father would almost certainly insist on doing that part alone. Trevor wondered if relief at the thought made him a coward.

They reached the porch off the kitchen. It was at the home's end, wrapping around from the rear to the expansive front, where deck chairs overlooked the edge of a mountain lake. Trevor had seen that view when he'd gone around to count bad guys, but it had barely registered. He was too worried about dying.

"What now?" Raj looked at the porch. They'd stopped

just off it, knowing that rising onto its stained-wood surface would mean moving into plain sight to anyone walking into the window-strewn kitchen.

"If we're lucky, the door will be unlocked. They carried supplies in this way a lot because the French doors give them twice the width to carry boards and stuff. But I don't think Garth has been doing much construction since he came back."

"What if it *is* locked?"

"Then we'll be unlucky." Trevor's dad was looking forward at the door, mumbling. But Raj was asking a serious question, and there was still a not-insignificant chance that Raj might be shot before this was all over. Meyer seemed to decide that he deserved a real answer. "Try the windows."

"And if the windows are locked?"

"Maybe we can break one. He has the TV up pretty loud. These are energy-efficient windows. Should normally be pretty soundproof, but I could hear everything back there."

Meyer didn't seem to like that option. If the windows were soundproof enough to muffle a loud television, they'd also be thick enough to create a louder-than-average noise when shattered.

Trevor watched his father creep forward, duck-walking to stay low. Still, he was entirely visible to anyone who wasn't blind inside the kitchen, and Trevor felt his heart ratchet up another pounding notch.

He gripped the handle, seemed to wish a silent prayer, then pulled down. The door sighed open. Meyer closed his eyes for a half second and exhaled.

"Now," he said, waving. "Hurry."

They scampered inside. The kitchen was large and bright, lit above from skylights. If not for the imminent threat of men in the other room and the blaring TV, it might be possible to believe this was just another day in paradise. Even with the threats, looking out the large bay window, Trevor found it hard to believe that a fleet of alien ships was on its way, that what he imagined as enormous brushed chrome ball bearings would soon be floating above, hanging as if on strings.

"The door. Get the door."

Trevor reached back and slowly pulled the glass door closed behind him.

One last time, Trevor tried to see the girls hiding at the tree line. They'd fallen back, perhaps to where he and Raj and his father had tied their own horses. Seeing nothing made Trevor feel unanchored. He wanted that final glance, one last look of assurance.

But they were gone. There were only trees and grass and rocks and mountain peaks in the distance. Quiet air. Birds chirping. Nature going about its business, oblivious.

Trevor closed the door, committing them.

Meyer said nothing. He crept quickly toward the closet, minding the mop and broom and dustpan lying on the floor at its foot. It struck Trevor as odd that the closet had been stocked, given that the rest of the kitchen wasn't even finished — entire walls of cabinets missing, nude wires poking through holes in the drywall above as if waiting to be connected to can lights in the ceiling. But the construction crew must have to clean things up from time to time, or maybe his father had put them in there — either because he'd swept out the bunker below, or to make the closet's disguise that much more convincing.

There was a panel already opened in the closet's rear. Raj leaned closer, curious. It had a keypad on its front, but there was also a futuristic-looking pad below, angled slightly forward. It had the shape of a hand drawn in white outline. Even in his fear Trevor couldn't help feeling intrigued by the hand scanner. His father might have planned for the ultimate doomsday scenario, and that was cool. But Meyer's presentation made it that much cooler.

He'd laid his palm flat on the glass when Trevor heard the distinctive sound of a toilet flushing behind him. The sound had fallen into a gap in the TV volume, and in the temporarily quiet kitchen, the everyday sound was down-right chilling.

Trevor spun. So did Meyer and Raj. There was a sound of a toilet lid closing behind the door in a small alcove off to one side — a door Trevor hadn't been able to see when he'd looked into the kitchen from the front.

"Go!" Meyer said, his voice more exhalation than sound. "Hurry!"

But the man who'd been in the bathroom wasn't a hand-washer, and he was sauntering out before they could take a single step, his belt halfway buckled. He was a man in his twenties, stubble haircut, a few days unshaven. He had a gun on his hip and a daredevil's eyes — the kind of person who started fights for fun and, Trevor suspected, was either too brave or too stupid to be afraid of anything.

His gun was raised before anyone could flinch. He was too far to lunge at, too close to miss.

He faced them with his fly still open, his partially buckled belt hanging to the side like a brown tongue.

"Well now," he said, a slow, maniac smile crawling onto his face. "Looks like we got visitors."

Chapter Thirty-Three

DAY FIVE, Evening
Axis Mundi

MEYER'S first instinct was to fight the man who'd confronted them — not because he was a warrior by nature, but because the adrenaline in his blood was insistent.

He'd been on alert — sure that something was coming, as he'd seen during his visions and felt, beneath his skin, for weeks after each ayahuasca ceremony — for months. He'd gone into higher alert when the news of the spheres' approach had broken on the news, just like the world at large. He'd ratcheted up another notch after their Land Cruiser had been stolen, and hadn't really settled since. Then he'd seen that his Axis Mundi was occupied. They'd broken into the kitchen, knowing the men in the house had guns and they did not — knowing that being seen might get them shot out of hand.

Meyer was amped enough to dive at the new man

whether he held a weapon or not. But he was also at the back of a closet, with two kids between him and the problem. Boxed in.

There were three men in the house. Not two.

The man was watching them, his expression stern but also slightly amused. His whole head seemed to be reddish stubble, from head to unshaven face. He had cornflower blue eyes that were far too soft for a criminal, and a baby face peeking beneath his stubble. He was probably in his midtwenties, maybe less. He looked like a good kid gone bad — one of those fabled young men who'd been led down the wrong path by a sour crowd. But whatever was down that wayward road, this kid looked like he'd found it suited him fine.

"I guess you're the lady's husband," he said, the gun at his hip, almost an afterthought. He looked down at his pants, laughed, took two protective steps backward, and went about the business of buckling up. He couldn't do it with one hand occupied, so he set the gun on the kitchen island. It was a casual thing, disarming in order to zip his fly. But to Meyer, who'd made a living out of studying people, it came off as confident rather than careless. He knew they'd see that gun leave his hand and think of springing forward. But he clearly also knew he could get it again before they got close, and wouldn't hesitate to use it.

Meyer noticed something else, too. Beside the gun, a white residue was clearly visible on the dark stone around the banked oven, below the new steel fume hood. It might be drywall dust, but Meyer doubted it. Not after seeing the kid's tiny pupils, and the way he kept pressing his nostrils closed and sniffing.

He wasn't just cocky. He wasn't just confident. He was also high, wired. If Meyer had to guess, he'd probably love to pull the trigger, just to see the blood flow.

Garth wasn't like that. Not even the *worst* Meyer had seen in Garth was like that. But he'd found an appropriate henchman to help him take the Dempsey house: a wild card willing to shoot first and party later.

"You gone deaf, then?" he said when Meyer didn't reply. The kid had some sort of an accent, but Meyer couldn't place it. It wasn't quite Western, Southern, or East Coast. It might be the accent of reckless youth — a way of clipping speech, somehow turning *cocksure* and *careless* into sound, then using it to shave edges from words. "Maybe I'll shoot you in the leg."

"Whose husband?" The shift in his group's position, as Meyer moved from the back of the closet, was subtle. But it put him at the front, the gunman's weapon pointed at his chest, rather than at Trevor or Raj.

"The lady we got."

"Is she alive? Did you hurt her?"

"Sure, she's alive."

There was an oddball item on the stove's other side, and it took Meyer a moment to place it: a tiny crystal candy dish his mother had given him when he'd seen her six months ago in Denver. Somehow it had ended up here; somehow it had ended up on the kitchen island; somehow the new, armed occupants had seen fit to bring it down and fill it with M&M's. Had they run out to buy the candies? It seemed a strange thing to do while occupying a house and holding a hostage, but it's not like Meyer had stocked the place with food. At least not outside the locked bunker.

The kid popped an M&M in his mouth, then spoke around it. "We ain't savages."

"Who *are* you?" Meyer asked.

"I don't think that's any of your business."

There were footsteps from behind the kid. For a second Meyer imagined Piper and Lila, somehow in the home's belly, somehow armed, somehow having skirted the other men. Ready to strike with baseball bats, maybe. The kid wasn't turning to look. He'd be easy prey.

But of course, Meyer had made it clear that the girls should keep their distance, and neither Piper nor Lila were any good in a fight, let alone a bare-hands hostile take-down of two armed brutes. With luck, they'd already be riding away — *to get help*, Piper would tell herself to make abandonment easier.

Meyer heard the other man before he saw him.

"Who are you talking to, Wade?"

Wade didn't answer. He popped another oversized M&M in his mouth with his free hand. Had to be peanut.

A second man came around Wade from the back, watching the kid rather than the open kitchen. He only noticed Meyer and the boys once fully inside. He stopped like a wind-up toy out of steam. It wasn't Garth. This man was sandy blond, Meyer's age, with quiet, pale-blue eyes that matched Wade's. Were they father and son? There was no other resemblance, but two home raiders with pretty blue eyes wasn't something a person usually expected.

"Who the hell is this?" The newcomer's voice had the faintest lilt, as if he'd been born in England and hadn't quite lost the affect.

"Dunno." Then, speaking to Meyer: "Who *is* this?"

"This the guy Garth was waiting for?"

"I don't know. Go ask Garth, you wanna know so bad."

"Where did they come from?"

"You got a lot of questions, Remy." Another M&M. The kid was rail thin, almost emaciated. Apparently, the drugs he was clearly on were a fair counterbalance to his high-fat diet. "I don't know. Found 'em in the closet."

"The … the *closet?*" Remy sounded like he didn't understand the word.

"Yeah."

"That one there?" He pointed.

"Yeah."

Remy stared hard at the kid — some understanding having percolated that Wade either didn't get or was too cool to acknowledge. He was dressed in jeans and an unzipped black hoodie over a plain blue T-shirt, but somehow the look seemed to be meant as understatedly stylish. Like he was trying to prove that he wasn't actually a slacker, but found the wardrobe attractive.

Wade didn't so much as look at Remy. Finally, he turned his head from Meyer's group — still just feet from the closet in question — and said, "What?"

"Goddammit, Wade. He was going into the … you know."

"Yeah, I figured."

"So why didn't you wait until he'd opened it?"

Now Wade turned to face his accuser. "I was taking a shit. I came out, they were here staring at me. Then I was like, 'No, please, continue,' but for some reason they didn't want to."

"Goddammit, Wade."

"I didn't know they were here! Where the fuck were *you*, huh? Maybe Garth can come in with his hearing aid and tell me why he didn't know they were in here either. With that fucking TV so loud, it's like you *want* mother-fuckers to sneak in."

"Dammit, Wade."

Wade turned the gun on Remy. He held it high, his arm cocked, the barrel inches from the other man's head. "You know, I don't have to be here. And *you* don't have to be, either." He nudged Remy's forehead with the muzzle.

Remy sighed, ignoring the gun. Wade must do this kind of thing all the time. He turned to Meyer, who felt like an intruder caught midprowl. He and the boys were standing with their arms at their sides, but to Meyer it felt like he'd been stalking across a dark room when the lights popped on, feet wide, arms out, eyes flicking back and forth and unsure where to move next.

"You. You're Meyer Dempsey."

Meyer said nothing.

Remy nodded, apparently taking his silence as a yes. He indicated the closet with a toss of his chin. "Open it."

"I don't know what you're talking about," said Meyer.

Without hesitating, Wade strode forward, his pleasant, boyish expression becoming one of pure id. He struck Meyer hard with the gun's side. Meyer blinked the sudden pain away, then opened his eyes to find the weapon's barrel pointed between his eyes.

"He said open it."

"It's open." Meyer looked at the ajar closet door.

Wade hit him again. Trevor made a small, inarticulate noise of fear.

"The hidey hole, asswipe. That panel in the back you were working on when I came out."

The simple sentence sent a chill up Meyer's spine. This was a game of seconds. If they'd entered the closet ten seconds later, they would have had the door to the spiral staircase open before Wade had come up behind them, and the intruders would have had what they wanted. But if they'd entered it thirty or sixty seconds earlier, Meyer would have what *he* wanted: in and out, armed and armored. It wouldn't matter if Wade was in the bathroom. The flush would have heralded his death cry. The Uzi could have cut him in half through the door's fine oak.

"I can't. It's locked."

"Unlock it."

"I can't. It's on a time delay. For exactly situations like this." Meyer lied without hesitation or hitch. He didn't know what a time delay would mean or why anyone would possibly want one on a place they might need to enter in a hurry. But he did know that in at least some small way, Wade believed him.

He made to hit Meyer again, but Remy grabbed his arm. Wade looked for a moment like he might leap on the other man, but then his vitriol seemed to settle.

"That's enough, Wade."

He yanked his arm away, hard, then went about adjusting his hoodie with angry little movements.

"Open it," said the older man.

"I can't. I'm telling you the truth."

"He's lying. He's just fucking with us. Maybe I should just put him out of his misery." The gun rose.

"Hey …" said Remy.

"Or maybe I should put this one out of *his* misery," said Wade, sounding inspired. The gun lowered until it was pointing at Trevor. Meyer wanted to grab the man's gun arm, but the weapon was too far away to grab with any advantage, and Remy wore a gun, too.

Meyer stepped between Wade and Trevor, moving his hands behind him.

"Yeah, you see that? *There's* how we get him to do it. Good. We won't have to kill the woman. I could shoot him in the leg right now. Give him two chances to …"

"Wade."

"*This* one," he said, using the barrel to indicate Raj, "is clearly the mailman's kid. Or the kid of the guy at the Quickie Mart. But I shoot that motherfucker, he'll know I mean business."

"*Wade!*"

Meyer realized how hard his heart was beating. He'd blocked it out somehow, but was feeling almost light-headed. Wade was right, and Meyer had been stupid. He'd come in with something to lose. If they shot Raj, he'd talk. If he threatened Trevor enough, he'd talk. And even if the boys somehow got away, there was still Heather to think about.

"Okay then, Remy," said Wade, scowling. "What's *your* plan — have a tea party and hope they get friendly?"

Remy looked from Wade to the open closet to Meyer and the boys hiding behind him. His tongue went to the backside of his front row of teeth — a thoughtful move-ment echoed in a side-to-side yawing of his jaw.

He walked forward, peeled Trevor from Meyer's grasping arms, and shoved him toward Wade.

"Dad," Trevor said weakly.

"We'll take him to Garth," Remy said. "You go first, and we'll follow you."

He eyed Meyer and Raj, making sure everyone under-stood one another. "If this one tries anything stupid," Remy told Wade, "kill the kid."

Chapter Thirty-Four

DAY FIVE, Evening
   Axis Mundi

HEATHER HEARD the TV turn off some time later. Thank God.

She wasn't into science fiction, but Meyer always had been. Tolerating the polarity, when they'd been married, had been murder. He was flat-out addicted to that one series, so she'd had to endure it when they'd lived together. She could probably recite the *Matrix* movies by heart. But for Heather, who liked romantic comedies and stupid, brainless entertainment, listening to talk of nanobots and networks and singularity was the poop icing on the shit cake she'd baked herself into.

Being held captive? Bad.

Being held and forced to listen to actors blab on and on about the future? *So* much worse.

She peered through the mesh at the front of her locked pantry, wanting someone to shout observant and witty insults at now that things were quieter. When she saw none of the three men, Heather turned back to the walk-in pantry itself. Why had Meyer put a pantry near the laundry room? Shouldn't it be near where — oh, she didn't know — near where the *fucking food* would be prepared? But Meyer had a reason for everything, and she'd learned to pick and choose the things she allowed him to be superior about.

Maybe it wasn't a pantry. Maybe it was a giant linen closet. Heather was deep into contemplating the ramifications of this interesting possibility when she looked up to see the blond man — Remy — attempting to wrench the screwdriver out of the jamb.

"Oh, is *that* what the problem is, keeping the door closed?" Heather said. "Thank God. I've been puzzling it out all day."

Remy didn't even look at her. This was disappointing. Usually, Remy offered the best audience of the three. She'd known Garth before he'd become a big bad asshole — just a bit, but enough that he seemed embarrassed to face her. The kid, Wade, scared her. But Remy? He was out of his element. He looked like a copier salesman who'd been laid off, let his hair and beard grow out, then decided it was finally time to start living life as a sad sack of shit. In Heather's opinion, he was doing it perfectly.

"So I guess you found me a TV? The service in this place is terrible."

Remy kept wrenching at the screwdriver, too focused and sweaty to reply.

"And the bellhops are sloppy as shit."

Remy's eyes flicked toward Heather for a second. Then he resumed jimmying. Finally, the screwdriver broke out of the wood. His momentum, when it popped out, nearly threw him to the floor.

Heather was about to make another witty rejoinder when Remy moved to work on the second screwdriver but a voice stopped her: Wade, just out of sight.

"Kick it."

Remy had the screwdriver in his hand, working it as he'd worked the other, stuck farther in and barely budging. His dark-blond hair swung in his face.

"Kick it. Come on, shit."

Remy kept working.

"Jesus Christ," said Wade, now stepping into view. Heather saw something that almost stopped her cynical heart. Trevor, with a gun to his side.

"Like this, idiot." Wade kicked at the screwdriver, but it didn't budge any more than it had for Remy. His hard eyes glanced at his companion to see if he'd have something to say about that, but then moved closer and stomped hard on the thing. It bent with a crack.

"Okay," said Remy, moving in to get it the rest of the way.

Wade stomped again, mashing Remy's fingers.

"I said, I got it!" Remy shouted.

"Come on." Wade looked over his shoulder at something Heather couldn't see. "I don't trust this fucker."

The screwdriver came free, and the door sighed an inch outward, the latch seemingly jammed or shattered. Heather's first impulse was to rush forward, bang into the door, throw it into Wade, and wrestle her son away from him. But they were already moving to open the door and shove Trevor inside — a good thing, since her move would've seen them both killed.

Heather wrapped her arms around Trevor. He was almost as tall as she was. She was pulling his head to her chest when something came behind him. She looked up expecting to see one of the bandits, but instead saw Meyer stumbling in with an Indian kid she didn't know.

"Meyer?"

His answer was perfectly Meyer Dempsey. He was bleeding from the lip, had a swollen cheek, and looked like his right eye was half-closed, the entire side of his face crimson with scratches. But he just said, "Hey, Heather." As if they'd run into each other at Starbucks.

She wrapped her arms around him anyway, shameless and unguarded. They made a tiny huddle: mother and father and son, safe and together for at least this moment.

Hammering noises came from the doorway. They were putting the screwdrivers back, the unimaginative bastards. Only this time Remy had a bunch of fat nails in his teeth as well, each pitch black and thick as a nightcrawler. Was the bunker the only place in the house that could be locked?

Four prisoners, now. Heather and Meyer and Trevor and …

"Who are you?" she asked.

Her tone must have been caustic enough to cut through the kid's fear. The Indian put a hand on his hip and said, "Who are *you?*"

"Heather, this is Raj." Meyer winced at the syllables. He looked up, watching Remy depart, then finished, "Lila's boyfriend."

Heather cocked her head, a rejoinder ready on her lips. You didn't date the infamous Heather Hawthorne's daughter without bracing for a stage show of shit.

"Raj, this is Heather. Lila's mother."

Raj extended his hand. It looked for a moment like he actually wanted to hug her in greeting — as if she might *enjoy* meeting the kid who was sticking his dick in her daughter — but he shifted to an offered handshake before making an ass of himself. Heather looked at the hand, then filled it with a box of crackers.

"Have something to eat, Raj. You're too skinny."

Seemingly unsure of what to say, the kid complied. Heather proceeded to ignore him and turned to her boys.

"How'd you get stuck with lamb curry?" she asked, nodding toward Raj. "Is Lila safe?"

Meyer looked toward the closet door, then turned Heather around before saying, very low, "She and Piper came with the three of us. But they stayed outside. They'll be fine."

"'Fine,' as in, 'they'll call the cops and come back to save us?'"

"I don't think the cops are going to be very responsive right now."

Heather sighed. She knew that, of course, but it was annoying that Meyer treated her remark as serious.

"Well," Heather said, "it's nice of you to stop by for a visit." She held Trevor out at arm's length, unable to repress the need to be an assessing mother even now. He seemed okay, as Lila was hopefully okay. Piper? Meh. Heather liked Piper fine, but she was also the new wife and could stay or go.

"How many of them are there?" said Meyer.

"Three. Unless the others are having a party, but are too shy to say hi."

Trevor shook his head. "I'm sorry."

"Don't be sorry," Meyer said.

"Sorry for what, Trev?"

"It's nothing," said Meyer.

"I wasn't asking you."

"I told Dad there were only two guys. If I'd seen the third ..." He looked for a moment like he might start to cry. Heather wasn't sure what bothered her more: that he felt responsible or that crying, at fifteen, would embarrass the shit out of him later. Either way, Heather pulled him back into a hug.

He was safe. Meyer was safe. Even Lila was safe.

Their situation could be better, but Heather had more or less resigned herself to the possibility that they'd all been killed — or at the least, waylaid and not coming. Having her ex-husband and son here, even wedged into a pantry, was strangely comforting. Apparently, misery loved company, and Heather had made a living out of being miserable. She was practiced, and almost at ease.

"What are they going to do with us, Mom?" said Trevor.

"Yeah, what have you heard?" the Indian kid added. *Raj*. Who was surely fucking her baby girl.

"I don't know, kid." She looked at Meyer, ignoring Raj. "Don't take this the wrong way, but why the hell are you here?"

"I told you we were coming here. I told you to meet us here before the ..." Meyer trailed off, apparently unwilling to add a forthcoming alien apocalypse to their current list of concerns. "I saw your car and their trucks. I wasn't just going to run away. I screwed it up, I know. But ... fucking *Garth*. Can you believe that asshole?"

"I mean here. In this closet."

"Oh. Well ..."

"They threw us in here," said Raj.

Heather stared at Raj for a long moment. Then she said, "We're going to discuss our situation over here. Go do some math."

"They caught us in the kitchen. We didn't have any weapons, but I thought if we could get into the bunker, I could get some. But the bald guy was in the bathroom —" He rushed on, not looking at Trevor, who didn't seem to have forgiven himself. "— and he stopped me before I could unlock it."

"Darling ex-husband of mine," said Heather, her voice saccharin. "Former love of my life."

"Yes?"

"I hate the need to be so specific and crass."

"When have you ever hated that?"

"But what I'm asking is, why didn't they kill you? Or chop off your hand and use it to open the door. Or …" She looked at Trevor, remembering the way Wade had been holding him as a bargaining chip. She didn't want to say what she'd had in mind, but Meyer got the message just fine: … *or threaten Trevor until you did what they wanted?*

"I told them there was a time delay."

"What does that mean?"

"I told Garth the door was on a timer. Like the safe in a convenience store."

Heather looked at Raj.

"It's a safety precaution," Meyer went on.

"So … wait … why would you put a time delay on something like that? What if you really needed to get in right away?"

"I didn't. I wouldn't. That would be idiotic."

"But Garth believed it."

Meyer nodded. "They …" He trailed off, eyeing Trevor, and Heather wondered if they'd threatened her son after all. "They kind of forced me to open it. Those two other guys. After they reported to Garth, who seems to be in charge. Which is amusing, seeing as he was barely in charge when he was just a foreman. You know — the kind of construction foreman who doesn't kidnap you?"

"He did manage to build you an apocalypse bunker."

"Garth thought … forcing me to open it was a grand idea." Again he looked guiltily toward Trevor. "So I did the whole routine. Scanned my hand. But then I entered the panic code instead of the one that opens the door."

"So it'll call the cops after all."

"It would if the cell networks worked. Which they don't."

"Oh."

"But it lit up the right lights. They seemed convinced."

"Are you sure they believed you?"

Meyer looked at Trevor and Raj as if to say, *Well, they're still alive.*

"While I was in there pushing buttons for show, I changed the clock."

Heather shrugged.

"It has a countdown timer."

Heather shrugged again, wishing he'd get to the fucking point.

"A countdown timer," he elaborated, "that shows when the lock can be opened."

Heather nodded. She could picture it: a lock of the type the workmen had never seen before, installed by one of Meyer's high-tech specialists. A ticking clock on the lock's face, counting down to zero.

"How long until it runs out?"

Heather looked through the open mesh at the pantry's end, through the room beyond, and at the sky outside, where the sun had finally slipped below the horizon at the end of a very long day. The *last* day, if projections about the alien ships hadn't changed during her amateur incarceration, that humanity would spend alone.

"Eight hours," Meyer answered.

Heather looked around at each of them, then at the door with its new nails. "Well, what do you want to do until then?"

Meyer's eyes became steely. He was looking outside too,

possibly wondering when people would be able to look up and see the ships without an app or a telescope. Wondering what might happen then, and if eight hours of waiting would give anyone time to run and hide.

"Figure out what to do when that timer hits zero," he said. "Before they realize I tricked them, and decide to come in here and start killing until I do it right."

DAY SIX

Chapter Thirty-Five

DAY SIX, Early Morning
  Axis Mundi

THE NIGHT WAS long and dark.

It had been nearly eight hours by the time Meyer finished his debate with Garth, doing his best to twist the man into a conversational pretzel. He'd acted irate — easy, because he was. He'd acted betrayed, which he also was — and which, surprisingly, he'd decided might be an effective lever against a man with blue-collar values and what he thought might be a Christian upbringing. And about that, he was right: Garth didn't shout when Meyer said he'd taken what rightfully belonged to the Dempsey family. Instead, he'd gone on the defensive — the move of a man trying to establish himself as right, rather than arguing why it was okay for him to do wrong.

But that was just filibustering, and Meyer had known it from the start. He was buying time, unsure what to do with it post-purchase. In truth, he had no idea how to handle the situation. There was really only one way to solve it — to let Garth and his crew into the bunker. The stubborn part of Meyer — the one that always had to win, and never surrender, because giving up was for cowards — wanted to resist just for the sake of resistance. But there was another, more practical reason to keep trying.

Garth knew that there was plenty about the bunker that he himself didn't know, because Meyer — like any smart man who wishes to keep a secret — had the lair constructed in pieces by discreet firms. One handled wiring for the lower level only; another handled network and computers; another handled rooms that Garth's crew only saw through caution tape. Only Meyer knew all of its tricks … and Garth, unless he was an idiot, knew that Meyer was the kind of man who liked tricks plenty. He'd have back doors. He'd have failsafes. It was all true. If Garth and the boys went into the lair, Meyer would know how to get them back out.

And of course, Garth knew that. Which meant that Garth, as much as it would pain his relatively moderate personality to act, couldn't afford to let Meyer or his family live. It didn't even matter that Garth wouldn't be able to pull the trigger himself. Wade would do it with relish.

Meyer sat in the dark while Trevor snoozed with his head on his mother's chest, Heather's abrasive mouth finally silent.

Eight hours.

He'd set the timer at around 8 p.m. That meant that at some time around 4 a.m., it would reach zero. It wouldn't ring or buzz, but it seemed too much to hope the invaders would just sleep until morning and give him extra hours to think. No, they'd be watching it. They'd know they could sleep in the bunker. And truth be told, Meyer thought that none of the three men truly believed the time delay thing.

They just knew that they could wait eight hours with impunity. Last Meyer had heard, the current projections said the ships wouldn't arrive until around noon, maybe later.

He sat cross-legged on the floor, watching the moon as it appeared between distant peaks. The moon was just a big rock in space. The Earth was just a big rock in space. Of course they weren't alone. They'd never been alone. They'd just been more anonymous life on the one planet in the solar system lucky enough to have a magnetic field to deflect the solar wind. It was luck, nothing more. Humanity wasn't special, and they were about to learn it.

Meyer thought of the bunker, trying to fight the growing certainty that they'd never get inside, and that something terrible would happen if they did.

He closed his eyes, keeping his spine tall, rigid enough that his tired mind wouldn't be tempted to sleep. If he started to nod off, he'd slouch, and that would wake him.

But he didn't think he'd sleep. Meyer's mind — his higher mind, not the lump of gray clay inside his skull — knew what he was doing, and what he was trying to access.

He breathed slowly. Tried to muffle the outside world. Tried to imagine the home's quiet as being the silence of somewhere else, far away. Outer space, perhaps. Or maybe not. He'd visited a place very like outer space again and again, when his individual mind found the universal mind, when he seemed to see the world from above (not literally, but conceptually), when he felt like he could see through all the things that others took for granted: the permanence of objects, the rigid and always forward-marching nature of time, the artificial divisions between *this* and *that*.

Meyer wasn't a party guy, not one to rely on substances. He'd smoked pot; he'd drunk; he'd smoked. A few years ago — right around the time he'd grown serious about his nutrition, his body, and whatever energy lay beyond it — he'd quit all three. Now the only thing he ever took into his system was what Juha prepared for him, and for Heather if she joined the ceremony with him. It wasn't a drug: it was medicine. To Meyer, ayahuasca felt more like a lens. Or a doorway.

He sat for ten minutes, trying to access that feeling of ascension and seeing beyond. But it was no use. It had been too long. The effects always stayed with him after the ceremony ended, leading to a long-tail high that lasted for weeks, sometimes months. The medicine was Windex on a windshield. Eventually, life's muck would cloud that view, and it would need another cleaning — but for a while, Meyer could finally see everything clearly, like stars outside of the city.

But not now. The lens was too dirty. He knew the ships were coming, same as everyone else. He knew there was more to the story, but could no longer remember what it was. He knew there were connections. There was universal knowledge, accessible only to his higher mind — the higher mind, he often thought, that belonged to everyone and everything. But right now he was only a man, in a body, trapped in a pantry.

He looked at the wall clock beyond the door. It was after midnight. Less than four hours to go.

They couldn't ram the door. Even without the new nails, it would take several hits — plenty of time for the men to hear and come running. They couldn't open the door in stealth; the hinges and screwdrivers were on the outside, and the mesh was too small to reach through. There was no one to help them. Piper and Lila would try to find a cavalry, no matter what he'd told them, but there was no one to help. The closest neighbors were miles away;

the streets were empty; anyone who *could* help, given their own surely pressing concerns, never would. Lila and Piper were on their own, and that meant that Meyer, Heather, Trevor, and Raj were, too.

He had no idea how to escape.

No idea how to get into the bunker.

No idea how to do anything but wait for time to expire.

And then, all of a sudden, he did.

Chapter Thirty-Six

Day Six, Early Morning
 Axis Mundi

Garth didn't like this at all.

He'd checked on the panel outside the bunker's entrance three times since midnight, but none of those times had done anything to improve his mood. In theory, he should feel relieved. The clock was ticking, and in just a little while, this would all be over.

He looked at his cell phone, eyes ticking toward where the service bars should be in the vain hope that Verizon might have suddenly and inexplicably stitched its shit together. It hadn't. And really, cell service had been hit or miss up at this job even before the aliens encouraged the world to start crapping its pants. That's why the house had been hardwired for phone service. It struck Garth as strange that anyone would bother with real phones anymore, seeing as his grandmothers were the only people he knew who still had one. But maybe this was why: because sometimes in the mountains it was the only way.

3:07 a.m.

Just over an hour left. Garth wasn't sure how he felt about that. He was almost positive that Meyer had been lying out his ass (who put a time delay on a panic room?), but hadn't been positive enough to start shooting kids. They could wait. At the end of eight hours, if it turned out Meyer was as full of shit as Garth thought he was, *then* they could start pulling triggers.

The thought turned Garth's stomach. He didn't have kids of his own, but he did have nieces and nephews. The kid with the bushy eyebrows wasn't as young as they were, but he was still just a teenager. Garth remembered being a teenager. He'd been stupider than a retarded idiot, and more ignorant than he'd have ever believed, driven by his dick and gluttony. He hadn't had as much sex as his friends, owing to his awkward manner and equally awkward appearance, but that hadn't stopped him from spending all of his time in pursuit. He'd broken laws, and a few heads. Even now, looking back as a man who was considering shooting kids to get his way, Garth wanted to groan at his teenage self's poor judgement.

He didn't want to shoot Meyer's son, and didn't particularly want to hurt Meyer. Or his wife, or that Indian kid. This was supposed to be straightforward. It was supposed to be bloodless. He'd been drinking with Remy on the day the news had broken. Remy was already dour, and started saying that if the world ended at the hands of the aliens, at least his pathetic life wouldn't be much of a loss. Garth had tried to talk him out of it, to tell him he'd done okay.

But what did it matter? Remy had wanted to know. They were dead anyway. There was no place to go, no place to hide.

Maybe Garth shouldn't have started talking about the Dempsey job. Maybe Remy shouldn't have agreed as readily. And *definitely*, anticipating trouble on the drive, they shouldn't have turned to his cousin, Wade, as necessary recklessness. But what was done was done, and by the time they'd found Dempsey's cunt of an ex-wife in the living room, it had been too late to go back. By then, Remy had decided that staying alive was a good idea after all. Garth never needed convincing. Wade was too hopped-up, young, and dumb to consider hesitation.

Kill her, Wade had suggested.

But Garth didn't like that idea, so they'd tossed her into the pantry. Now the fucking pantry was full, and he might have to shoot a kid to close the door on this mess. It was out of hand. But they'd come this far, so it wasn't like they could walk away now. Wade, for one, wouldn't have it. Garth, too, kind of wanted to keep on living. And at this point, it wasn't like Meyer and his family would just let them hang out in peace, as they very well may have if this had been handled differently.

Garth stood. Wade and Remy were in bedrooms, maybe asleep. Garth couldn't do the same. Even if he didn't have to kill the kid himself, he'd have to order it. Even turning his head would be tacit agreement. Wade was an animal; it was the owner's fault if a beast got off its leash.

But as much as Garth didn't want to do what had to be done, he wanted to get into that bunker. He knew what was in it. He'd watched, between nailing boards, while Dempsey had stocked the thing on his last visit. He'd brought case after case of food through the doors off the kitchen, then dumbwaitered them down himself. There was some sort of mechanical unloading thingy at the bottom, it seemed, because Meyer was able to keep sending more and more stuff down without any help.

Food.

Water.

Mysterious cases with no labels.

Garth knew what was in at least some of those cases. He'd even considered calling Meyer on it, joking that he was breaking all sorts of laws. A man couldn't own those things. Only armies could. Normal people wouldn't even recognize some of the stuff Meyer was sending down the chute, but Garth, thanks to his time with the Army, knew plenty.

Electronics, for entertainment.

Survival supplies.

Body armor, gas masks — paranoid shit that Garth wouldn't have a clue how to find.

It was all down there, just waiting in the enormous bunker under the well-paced floor. His crew had only built parts of it (and had been specifically barred from other parts by polite men who seemed an awful lot like private security), but he knew it was big, comfortable, and well stocked. He'd even had the place furnished like the ultimate man cave before they'd capped the last corner, lowering couches and beds from above on cranes.

It was all right below his feet, and he wanted it. He'd thought they could waltz in and steal it, but he'd had no idea they'd be cockblocked by such nasty security. But they had, and so maybe Dempsey's arrival, as unpleasant as it might get, was a blessing. He still believed in blessings, when they served him. So yeah, maybe this was meant to be. Maybe Garth Wrigley was destined to survive the apocalypse. Maybe God had arranged this. Didn't God occasionally kill his own people? Garth's Sunday School was rusty, but he was pretty sure he had. Maybe this was like that.

Or maybe Meyer would make it easy. Maybe he'd just tell them the code. Maybe he'd open it up without any fuss.

But then he'd be a threat. No, he'd probably need to go. They all would.

It would be okay. Wade could do it. Or maybe they could just reinforce the pantry and leave them in there forever. But of course, that would mean they'd die of thirst and starvation, and that sounded worse than a bullet. Maybe he'd be doing them a kindness.

He looked again at his phone: 3:18.

The room was too quiet. It was impossible to believe any of this was real — either the approaching doom from above (that would, by the way, forgive extreme acts like kidnapping and killing in self-defense, which is what getting rid of those in the pantry would be, when you thought about it) or his new position as a home invader. The silence and darkness were their own presence.

He walked through to the kitchen, peeked at the clock on the supposed time lock, then backed away again, wishing time would hurry the fuck up.

He looked through the bay window. The moon was huge, perched between two distant peaks. Was it full? Well, there was only one way to be sure.

He walked to the French doors, then unlocked them by turning the lever that Remy, retard that he could sometimes be, had left open earlier. He stepped out onto the porch, then walked out to its middle.

No, not a full moon, but close.

He looked up. Garth wanted to see the stars, but the moonlight had washed most of 'em out. All he could see were a few of the brightest blips, including the really bright one that he seemed to remember wasn't even a star. It was Venus. Sunlight simply bounced off it just as sunlight bounced off the full moon, and ...

Garth staggered back and almost fell to the deck. He had to grip a chair to recover, then give himself a moment to find his balance.

The air was peppered with dozens of tiny round blips, each lit on one side like miniature crescent moons. They were disturbingly obvious, once Garth's eyes began to adjust. If he'd held a marble at arm's length, it would be about the same size to his eye as the alien spheres in the sky.

Garth looked up for a long time, feeling like he was tumbling upward. That was them. It had to be. The sight of what looked like half-lit ball bearings in the sky was pure, blood-chilling menace. Something that odd should have a soundtrack or at least appear to move, but as long as Garth watched, the spheres appeared silent without motion. It was quietly ominous — the way a person with feet in concrete might feel watching a steamroller creep forward.

Which, really, was a fair analogy for what was happening.

There was a sound from the lawn, opposite where Garth had been looking.

He whipped around, his hand automatically going to the gun on his hip. For a moment, he stared into the dark, waiting for his eyes to adjust. But the home's rear side was thick with trees and hills; much was shadow even in moonlight.

He didn't like turning his back on the ships in the sky. They were just hanging there, surely still thousands of miles away or more. Slowing down, if the NASA people were right. But still Garth felt them like a cool hand on his shoulder — a boogeyman waiting to strike the minute he stopped looking them in the eye.

He couldn't see anything that might have caused the noise he'd heard. Or *thought* he'd heard. Because he might not have heard anything. It might've been his imagination.

"Fuck you, squirrel," he said aloud.

Joking — even with himself — should have calmed Garth's nerves. But all it did was remind him that he was all alone, whistling in the dark to keep the spooks at bay.

He turned back to the house, and heard that sound from the front yard again. This time, he took a few steps forward, forcing his feet to move in an attempt to defeat the stupid, childish fear he felt threatening to suffocate him. He squinted.

A pair of pickup trucks, yellow moonlight glinting from the hoods and bumpers.

The place where the driveway broke through the trees, headed to the main road, looking like a shadowed archway in a fairy tale.

Nothing else.

It must be an animal. A deer or something. They were up in the mountains, after all, and just last night he and Remy had sat on this deck, huddled in blankets, happy to get out of earshot of the woman's loud mouth. With Wade sleeping something off, they'd felt they could go outside without him deciding to shut her up in an obvious way. And they'd found all sorts of natural sounds: owls, wolves, or coyotes in the distance, the wind's heavy sighing.

Still, Garth continued to stare at the shadowy yard for an extra few seconds. Then he seemed to feel the spheres in the sky watching him and turned to look, sure they'd have grown to the size of basketballs. But they were no larger than they'd been, no more of a menace.

He turned, reasonably sure he was choosing to leave

rather than being frightened back into the house. But when he reentered the kitchen, Garth found himself looking at someone's back. Someone who shouldn't be where he was, covered in drywall dust as if he'd found something sharp, then dug his way through a locked pantry wall.

Someone who, in going to the bunker lock before the timer expired, had just shown his hand.

Garth wanted to wait until Meyer Dempsey finished his business at the lock, but Dempsey must have heard the doors open. He turned slowly, the two men facing each other like gunslingers in a standoff.

"Meyer," Garth said, reaching for his gun.

Before Meyer could respond, there was a tremendous wrenching from outside. A long, cacophonous rattling. A bone-shattering crash of metal and glass.

Garth's head twitched toward the yard, toward the sounds he'd so recently dismissed as an animal's.

Meyer leapt.

Chapter Thirty-Seven

DAY SIX, Early Morning
   Axis Mundi

IT TOOK Lila far too long to figure out how to put the first of the old trucks into neutral.

She'd been able to drive a car in manual for over a year, but was a New Yorker, and her opportunities to hit the open road were few and far between. Even then, you almost never needed to take a car out of autodrive, and Lila, other than for instruction, never had. And even *THEN* she'd only driven Dempsey cars: rich girl cars, top of the line. If they even had neutral, it would be a utility.

But these trucks were ancient. Beater vehicles, owned by blue-collar guys and kept until they fell into piles of rust, meant for hauling wood and reeking workers. They had a big stick between the front seats, and you could yank it down to take something out of gear. That's what Piper had said, anyway, but Lila wasn't sure Piper had ever driven a manual car much before this trip, either. If Piper knew "neutral" and "out of gear," it was from movies.

Lila could feel the seconds ticking away. She'd lost track of Piper some time after they'd left the cover of shadows, when they'd both sprinted out into the moonlight toward the house. This was all taking too long. She saw the stick; the doors of the first truck opened without a lock. But the stick didn't want to move, and Lila was afraid she'd break something. Or make the old truck run her over.

Lila felt dizzy, her heart beating in her ears like a tympani.

How much time had passed? She had no idea, because every minute was like a quickly passed second. It was especially disorienting because up until they'd seen her father pass the window covered in what looked like powdered sugar, time had been dragging. She'd stopped checking the time because seeing minutes freeze was so disheartening. She'd check it at midnight, then feel hours pass as they huddled in the trees — and find it was 12:15 the next time she looked. It was excruciatingly boring, and yet the attention needed to watch the windows through her father's binoculars had drained her energy.

It was dark and creepy. She'd seen the ships through the trees once, then had moved into an area with a thicker overhead canopy so she wouldn't have to look up by mistake and see them again. It was boring and exhausting, worrying without being able to do a thing. She'd felt guilty disobeying her father's wishes. And on top of all that, she'd been cold this high in the mountains, without even horses to keep them warm. They were tied farther up. Piper thought their movement or noises might give them away.

They'd seen Meyer walk past a window, slow and creeping, clearly having freed himself from something, someplace where he shouldn't be.

Then they'd seen the guy with the dark hair and the mustache in the kitchen. They'd watched him go outside, then watched Meyer enter the kitchen, apparently with no idea the bad guy was there.

It had taken maybe ten seconds for Piper to tell Lila what to do. Another ten to reach the trucks when the bad guy was looking away, sure with every running step that she was about to be seen then shot. She almost had been; she'd peeked through the truck's windows and seen him standing there, practically staring right at her. But then he'd gone away.

He'd gone *inside*.

Liquid seconds ticked. Lila fought panic, a strangely insistent part of her mind arguing that it was all too late anyway and that she should just give up. But eventually, the big stick between the truck's seats came free as she tugged it, dropping into a wiggly position. She only had a moment to wonder what she was supposed to do next before the truck began to roll.

Lila jumped back, nearly clocked by the still-open door. The house had been built on a small rise — possibly built artificially, so rainwater would run away from the house rather than toward it — and the bad guys had driven through the raggedy lawn's edge to park against it. Now she understood why Piper had said she really wouldn't have to do much after getting the truck into neutral. She asked, *How am I supposed to move a truck with the engine off?* But Lila *didn't* have to. With gravity's help, the truck was moving just fine.

Lila stood dumbly in the truck's vacated spot, watching it clatter and bounce down the short, shallow hill. It gathered speed, going at a good clip until it smashed into a tree at the bottom with a sound that rattled to the mountains.

Something happened in the windowed kitchen, visible as a blur in the corner of Lila's eye.

Dad.

Before she could do something even more foolish than run toward the bad guy in the kitchen, a pair of lights popped on inside the mostly-dark house, almost at the same time.

Move, stupid! she told herself. *The whole* point *was to attract attention.*

Lila ducked to the right, toward the porch where the bad guy had been watching. She tried to tell herself it was because the other truck was still there to hide behind, but it was more likely a little girl's unthinking need to find her daddy. Who, really, might already be dead.

As if someone had read her thoughts, Lila heard a gunshot, maybe from the kitchen.

She ducked low, squatting behind the second truck's tailgate. The front door burst open. The two other men ran out, the blond's hair in corkscrews. He looked lost, baffled by the wreck at the bottom of the incline. But the other — the one with the buzz cut — didn't look lost at all. He looked like he knew exactly what was happening, angry as a kicked nest of wasps.

His head ticked toward Lila. She slunk back, hopefully out of sight. She had no idea if he'd seen her, and couldn't peek to check. Lila was blind. And he might be coming after her. She had to stay frozen, waiting to be taken like prey.

Where is Piper?

Lila had no idea. She might have run forward when Lila did, but if that was the case, wouldn't she have gone for the second truck?

Lila looked around the truck, toward the kitchen and away from the shaved-headed man. The door was closed, and she could see the cab's upper half, angled up from below. Unless Piper had slipped into the truck, closed the door, and ducked into the footwell, she wasn't here.

Lila saw movement: a blur, running at an angle toward the trees.

Dad!

She kept the cry in her mind — good because after another gunshot splintered a wooden post on the deck beside the runner, Lila realized it wasn't her father. The bad guy was about to run right by her, and would see her clear as day if he turned his head. But she didn't think he'd be turning; back at the kitchen door, her father was still aiming the man's weapon at him.

Another gunshot. Another miss. But Lila didn't think her father was trying to scare the man. She guessed he was aiming to kill.

Time dilated, everything slowed. Lila caught it in manic strobes.

The two-man crew on the truck's other side fanning out, now pointing around the yard with flashlights they'd either grabbed on their way out or gone back inside to retrieve. She peeked out once. In the hands without flashlights, each man held a pistol.

Activity in the house behind Lila, visible as darting shapes through the windows. More men? No, it was Trevor. Trevor in the kitchen; Trevor emerging with a hammer wielded like a weapon.

But before Lila could confront that absurdity (how was a hammer any good in a gunfight?), there was a blitzkrieg shout from the doorway. Both men turned, and the shaved-head man fired. Raj emerged, holding what looked like a fireplace poker as if it were a sword, trying to storm the men before they could turn. There was no way he'd make it.

The first man turned with time to spare. He sighted on Raj's head (not even his chest; he was about to paint the front door with her boyfriend's brains while she watched), the pistol arm firming. She could see the small muscles in his bare forearm flex to pull the trigger, watching Raj run at him, brave and stupid, the poker raised, his brown eyes hard even from where Lila was hiding, the man's face turning to a scowl as he aimed.

A new sound, from behind, a gunshot with the same echoing report as the first. Lila turned to see its source and saw her father standing like a statue, his own weapon held with both hands. It was the opposite of the showy way the man had been preparing to shoot Raj: both arms strong and firm, both hands wrapping the gun's grip. Like someone who'd trained to shoot, and knew the value of aim.

Her head darted back in time to see Raj reach his target, but the man was already falling. Shot through the chest, not the head. The bigger target — less dramatic, but far surer.

Raj couldn't arrest his momentum. He saw the man crumple but was unable to stop. He managed to hold the fireplace poker away and not spear himself to death, but tripped and fell hard on the pile, striking the grass with a shattering impact that Lila could feel in her bones.

"Lila!"

She turned, suddenly aware that at some point, her tears had fallen. "Daddy!"

Raj was scrabbling like a crab, apparently unhurt, then crawling toward the man's gun, jarred loose. The other bad guy, the blond, was running behind a small rock wall.

"Get down!"

Meyer pushed Lila behind the truck. The shove was hard; she racked her head on the metal and fought the urge to cry out. A second later, there was a loud pop, and Lila realized she'd narrowly avoided being shot. Her father was behind her, beside her.

"What the hell are you still doing here?"

"Creating a distraction," she managed to say.

"Jesus Christ, Lila. You almost got yourself killed."

His chastising voice outweighed his thanks. She felt like a little girl again, called on the carpet for doing something naughty.

"Where is Piper?"

"I ... I don't know."

Another gunshot. Dirt popped near the truck's tire.

Another shot, then another. From somewhere else. They both peeked out to see Raj holding the dead man's gun. To Lila's knowledge, Raj had never fired a gun. It showed. She watched him pull the trigger a third time, and the recoil looked like it surprised the hell right out of him. There was a ding near the house, very high, as if he'd shot into the roof. He wasn't remotely close to his target, and after another shot (also into the roof), the blond seemed to realize it.

He stood.

Meyer stood.

"Hey!"

Another shot, very loud, from above. Lila's ears were ringing, though her father's shot hadn't done more than force the man to duck back.

Instead of falling back himself, Meyer ran toward Raj. He tackled him mercilessly, flattening him and seeming to say something before rising — something that, if Lila had to guess, was about Raj's stupidity and how nobody wanted his death on their hands.

The blond, sensing an opportunity, sprung up again like a jack in the box. But he wasn't fully upright before something hit him from behind. Lila saw her mother, looking ridiculous with a frying pan in her hands of all cartoonish things. But the pan didn't do what it did in cartoons, and the man only spun, now aiming at Heather, who ran around the side of the house.

The blond took off after her.

Raj remained dutifully where he was, but Meyer became a blur. He crossed half the distance to the man before the runner could reach the home's edge. He shouted again, and the man turned, apparently realizing he wasn't going to make it.

His hands were at his side, the pistol not pointed. There was a split second where Lila thought her father might let him surrender. Instead he took two strong steps forward and, without a second's hesitation, fired a slug through his chest.

"Get your mother," he said. "Go!"

The way apparently clear, Lila ran, trying not to look at the dead man or consider how surely her father had dropped him. He was going to give up. But then again, he'd have done the same to his target. The world's rules had changed, and Meyer Dempsey wasn't a man to flinch at convictions.

Lila was halfway there when she heard a shout — another male voice, not her father's. She turned to see the first man — the one who'd gone out onto the porch, just beyond where Raj had been tackled. He seemed to be looking for something even after the shout, but Lila could already see that he was seeking the gun.

The final man had reached it first, after her father had knocked it loose from Raj's hand. He was holding it now, at Trevor's head.

Lila felt her heart break. She wanted to run to her little brother, but the man had an arm wrapped around him from behind, holding Trevor like a human shield. The gun was pressed to his temple. The knife he'd been holding was gone. Trevor looked beaten, sad, terrified. His eyes were streaming — something that hurt Lila's heart most of all.

"Drop it, Meyer!" he yelled.

Lila watched her father. He'd swung around when the man had shouted, and the gun was leveled rock steady in the bandit's direction. She knew him well enough to know that he was calculating aim and odds. They'd crossed the country to come here, and they hadn't turned away when they'd found the home under siege. If this man won their encounter, even if Trevor lived, they'd have lost. All in all, Meyer would prefer to win. Lila could see wheels turning, assessing the odds of pulling his trigger and landing a head-shot.

"Do it!" He ducked behind Trevor's head, probably realizing what Lila had.

Meyer lowered his weapon. Reluctantly, he dropped it to the dirt.

"Kick it toward me! Now! No fucking around!"

Meyer did. The move was almost petulant, like a child. The weapon bounced past the man and Trevor, toward the wrecked truck. Lila watched him stand in the middle of the open, defenseless but seemingly unafraid. He was looking at Trevor rather than the man holding him. It was a look of apology.

Now that Meyer had discarded his weapon, the man's demeanor changed. The gun moved an inch or more away from Trevor's skin, whereas the muzzle had been branding his scalp before. His face changed, more desperate than scowling. His voice lowered.

"I didn't want any of this."

Meyer said nothing. The man went on, speaking to his mute audience.

"I just wanted a place to stay. I knew you had this house, and that it had a bunker. I didn't even think you'd come here. Hell, I didn't think you'd be *able* to come here. You live in New York, for shit's sake."

Lila watched her father's lips form a pressed line.

"I just needed a place to hide." He looked at his two dead henchmen in turn: the younger one past the stoop, the blond up near the home's left side. Lila had watched both men all evening, seeing them go about their human business of walking, speaking, eating, presumably sleeping. Now they were meat. "I never wanted anyone to get hurt."

"Is that why you kidnapped Heather?"

"Would you rather I'd killed her?"

"You could have sent her away, Garth. But you didn't want that, did you? Because she's a loudmouth, and I'll bet she went on and on about how we were coming to meet her. You couldn't get into the bunker without me."

Garth didn't acknowledge Meyer's point, but his eyes seemed to.

"You could have just asked me, Garth. You could have come alone, without …" his eyes strayed to the dead man with the shaved head, " … reinforcements," he finished. "I would have let you in. There's room. Plenty of supplies."

Now *Garth* looked like he might cry — a strange thing to see on the face of a man holding a gun to a fifteen-year-old boy's head. He was scared more than Lila had realized. Like her father was surely scared more than he let on. Meyer would do anything to protect his family. Garth, it seemed, was obeying his human impulse to do the same for himself.

"I have to do this," Garth said. "You won't let me in now. I can't leave." His lips pressed into a frown: *You're damned if you do, and you're damned if you don't.* Nobody had to like it, his look seemed to say, but that's how it is.

"Just let him go. Let me have my son."

He seemed to firm his resolve. "Open the bunker. Just do it." He twitched his chin toward the open porch door, seeming to indicate where Meyer should go.

"Let him go, Garth."

Garth's hand shifted on Trevor's chest. Then Trevor did something Lila remembered from their shared past, when she'd been six and he'd been four: he took the hand on his chest with both hands, yanked it up to his mouth, and bit it hard.

Garth yelled out. Trevor ducked and ran.

Garth swiveled on the spot, unsure where to point his weapon. There was a strange moment of indecision, and for a second Lila could see him trying to figure out whether to keep aiming at Trevor or take aim at her father.

Before he could do either, another gunshot thundered.

Lila blinked toward the smashed truck, not ten feet from Garth's collapsing body.

Piper was standing beside it, a pistol in both hands and terror on her face.

Chapter Thirty-Eight

THEY LEFT THE BODIES OUTSIDE.

Piper didn't want to think about any of it. She let Meyer do his manly thing, taking over for her and doing what had to be done. After she'd shot Garth, she'd hugged Trevor and Lila, then walked to Meyer and hugged him hardest of all. Meyer took a double brunt of meaning: affection and gratitude as intended in the kids' hugs, but something else as well. Something Piper couldn't articulate. Something that was more about her than Meyer. She hadn't really cared if the kids, under the circumstances, hugged her back. But Meyer needed to, and she wouldn't leave until he did. Fortunately, he seemed to understand, and pulled her hard to his body.

Then he'd kissed her cheek, and she'd walked back toward the porch, sitting in the kitchen while he'd done something that took about ten minutes. Probably dragging the three dead men into the trees, maybe freeing the horses from their tethers.

He came into the kitchen with Trevor and Lila at his sides, each holding one of his hands like toddlers. Heather brought up the rear, but said nothing sarcastic. She simply came to where Piper sat in her chair, stooped to wrap her arms around her, and said, "Thank you."

Meyer went to the kitchen sink, overlooking the lake out front, and took a moment to stare out across the moonlit scene. Then he washed his hands of red and brown grime, and said, "Let's get inside."

Piper didn't reply. She just wanted to sleep.

Hours passed.

Day must have dawned outside, but the bunker didn't have windows, and they could only guess. Meyer locked the bunker door, flipped a few switches that made machines hum and putter behind the concrete walls, and suggested everyone rest. He himself hadn't slept. Heather and Trevor seemed to have nodded off for a few hours, but despite Meyer's trying to conceal the tunnel he'd dug through the pantry's drywall, it hadn't taken much detective work to find it once they'd woken and found him gone. Piper hadn't slept either. She'd been far too nervous, too worried about what might come next, and that someone might die. Lila must have been the same; she'd wanted to take her turns faithfully on the binoculars rather than attempting to bed down. Piper couldn't blame her. It was tiring to surveil the house, but so much worse to simply sit in the quiet darkness with the dots of alien ships overhead, and wait.

So they bedded down. Meyer had done his usual paranoid best, and outfitted their space in the best manner that a rich man's money could buy. Five bedrooms for six people. If Lila and Trevor had shared a room (blessedly, Lila and Raj didn't ask to do the same), there would even have been room for Garth.

Piper didn't think she'd be able to sleep.

But she did.

PIPER WOKE to the sound of a television. How long had it been since she'd watched a TV? Not an Internet stream, but an actual TV on a genuine wall?

It had been a very long time. The last time Piper had watched TV, the world had been a different place. Piper had been a different person. She'd been so much younger. Trevor and Lila had been innocent. She'd lived in a totally different life, caring only about foolish things like yoga and her own entertainment.

How long ago had that been? Ten years?

But no. It had only been a week.

The bunker had been built to mirror the floor plan of an ordinary home, and despite the gray concrete walls (they were due to be painted at some point, but the apocalypse had called first), it almost looked like one. There were attractive track lights mounted to the slab overhead; there was plush carpeting and hardwood in the kitchen; Meyer had furnished the place in an inappropriately lavish (but very Meyer) style.

She entered the living room, trying to think of it as a real living room. She found Heather on the couch, flanked by Trevor and Lila.

Heather gave her a very un-Heather smile. They'd met many times, and even taken a few vacations en masse "for the kids' sake." On those family vacations, Heather was supposed to be the hanger-on, but Piper always felt like the odd woman out. They'd got along fine. Heather was hard

not to like, once you were used to her always-on personality — and this despite Piper's suspicion that she was still
sleeping with Meyer.

Heather and Meyer shared history that the two of
them never could. Piper liked to think she was mature
enough to respect different kinds of love for what they
were, but suspected she might be pitying herself.

Maybe she wasn't enough for Meyer. He certainly had
much more in common with Heather — and that
extended to memories and preferences, not just hobbies.
Maybe he needed Heather. Maybe she was just too
bedraggled, being raised by a mother who served her
husband, to stand up and put an end to it.

Heather held her small, uncharacteristic smile. The
room was quiet despite the TV, and they all seemed reluctant to break some sort of a spell that had descended on
the room.

They were safe. The fight was over, and they'd reached
their destination.

They could bask in that feeling for a while before
facing the next thing.

"How are you feeling?" Heather asked.

"Tired."

"Sleep well?"

Piper hadn't slept *well*, but she'd slept *some*. She
nodded.

"Did you sleep at *all?*"

Heather shrugged, seeming to indicate the children at
her sides. They looked sleepy but not asleep. She must have
stayed up with them. Like she'd once chased away their
nightmares. Piper had never done that. Lila and Trevor
had both been grown when she'd entered the picture.
There was a moment of jealousy, and then it was gone.

"Not really."

Piper sighed, then sat. She wanted to say something conclusive to cap their adventure (even "Well, we made it" would do), but her lips betrayed her. She found herself watching the screen, hypnotized by its glow, its soporific, low volume.

Heather was watching the news. The kids, at her sides, looked like zombies — their eyes open and mesmerized.

"How do we get TV down here?" said Piper.

"I don't know. There was a TV. I turned it on. It worked."

"Satellite," Piper guessed. There was a humming behind one of the walls. It might be a heater, but it also might be a generator or three. There might be line power to the house, but there were also solar panels on the roof and huge wind turbines visible farther up the hill. If there was line power and it went out, theirs, down here, never would.

"You know Meyer," said Heather. "He's probably got his own satellite up there. And armed guards outside protecting the dish. Did you know that when he started Fable, he was so paranoid about other movie studios stealing his techniques that he had decoy studios built, so it would be harder for spies to know where the real action was taking place?"

Piper shook her head. She hadn't known that. She thought of how Heather had started the story by saying, *You know Meyer*. But Piper, hating herself a little, thought instead, *YOU do*.

She looked over at Heather, sitting between the children Piper had spent the last few years raising. Heather looked tired and rumpled — not at all the polished, primped woman with the outrageous dresses she usually wore in her comedy specials. But Heather dressed down exceedingly well. She looked good casual. Comfortable. Even normal. It was hard to fathom her reality, but oddly enough Piper found her conversation with Heather oddest of all. Heather wasn't being her usual self. They were talking like old friends. Which, under different circumstances, they probably would be.

"Have you been watching all night?" Piper said, nodding toward the TV.

"Mostly."

"Mom made us watch *Friends* for a while," said Lila. "Just like you do."

"It makes us think of our youth," said Heather, smoothing Lila's hair. But Piper had been far too young to remember the show. She liked it in the way Heather liked older shows before her time — with a sense of days passed, times she'd missed out on.

"What's going on?"

"The ships are starting to settle over big cities."

"'Settle'?"

Heather nodded. "Just hanging there. Floating. Like in *V.* Did you ever see *V*?"

Piper shook her head.

"Lucky. Meyer made me watch it a few times." She pointed at the screen. "There. Like that."

Piper put her hand over her mouth, feeling her wide eyes bloom wider. The picture on the screen was surreal. She saw the familiar New York skyline, now circled with what seemed to be an unusual number of helicopters. But smack in the middle, eclipsing the screen's top half, was the curved bottom of a huge silver sphere. Then the screen changed, an announcer babbling on in words Piper could barely hear. The new shot was from several miles farther back, taken from a helicopter, judging by the high view-point and slight jostle. It showed the sphere in its entirety, just hovering above Manhattan like a giant brushed steel bowling ball.

Piper looked at Lila and Trevor, feeling a strange urge to shield their eyes. They shouldn't have to see this. Then again, it was their new reality. And they'd seen so much worse already.

Heather reached for the tablet on the back of the couch, tapped the screen, and killed the picture.

"I know that look," Heather said. "It's how I think I looked a bit ago, when they first started showing footage of the things arriving."

"They're not doing anything?"

"Not as far as I've heard. Just waiting."

"For what?"

But Heather could only shake her head.

DAY SEVEN

Chapter Thirty-Nine

Day Seven
  Axis Mundi

THE FIRST TWENTY-FOUR hours were hardest.

Piper was used to being out and around. She was a New York girl now, and living in Manhattan meant constantly walking. Meyer had had the foresight to equip a small gym, but walking on a treadmill wasn't the same. She craved fresh air and felt slightly claustrophobic — a fear that seemed to magnify if she considered tomorrow and the next day, knowing that depending on what the ships did, they might be here for a long time. Knowing Meyer, "a long time" could provide sustenance for a decade. The idea of staying inside this bunker for a decade was suffocating, and when she thought about it the first time, Piper retired to her room while Meyer was playing a game with the kids, closed the door, and cried.

There was a floor area in the gym, and Meyer, bless his considerate, forward-thinking heart, had floored it in bamboo so that Piper could do yoga. Doing a few sun salutations calmed her mind, so she pulled up some of the stored routines on the small juke in the gym and played through a few longer sessions as led by her favorite video instructor, Heidi Bleue. That helped more. But even after the invigoration of a long and tiring session, she found Savasana, the moveless pose that always closed her routines, hard to stomach.

Piper was supposed to be clearing her head, breathing into universal intelligence with her body and mind. But now her universal intelligence was polluted with Meyer's visions — with the premonitions he'd seemed to have about all of this, as spied when he'd taken his drug. The aliens seemed to be out there somehow, visible when one cleared his or her mind. And now they were all Piper could imagine: gray skinned with black almond eyes like in the movies, or green and dripping with slime.

She looked longingly at the spiral staircase, wanting with everything she had to go up. The ships might be above Denver, but they wouldn't be above Vail. This was the back country. It's why Meyer had chosen the land, why he'd bought so much to assure isolation. So why *couldn't* she go outside? The bunker's air felt stale, almost suffocating.

She'd known Meyer wouldn't want anyone to leave, so feeling reckless one day, Piper quietly climbed the stairs with her walking shoes on, vowing to only taste the air for a few minutes.

But the door was locked, the access code changed.

He'd sealed them in.

IN THE AFTERNOON (Piper didn't know when and didn't care; time didn't matter in a world where sunshine was rumor), Piper found herself preparing an argument for Meyer.

They couldn't hide for the rest of their lives, especially when there wasn't even anything menacing going on. Maybe the ships were there to stay, but maybe they'd only hang there forever without disembarking. Maybe they were stranded. Piper hadn't seen *V* as described by Heather, but she'd seen another of Meyer's favorites: a rather violent film called *District 9*. Those aliens had basically run out of intergalactic gas and parked their ship above Johannesburg. Maybe this was like that.

Or even if this *wasn't* like that, why couldn't they wait until there was something to fear before hiding? They'd have time to react if a war began. Piper didn't want to drive to Dallas; she wanted to take a walk around the house. She wouldn't even enter the woods if he didn't want her to, and he could come with her if he insisted on babysitting. They wanted protection, sure. But there was no reason to voluntarily turn themselves into prisoners.

Piper found Meyer in the living room, which after just a day had already become the underground home's clear nexus. They'd eaten dinner and breakfast from TV trays rather than at the table, and thus far the kids' only slumber had been on the living room couches, passing out from exhaustion rather than truly falling asleep.

"Meyer," she said, her spine tall and her hands uncomfortably near to perching on her hips, "I think we should talk about …"

He shushed her. Piper didn't like that at all and was about to call him on his rudeness, but then she saw his eyes. He, like Trevor, Lila, Raj, and Heather, was staring at the TV, transfixed.

"What?"

"Shh, Piper," Lila said.

Piper looked at the screen and saw what had already become a shockingly familiar sight: a massive silver orb hovering above a city. Judging by the Slavic architecture (all swirls and onions), she thought it might be somewhere in Russia. At the bottom of the screen a red banner said, SATELLITES SHOW MOSCOW HEAT BLOOMS.

"What's a heat bloom?"

"Shh!" This time, it was Trevor.

The announcer was going on, but Piper was coming to this party late and didn't have the background the rest of them, who'd apparently camped in front of the TV like drones, had already absorbed. For some reason, being shushed a third time made her furious.

"Don't you 'shh' at me, Trevor! Someone tell me what the hell is going on!"

Heather looked up. For a second Piper thought she might bark at her for yelling at Trevor. Instead, her usual sarcasm still mostly absent, she said, "It's what happens when they launch missiles."

"Who's launching ... what kind of missiles?" She heard her voice falter.

The screen seemed to come alight all at once. Whatever had struck the sphere was massive. Piper didn't know much about weapons of war, but the explosion looked like something from Cold War footage — a kind of awkward mushroom that shook the enormous sphere like a piece swinging in a Newton's cradle.

"Was that one of the big ones?" she asked, now desperate. "They can't do that, can they? Wouldn't it destroy the city? Wouldn't it give them all radiation poisoning?" There was more, too: where was the camera showing this footage? It looked like a helicopter. Had anyone told the pilot that nuclear action might be afoot?

Nobody answered.

Maybe the city had been evacuated.

Maybe a rogue faction had managed to launch something, not strictly authorized by the government.

Or maybe the world had gone to shit inside a single day.

"What's going on in the rest of the world?" she asked, panicked, feeling her legs start to wobble. She grasped the back of a chair for support as a torrent of rapid-fire questions spilled from her lips.

"What about New York? Is there one over Denver? Did they say if they've done anything to us? Is our government talking about launching missiles too? Oh Jesus. Oh shit. What about the president? Has the president made any …"

The entire bottom half of the sphere turned bright, like a down-facing lamp. Even with the set's downturned volume, she could hear a loud, low *fwump* like a fire suddenly coming alight.

A few seconds later, some kind of shockwave must have struck the camera and killed the feed.

In those seconds — between the massive light beam and the loss of signal — Piper could clearly see that Moscow's city center was gone.

THE TV WAS OFF. They sat around the coffee table in the quiet the way they'd sit around a campfire, with the lights low. Nobody had wanted to watch the news after satellites started showing overhead shots of the damage. The ground seemed flat and burned, no structures standing within a radius of a dozen miles or more. And most ominously, front and center on the satellite image was the ship itself — an impossibly large silver circle above the debris, again unmoving and silent.

After that, the huge Moscow ship had moved on. Without a city to watch, it seemed to feel it had other business to attend to.

They'd watched sporadically after that, checking for new and horrible updates in the way Piper remembered her grandparents describing 9/11. Nobody, they'd said, wanted to see more of what had happened that day. And yet few had been able to look away.

Piper could relate. She told the kids to keep the screen off but found them with it on a few times, Heather disobedient in their midst. But she herself had been peeking too, ducking into rooms to watch on a tablet, staying too long behind Trevor, Lila, and Raj before laying down the law. It was impossible to turn from. Her desire to go outside had evaporated, and she was quite sure, now, that they were all going to die. But she still wanted to know *when* she was going to die. *How* she was going to die. And to be as frightened as possible in the meantime.

None of the other ships struck. Other nations, apparently having learned Russia's lesson, stood down. Even the amount of helicopters circling the things decreased their numbers and increased their distance. There were addresses from the president, promising that the government was doing all it could to communicate and keep the people safe. Pundits pointed out that Russia had struck first, though there was no information on why, or if the action had been official.

Sometime later, a few of the ships opened ports and released much smaller ships, like hovercraft. The smaller ships were like the larger ones: polished silver spheres perhaps a hundred yards in diameter. They moved from one location to another, sending thin rivulets of energy down to the ground. Nobody was sure what they were, because cameras seemed to blitz out whenever they got close — some sort of electromagnetic interference, said those who seemed to know. Conspiracy nuts rushed to cobble two and two, theorizing that the green beams meant abductions in progress.

They were *harvesting*.

After one such conspiracy theory report, Piper looked down to see that Trevor had turned pale. That broke both her trance and addiction. She turned the screen off and vowed that for a night, at least, they would just be people. Not *hiding* people, but *people*.

"Did you know," said Heather, running her fingers through Lila's dark hair, "that your father and I named you after a song?"

Lila, safe in Raj's arms, looked up at her mother. Piper, watching, felt it impossible that Lila wouldn't know the origin of her own name. But maybe she did know, and it didn't matter. Maybe she just wanted to hear the story again, and be young for a while.

"It was one of our favorites," said Heather, looking over at Meyer with a nostalgic, almost bittersweet expression. "An old song, called 'Hey There, Delilah.'"

The evening passed as if by candlelight. They told tales — each taking their turn, each free to go wherever he or she wanted, into authentic past or spinning fiction. Slowly, the room began to feel small again ... but this time, the aura was more intimate than confining.

They would be safe.

The world had become a perilous place, but they'd made it to the ranch — to the somehow spiritual Axis Mundi that Meyer had been going on about for years. It was small, and they might be in it for a long time while the dust (hopefully more metaphorical than literal) settled beyond the bunker's walls. But they would adjust. Piper would learn to walk on the treadmill. She'd do her yoga.

She had millions of books stored on her Vellum; they had years of entertainment on the bunker's various jukes. They had endless power (wind, solar, generated if need be), enough food, and three protected subterranean wells for water.

It would be okay. Somehow, because they were safe and because they were together, it would be okay.

Story time ended with the feeling of a fire's coals glowing slowly to ash. Piper retired for the night, repeating that single refrain over and over inside her head, making herself believe: *It will be okay.*

She and Meyer made love that night. And when they did, Piper found herself wishing they'd had the history he shared with Heather — the kind that featured a song special enough to name a firstborn daughter.

DAY TEN

Chapter Forty

Meyer's eyes opened.

Something had changed.

He watched the concrete ceiling above the bed he shared with Piper before rising, suddenly realizing that the gray mass was actually a vibrating matrix of molecules, apparently solid on a macro scale but entirely permeable once you got down small enough. The concrete was composed of sand and cement, which in turn were composed of quartz, silica, and dozens of other components. Each of those were made of elements, and each of the elements were made of atoms that were all the same. But even then, those atoms were mostly space. A nucleus with electrons somewhere around it, not so much *orbiting* as *existing*. Between the solid cores of the elements and the electrons was nothing.

Like outer space.

He sat up.

He understood.

There had been a time, making a wish list for his bunker at the end of the world, that Meyer had considered ayahuasca — his medicine. But you couldn't just store it like pedestrian drugs, like coke or even weed. Ayahuasca was brewed by a shaman. If he wanted to go on his spiritual, other-level voyages while waiting out the apocalypse, he'd need Juha. But getting just his family here had been hard enough.

That, he saw now, had been a pointless thought. He didn't need medicine to see the core of truth within him — or perhaps more accurately, far outside. It was a lens — or a rag used to wipe his lens, and he no longer needed that rag to see.

Something had changed.

Now his vision was clear.

Meyer could imagine his mind as an extension of a universal collective. He imagined himself as a blip of existence peeking beyond some kind of veil. Behind the veil, though, there was more of him. Like the tip of an iceberg. Other people might peek out farther down the veil, but behind the scenes, where few ever looked, they were all connected.

They were all part of one larger thing, with many heads.

And still, Meyer was himself. He was both things. They all were.

He saw the emptiness all around him, baked into even the most solid of objects.

The ceiling was space.

The floor was space.

Piper, still asleep beside him, was space.

If you peered close enough, everything was nothing.

And if you pulled back enough, nothing somehow became everything.

Images that had been just beneath consciousness began to clearly rise inside his awakening mind. He saw a sun. A planet. A thing that was like a hole in nothing, leading great distances to another place.

Of course he'd known they were coming. It's why he'd run. It's why he'd come here. It's why he'd protected them all. Because what had happened in Moscow? That was the beginning.

He could see their purpose — the visitors' purpose — as clearly as he saw his own feet sliding into slippers at the bed's side, standing up, leaving the bedroom to enter the quiet nighttime living room.

He knew what they wanted.

He knew why they were here.

He knew what the shuttles were doing. Why they were breaking homes open like nutshells. Why they were pulling people from their beds, so many screaming. He knew that fear. It percolated beneath his awareness like an unscratchable itch.

He knew why he'd fought so hard. Why he'd risked them all dying, if the alternative was to not be here, to not be inside. Of course they'd had to be here, now. It was ludicrous that he'd ever, ever hesitated.

Meyer crossed the living room, now quiet. The kids were asleep in three rooms. Heather was asleep in a fourth. This was their sanctuary. Their place of sanity. The place where, in discreet doses, they could see what was happening in the larger world without having to fear it.

If only they truly understood.

But how could Meyer explain? He'd never understood it all until now.

He watched the dark screen for a full minute, aware as

he did it that he must look like a lunatic. If Heather or Piper came out and saw him gazing at the blackness, they'd worry for his sanity, thinking him sick with some kind of cabin fever. Yesterday, they'd think, he'd been normal. They were all settling into routine as more and more shuttles ventured from the motherships, as more and more desperate and fearful factions struck at the ships and were reduced to rubble. The shuttles would take whomever they wanted, and there was nothing anyone could do to stop them. But that was a hard thing for humans to accept — that there were powers in the universe that found their force and aggression not just laughable but unworthy of notice. And so there were always reports of someone fighting back. Always reports of that someone — be it a lone man with a shotgun or a nation with artillery — getting smacked away like a fly.

Still, Meyer stared at the screen. Within it, he saw space. Beyond it, he saw space.

The notion was fascinating. If he were reduced to small enough size — as large as one of those electrons, say — he could fly through the television and all of the bunker's walls as easily as a ship flying through the vacuum of empty space.

Finally, he turned away, grateful for time to gaze without being watched.

They wouldn't understand. They'd think he'd lost his mind.

He moved to the spiral staircase, put a hand on its cool railing, and began to move upward.

He opened the kitchen door, and found the air strange. Compared to the canned, filtered, and scrubbed air below, the home's atmosphere was almost electric. Too cool, too raw. Naked air.

He closed the door and crossed the kitchen.

It was dark. There should still be a partial moon tonight, but it must not have risen. He opened the French doors to the porch, taking a moment.

His skin adjusted to the cooler air. His eyes adjusted to the dark.

After a few minutes, he found that the black wasn't pitch after all. Maybe the moon was up beyond a rise, and it was reflecting off the atmosphere. Something was letting him see, even if it was merely the scant candle cast by the stars.

Meyer went to the lake.

For a strange moment, he wondered at himself: still in pajamas, still in slippers, his hair a mess, outside as he'd told the others never to be — having locked them in until now. And he was standing by a lake without moonlight. Was he going to go swimming? It was strange to realize that his mind wasn't entirely his own.

Meyer looked up.

Above him was a perfectly smooth silver object, large enough to fill the small lake's basin if it chose to. He could see it clearly despite the dark, as if the sphere cast its own light. And with that realization, he found himself looking through it as he had the ceiling and the TV screen. He couldn't literally see space above the ship's bulk, but could imagine it perfectly. As if he were but a particle, able to zoom through apparently solid area to find it as cavernous as outer space.

There was a soft clanging, and a round hole on the ship's underside opened like an old-time camera's shutter. Inside was a light: *green*, like he himself would ask a director to color it, in one of his films.

He knew what this meant.

He knew why he'd come.

Meyer spread his arms and looked upward, closing his eyes as a soft, warm glow surrounded his body.

He felt his feet leave the ground.

Sometime later, Meyer Dempsey and the ship he'd entered were gone.

The mountain was still and quiet, as if vowing to never whisper a word of what happened.

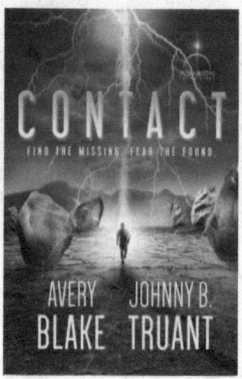

A Quick Favor...

If you enjoyed this book, please take a moment to write a short review on your favorite online bookstore so other readers can enjoy it, too.

Thanks so much!
   Johnny and Avery

About the Authors

Avery Blake doesn't want you to know where she lives, or what she does. She travels the world, moving from place to place quickly to ensure she can't be tracked. It's safer that way.

When she's not looking over her shoulder, you can find her in the corner of a cafe, facing the exit, typing as fast as she can.

~

Johnny B. Truant is co-owner of the Sterling & Stone Story Studio, an IP powerhouse focusing on books and adaptations for film and television. It's the best job in the world, and he spends his days creating cool stuff with partners Sean Platt and David W. Wright, as well as more than 20 gifted storytellers.

Johnny is the bestselling author of over 100 books under various pen names, including the Fat Vampire and Invasion series. On the nonfiction side, he's also co-author of the indie publishing mainstay Write. Publish. Repeat. and co-host of the weekly Story Studio Podcast.

Originally from Ohio, Johnny and his family now live in Austin, Texas, where he's finally surrounded by creative types as weird as he is.

Also By Avery Blake

The Hidden

The Saved

The Next Evolution

Transition

Convergence

Evolution

Stand-Alone Novels

Analog Heart

Family Royale

Ruthless Positivity

Vicarious Joe

Also By Johnny B. Truant

The Dead World Series

Dead Zero

Dead City

Dead Nation

Dead Planet

Empty Nest

The Fat Vampire Series

Fat Vampire

Fat Vampire 2: Tastes Like Chicken

Fat Vampire 3: All You Can Eat

Fat Vampire 4: Harder, Better, Fatter, Stronger

Fat Vampire 5: Fatpocaplypse

Fat Vampire 6: Survival of the Fattest

The Fat Vampire Chronicles

The Vampire Maurice

Anarchy and Blood

Vampires in the White City

The Beam Series

The Beam Season One

The Beam Season Two

The Beam Season Three

The Target

The Island

Devil May Care